death DROP

A KILLER QUEEN mystery

by
Greg Herren

death DROP

A KILLER QUEEN
mystery

by
Greg Herren

golden
NOTE
BOOK
PRESS
Woodstock
New York

Death Drop: A Killer Queen Mystery
First published in 2023 by Golden Notebook Press
Copyright © by Greg Herren

First Golden Notebook Press Printing: October 2023

Golden Notebook Press, LLC
29 Tinker Street
Woodstock, NY 12498

goldennotebook.com
goldennotebookpress.com
@goldennotebookbookstore

ISBN: 978-0-9675541-5-0

Designed by James Conrad

Printed in the United States of America
1 3 5 7 9 10 8 6 4 2

First Edition

*This is for
James, Alison and Wendy—
thank you, this wouldn't exist
except for you three*

PROLOGUE

"Are you sure you want me to let you out there?" asked my Lyft driver Shawna in a skeptical tone.

I looked up from my cell phone and over the front seat. The light was red at the corner of Nashville and St. Charles. There were three cars ahead of us. I looked past the glare of their red tail lights and could see a crowd out in front of the enormous stone wall encircling the business on the corner, Designs by Marigny. Some were carrying signs. There was also a police car parked in front, the blue lights flashing.

My heart sank. This wasn't good.

"Well, that's where I'm going," I said, making it sound more like a question than a statement of

1

fact. Hadn't I just made a joke that very morning about this show attracting anti-drag homophobic protestors?

"I don't know if I feel comfortable letting you out in that crowd," she replied as the light turned green and the cars ahead of us started moving. "Maybe I can take you down to the next house?"

I started to say *but I'd have to walk back anyway* but decided to just go along with it. "That's fine."

"I said when I saw her last night on WYES talking about her fashion show she was begging for a protest," Shawna started moving towards the intersection. "The way things are now? I'm surprised they aren't showing up at the gay bars when they have drag shows now."

"Well, I'm not a queen, so I should be okay," I said dubiously as the car moved through the intersection at Nashville.

But were hostile homophobes capable of making that distinction? They didn't know the difference between a transwoman and a drag queen, after all.

Shawna slowed as she reached the opposite corner. Some of the protestors were standing in the street, and there was a lot of pushing and shoving and yelling going on near the gate to the mansion that housed Designs by Marigny. The light was fading, and the streetlamps were coming on. It rained earlier in the afternoon, so the streets and sidewalks were slick and shiny. The crowd looked like about twenty people, maximum? One of them was carrying that massive sign that always shows up at the corner of St. Ann and Bourbon during Carnival and Southern Decadence—listing all the sins that would send someone straight to hell. They usually had someone with a bullhorn shouting at everyone partying to repent. The list on the sign was thorough and included all the usual slurs: *faggots, adulterers, idolaters, fornicators, masturbators* and so on. I could see two uniformed cops standing in front of the gate, while a man—most likely the Reverend Graham Steuben, was yelling in their faces. Steuben was pastor of an evangelical church somewhere on the West Bank and had become kind of a local fixture, as a kind of D-List Westboro Baptist Church. He and his flock always turned up looking for headlines and news cameras, usually with a group of people wearing black jeans and black T-shirts with the word FAG on the front in red, inside a circle with a line through it. It looked like the usual group I'd gotten used to seeing protesting any and every gay event in the French Quarter.

I should have known they'd jump all over the "drag queens are groomers" narrative. Anything to hate on queer people.

Shawna pulled the silver Taurus over in front of the house just past Designs by Marigny. "Thanks," I said, opening my door and lifting my rolling makeup case out of the backseat and onto the walkway. "Have a safe night."

I shut the car door and tipped her twenty percent on the app. I shoved my phone back into my jeans pocket and rolled the case up the walkway to the sidewalk. This house didn't have a fence and was enormous. The upper floors of Designs by Marigny, housed in the enormous plantation-style mansion on the corner, were visible above the massive stone fence running around the property. The purple, gold and green awning stretched from the front porch down the walk all the way to the gate.

I glanced at my watch. I didn't have to be there until seven and it was about twenty minutes till. I sighed as I drew nearer the people blocking the sidewalk. The cops were still standing, stone-faced, in front of the gates. Just as I was about to start saying "excuse me" on repeat as I pushed my way through, a van bearing the logo of our local ABC affiliate pulled up right where Shawna had let me out and the back opened. A local news reporter whose name I could never remember climbed out, smoothing her skirt and adjusting her jacket. It was a bit muggy for a jacket, but the night was cool. A heavyset man with a neckbeard also got out, carrying a massive portable film camera.

"Reverend! The news is here!" someone shouted, and the Reverend Graham Steuben himself separated himself from the group and bounced along the gutter to where she was standing, talking to her camera man. As if on cue, the group started chanting "*Groomers! Groomers! Save our kids!*"

4

It didn't even rhyme.

I rolled my eyes. They could have at least put some effort into their homophobia. I've heard better chants from junior high school cheerleaders.

I didn't even have to say excuse me once. The group magically parted as I rolled down the sidewalk towards them. I doubt that my battered old Louis Vuitton make-up case impressed them very much. My guess was if they touched or tried to block anyone from entering Designs by Marigny, the two cops would leap into action.

Here we go, I said to myself and started rolling my case behind me over the broken, tilted flagstones and over the roots of a massive live oak tree. Before I made it to the gate an older woman stepped in front of me, smelling like liniment, watery roses, and peppermints. She was short, with graying hair handing loosely to her rounded shoulders. She was wearing a pair of black yoga pants, ballet flats, and a black T-shirt with the words *Stop Grooming Children!!!* written across the front in gold.

"Are you one of the pedophiles?" she hissed at me, her bloodshot eyes staring at me intently.

I recoiled from her in distaste. "I—"

"I said you couldn't bother anyone." One of the cops said before I could finish. He'd moved rather quickly from the gate.

She flinched away from him. "I wasn't bothering anyone!"

"Go on, move along." He went on casually. "I don't want to have to arrest you as a public nuisance."

I bit my lower lip. *Typical cops, siding with the oppressors and not wanting to upset the nice straight white lady.* "Actually—" I started to say, but she shoved a piece of paper in my hands and ran off, disappearing around the corner of the fence and up Nashville Street.

I looked down at the paper. It was a flyer, an anti-drag one, with the expected bad grammar, misspellings, and overwrought capitalization. Whoever had made it hadn't skimped on the exclamation points, either. There was a website listed at the bottom, as well as a listing of social media accounts. I started to toss it but stopped myself.

I've always believed it was wise to know what the haters were saying, so I folded it and slipped it into my front pocket.

I tried not to make eye contact with anyone as I made my way through the chanting people. I glanced back over my shoulder. The reporter was interviewing Reverend Steuben, the cameraman holding the camera on one shoulder and a handheld spotlight in the other. *Perfect,* I thought, irritated. *As usual, they get to tell their side on television. Bet she's not going to interview any of the queens.*

As I looked, Reverend Steuben made a gesture and the chanting stopped.

Can't have the chants on the news, I thought

cynically as I approached the gates. There was a tall, cadaverous looking woman on the other side of the gate, holding a clipboard.

"Hi," I said to the cops. One was Black and in his mid-thirties and knew his way around the gym. The other, the one who'd chased off the protestor, was older by several decades, white and balding with a healthy paunch over hanging the waistband of his uniform pants. He spat chewing tobacco into the grass and gave me a gruff look. "I'm working on the show tonight? Make-up?"

"Name?" the woman from the other side of the gate barked.

"Jem Richard," I had to shout because they'd started chanting again. The interview must have ended.

She found my name on the list and checked it off, opening the gate from the inside. The cops moved so I could maneuver my rolling case through the gate. Once inside, she closed it again. "The dressing room is in back on the first floor," she directed me. Tall and thin, she was one of those women who looked like she was always hungry but could make do with a lone almond. She was wearing a sleeveless red silk dress I could tell was a "Design by Marigny" by the way it emphasized flaws a properly fitted dress would have hidden. Her shoulders were bony, her arms sinew and muscle and skin. Her hair was pulled back into a ponytail so severe that it looked like it hurt. "Same place as the last time you were here." She gestured for me to continue walking. "Service entrance in the back," she added as I started walking again. "The walk will take you around that way."

I bit my tongue. The last time I did glam for one of Marigny Orloff's fashion shows I'd sworn it was the last time. Her check had bounced, for one thing, and it took me weeks to get her to make the check good. The only reason I agreed to break that vow was because someone guaranteed my pay, and it was already deposited in my bank account.

I started pulling the case up the walk and made a right at the front steps, following the walk around to the back.

"*Save our kids!*
Save our kids!
Save our kids!"

I sighed as I reached the back steps. I could make a break for it....

Knowing I was going to regret it, already regretting it, I dragged my make-up case up the stairs. *Just a few hours, put some highlights on some drag queens, and you can get out of here.*

If only I could go back in time to last night and tell myself not to say yes....

CHAPTER ONE

"I don't know, Jem," Lauralee Dorgenois said, frowning and raising a perfectly plucked eyebrow as she looked back over her shoulder into the three-way mirror set-up in her dressing room. "You're sure that this dress doesn't make my butt look big?"

Okay, I'm going to take a sidebar right here to give y'all some free-of-charge advice that is more than worth its weight in gold. There is only one correct answer to be given without pause or hesitation any time a woman asks you if something she is wearing makes her butt look big: "No."

You always, *always*, ALWAYS say no.

If that is, in fact, a lie—you say "I don't know if that cut drapes right" or "I don't like what that color does to your skin."

There are literally a thousand other options besides making the incredibly foolish mistake of saying 'yes' or the seemingly safe, non committal 'maybe.' Marriages, engagements, friendships, and relationships have all ended over this question being answered incorrectly—and no, it's not a trap question. Women are bombarded from childhood with images of what they are supposed to look like and what they are supposed to wear. They are taught to fear fat cells and fatty foods, spend millions on diets and gym memberships and personal trainers. They are gaslit into thinking that being any size larger than zero and not having big firm breasts and not having a wrinkle-free face aglow with the dewiness of youth means they are doomed to grow old alone and unloved. So, they try to fight aging—and the fear of being traded in for a younger model—by having poison injected into their faces, excess skin surgically removed, and their hair constantly colored and touched up. Centuries of societal and systemic misogyny, of telling women they don't measure up, echo in those sad, simple words: *does it make my butt look big?*

My heart breaks a little every time I hear it.

However, I get paid to make them look good. My opinion must be honest, but I still need to be delicate. Why be hurtful when you don't have to be?

I tilted my head to one side and brought my eyebrows together as I looked her up and down yet again. "You're curvy, Lauralee," I replied finally, fluffing the peacock feathers on her shoulders to spread them out further. It was true. Lauralee was about five seven, and maybe could stand to lose a pound here and there. Her hourglass figure had thickened a slight bit once she hit forty, but it was barely noticeable. I'd picked out a green silk dress for her because the color made her green eyes sparkle like emeralds. It clung perfectly to her hips and was cut low in the front to shove off the ample bosom, highlighted by an emerald pendant handing from a gold chain just above the cleavage. I'd braided her long auburn hair into a French braid that dropped about half-way down her back. I'd woven some extra pieces of auburn into the braid to make it thicker. "And there's nothing wrong with that, you know. We'd put Marilyn Monroe on a diet today."

"You're sure?"

"*Of course*, I'm sure! That's why I picked out this dress with the slight shoulder pads and these gorgeous feathers to broaden your shoulders out a bit more, to offset that juicy booty and make your waist look even tinier than it is." So much of beauty is an illusion, I added to myself as I gently tugged a bit on the neckline to bring it down just a smidgen lower on the shoulders. I stepped back away to get a good look and smiled in triumph. "*Voilà!*" I said dramatically with a snap of my fingers. "You look gorgeous, Lauralee. Right off the cover of *Bayou Vogue*. Anna Wintour would approve." Okay, that was an exaggeration, but she did look beautiful. What's a little harmless hyperbole between friends?

"You really think so?" she asked in the voice of a fourteen-year-old girl worried no one will ask her to dance, spinning back around to take another look at herself in the three-way mirror. A happy smile started tugging on the corners of her lips.

"I don't say things I don't mean," I lied, snapping my fingers to give my words more emphasis. Sometimes, you've got to "gay" it up a bit for the straight ladies. "Besides, who wants to be one of those bony-assed skinny popsicle sticks, anyway? Barry Dorgenois didn't marry you because you were built like a pencil, girl. He wanted a woman."

She flushed with pleasure. Her smile widened, dimples appearing in her cheeks. She really was beautiful when she had the confidence to lean into it. "Where were you when I was in high school?" She air kissed my cheeks and booped my nose. "Or college, for that matter." She glanced at her gold Tag Heuer watch and frowned.

"I told you, don't frown. Frowns are the enemy of the best make-up artist." I reached for a brush and smoothed out the little wrinkle she'd put in her perfect make-up above the bridge of her nose. I stepped back and smiled, raising my arms in triumph. "You know, you are just stunning, Lauralee. That green sets off both your eyes and your hair. If you aren't the hottest wife at this party I'll—I'll—"

"Eat your brushes?" Lauralee smiled back at me. "No, no need for that." She turned back to the three-way mirror, checking herself out from every angle and giving herself permission to like what she saw. "What did I ever do without you?"

"Only the Lord knows, and His lips are sealed," I said in as somber a tone as I could muster, but I couldn't keep my face straight once she started laughing "But let's just make sure you never have to find out in the future, okay?"

She beamed at me. "Let me get my checkbook." She checked herself out in the mirror one last time with a pleased smile before heading from her dressing room into the massive master bedroom.

Lauralee Dorgenois was one of my favorite clients, and not just because she was married to one of the richest men in New Orleans—but that didn't hurt, either. I was lucky. She usually wanted my glam expertise at least several times per month— so often she could have listed me as a dependent on her tax returns. She was always texting me photos of clothes she was considering buying, sometimes having me head to the Saks at Canal Place with her so I could give her my expert opinion on everything. I kept hoping she'd take me on one of her Paris shopping trips, with no luck thus far.

Lauralee was at that dangerous age for rich men's wives when they start worrying about getting older, spend hours staring in mirrors looking for new lines and wrinkles, and watch their butt to see if it's started sagging. There's always someone younger looking for a rich older man, after all, and when men start feeling like they're on the downward slide into the grave they think a younger woman will somehow make them magically young again. Lauralee herself was a second wife—I'd never really known what happened to the first Mrs. Barry Dorgenois and wasn't sure how to ask politely. Barry didn't seem like the type who'd want to trade Lauralee in for a younger model, but they never do until it happens. You only had to be around them for about five minutes to see he clearly worshipped the ground she walked on, and *what did I ever do to deserve her* was written on his face every time he looked at her. I'd be willing to bet that the Mississippi River would run dry before Barry Dorgenois would even glance at another woman, let alone think about replacing Lauralee.

But . . . she was his second wife, and Barry had about ten years or so on her.

He didn't *seem* the type to have a mid-life crisis.

I took a deep breath and sat down in a very comfortable wingback chair and pulled out my phone. No messages. No new emails. No missed calls. I opened my social media apps to look at my notifications.

I exhaled. Of course, nothing from Tradd. He was ghosting me.

I'd thought he'd had potential, too. I always think they have potential.

Forget about him, he's not worth it, I reminded myself, he's doing you a huge favor by ghosting you before things might have gotten serious.

Serious, what did that even mean anymore?

It wasn't yet eight o'clock on a Friday night and once Lauralee handed me my check for services rendered, I had no plans for the rest of the night. I'd like to think that even if Tradd had answered one of my text messages I wouldn't have jumped at the chance to see him.

Lord, how many texts messages had I sent him?

I checked and inhaled sharply. *Had I really sent him that many text messages without getting an answer? One, two, three…ten? You texted him ten times without an answer? Yeah, I would run for the hills if I were him, too. Desperate and pathetic, party of one, your table is ready.*

I'd thought Tradd Matherne would be different.

For one thing, I hadn't met him in a bar or on Grindr. We'd met at a birthday party for some girl who worked with my best friend and roommate Kyle Lamothe. I was getting another glass of wine from the flimsy poker table where the haphazard bottles of liquor and wine everyone had brought were placed when a hot guy held out a red cup with a pleading look on his face.

He was handsome in almost nerdy kind of way, with an attractive face and a slender body. His stretch jeans were skintight on his nicely shaped legs.

"Tradd," he said, shifting his cup to his left hand and shaking mine with his right. He gave me a flirty grin. "Where have you been hiding, good-looking?"

"Just standing here waiting for the hottest guy in the room to need a drink," I grinned back at him. "What are you having?"

He leaned in close enough to me that I could smell his cologne and feel his breath on my neck. "Red wine for now." His right hand brushed against my backside as I filled his cup. "Thank you," he said, giving me a slight bow as he took the cup from me. "Want to find a quiet place and talk?"

We found a couple of empty chairs in the back-yard and moved them to a secluded corner. For once, I wasn't fumbling for things to say or worried I was making a fool out of myself. He was smart and funny and sexy, with his brown hair gelled upwards and his almond-shaped brown eyes and thick red lips. I didn't realize how long we stayed out there talking until his friends told him it was time to go.

He asked me for my number, and I figured that was the end of that.

But he called the very next afternoon and asked me out. Our first date had been dinner and a Marvel movie (I'd been right about the nerdy thing—he knew a lot about Marvel and comic books). I was a little surprised when he gave me just a light kiss goodnight, but liked that he was taking it slow. Most guys just hop in the sack and don't want to give you their last name, let alone their number. It seemed romantic. On our second date he'd made me dinner—a kind of tasteless lasagna, but I ate two helpings before we streamed *Guardians of the Galaxy*. Our third date had been nice, too. We went out for a nice dinner—he paid—and then back to my place to watch *Now Voyager*, which he had never seen. On each date we went a little further than the time before.

On the fourth date, after he made me dinner and we watched *The Philadelphia Story*, I knew I was ready. I bit the bullet and spent the night. The next morning, he kissed me goodbye when my Lyft arrived, said he'd text me later . . .

And I hadn't heard from him since.

I sighed again. I was sitting at Lauralee's vanity, her little make-up table with light bulbs all around the mirror. I took a long hard look at myself in the mirror. Okay, maybe I wasn't the best judge of my own looks, but I wasn't that bad, was I? I didn't have snakes for hair and men didn't turn into stone when they looked at me. I had a long oval face with a widow's peak that cursed me to side parts for life. I usually wore my thick brown hair long because it was wavy when shoulder-length. It was cut down close to the scalp because on a wild whim I'd dyed it bright pastel blue a few weeks earlier, regretting it the minute it dried. I gave it a week before buzzing it all off. My best feature was probably my eyes. Big and round and expressive, they were a rich brown with golden flecks, framed by long thick lashes. My nose had a bump in the middle from being broken when I was a kid, but it wasn't offensive.

So why can't I meet someone special? Who wouldn't ghost after spending the night for the first time? Was that *really* too much to ask for?

Gay men are the worst.

Another lonely Friday night. I could sit home watching movies in sweats while eating a tub of ice cream feeling sorry for myself, or I could head out to the Quarter gay bars and look at the same gay men whose faces I saw in those bars every weekend, hoping against hope that this time would be the time I would meet my Mr. Right instead of the usual Mr. Right Now.

I glanced at the vanity surface. Her mail was stacked up in a corner. Being nosy, I sneaked a look at the invitation on the top of the stack and felt my blood pressure rise a little bit. It was an invitation to a fashion show at the Designs by Marigny shop the following night. Designs by Marigny was about as close to couture and high fashion as you got in New Orleans. For a certain class of women in New Orleans, a ticket to one of Marigny's fashion shows was *de rigueur*, although I couldn't see why. I didn't like her clothes. I'd talked Lauralee out of buying a Marigny Orloff original so many times I'd lost count. The clothes didn't flatter women's bodies.

Marigny was also an incredibly unpleasant woman.

She'd hired me to work on her spring show last year. Her check bounced. It took me weeks to finally get my money from her, and I'd vowed to never work for her again.

Fool me once, etc.

I picked up the invitation. It was a dark cream vellum, with black script lettering and the Designs by Marigny logo across the top—three swords crossed over a *fleur-de-lis*.

As I was setting it back down, Lauralee came up behind me and pressed her check into my hand. I folded it, sneaking a glance at the amount before slipping it into my wallet. I kept my face impassive. I wasn't cheap and Lauralee always over-tipped, but *fifty percent*?

Her check would take care of my pending bills, with some left over. I felt a gigantic weight lift from my shoulders. Note to self: always make her up in some variation of tonight's color and palette combinations.

"Have you got big plans for the night?" She asked as I started packing up my make-up case. She'd hated my old case, so she bought me an alligator-skin one from Gucci.

I was too afraid of the answer to look up how much it had cost.

If you can't be rich yourself, you need rich friends.

"Honey, I never have big plans on any night." I replied, snapping the clasps shut. "Probably just me, TCM, and some ice cream like every Friday night."

She was fiddling with her phone, summoning my Lyft.

"Are you going to Marigny's show tomorrow?" I asked innocently.

"Your Lyft is on the way and should be here soon," she said, looking at her phone. "White Prius, driver named Trevor. As for Marigny's show, I doubt it." She shrugged. "You know Marigny's designs just don't look good on me. I want to support a local designer of course, but—" she shuddered. "You'd never let me be caught dead wearing one of her dresses anyway. And after the way she screwed you over last year—"

"Tried—*tried* to screw me over." I corrected her gently, while moving a stray hair away from her forehead.

"It wasn't cool."

"You don't have to hold a grudge against Marigny for me, Lauralee." I winked at her. "I can do that just fine on my own." I air kissed her again and patted her on the arm. "Have a great time, Lauralee—you're going to be the most gorgeous woman there, you know."

I really do love making women feel beautiful.

Lauralee and Barry Dorgenois lived in a brick Georgian style townhouse on Camp Street, about a block or so from the World War II museum in the

Warehouse District of New Orleans. Barry's family money came originally from cotton and sugar, but eventually moved on to oil, shipping, and real estate. He currently was president of their shipping company—they had a fleet of about twenty tankers. The enormous Dorgenois mansion in the Garden District was a historic landmark, but it also came with Lauralee's mother-in-law, Thérèse. It didn't take Barry long to realize that the best way to keep the two most important women in his life happy was by keeping them apart as much as possible, so he bought and renovated this gorgeous place for his wife. Lauralee was talking about selling the townhouse and moving into something smaller, now that her youngest had left for college at Northwestern in Chicago. But I couldn't see her being happy anywhere else. Barry had given her *carte blanche* on how to do the house and she'd made sure it was exactly what she wanted. If I had a dollar for every time she told me how much she preferred the townhouse to "that old barn on Third Street," well, I could retire.

I think it also aggravated Thérèse that her oldest son refused to live in the mansion with her, making Lauralee even happier.

I went out the front door just as a white Prius pulled up and double-parked, the passenger window coming down. "Jem?" The driver was in his late twenties, cute in that way only straight girls understand. He was already past the flush of his youthful beauty, but it hadn't completely gone yet—but it was making a good start at a getaway. His brown hair was thinning on top and his wire-rimmed glasses were smudged and bent a bit. He was wearing a purple LSU T-shirt.

There was a lot of traffic on Camp Street heading to the Quarter, and no sooner had the Prius stopped before a cacophony of horns started blaring.

"Trevor?" I opened the back door. "Or would you rather I sit up front?" Kyle always takes the passenger seat, and will know the driver's entire life story by the time the ride is over. I always ask—but if I'm paying, well, Lauralee is paying, I think I should sit in the back seat to keep a professional distance. I preferred my ride-share drivers to be talking on the phone, to be honest. Then I don't have to worry about whether I should make conversation or not, how friendly I should be, should I tip more if he doesn't talk than I would if he did . . .

Kyle says I worry too much. He's probably right.

"Front's fine," Trevor shrugged. "Don't matter to me."

I sighed and hoisted my make-up case into the back seat, pushed it over, and slid into the seat. Once I'd snapped the seatbelt in place, I pulled out my phone again as he started driving downtown. I went through my social media accounts, liking some things, rolling my eyes at others. The Central Business District was hopping. The sidewalks were clogged with couples and small groups, people jogging or walking their dogs. The outdoor seating areas at restaurants and clubs were packed, and there were cars everywhere.

"Crazy traffic tonight," Trevor said as he turned left onto Poydras. "I think it might be faster to get to the 7th Ward by getting on I-10 and getting off at Claiborne?"

"Makes sense," I nodded, scrolling through my emails. Nothing but junk, so I started deleting them as he swung left onto Loyola and headed back towards the highway. I was tired and stifled a yawn. It had been a long day. I'd gotten up early and taken care of the yardwork before it got too hot, and then I'd cleaned and done laundry before heading over to Lauralee's. Too tired to go out? Of course I could always just take a nap . . .

That was the great thing about New Orleans being open 24/7; you could easily not feel like going out around eight . . . but you could change your mind no matter how much later it was. Some people thought midnight was too early to go out, especially on a weekend.

I closed my eyes as we took the on-ramp past Loyola. It hadn't been a great month for me client-wise. Sure, I could always count on Lauralee needing me once or twice a month (and generously over tipping the high rate I already charged her), but I generally booked more than three or

four other gigs a month. But nothing was film-
ing in New Orleans currently, I'd missed out on a
job working with the touring company of *Mamma
Mia!* playing this weekend at the Saenger and was
beginning to worry I might have to start looking
for work in a salon again—long hours on my feet
washing and cutting and setting hair. Being a freelance make-up artist was better than doing hair
full-time.

Not that there was anything wrong with doing
hair. My grandmother's salon on Magazine Street
had put my father through college and paid for the
house I live in currently. Mee Maw had left me the
house in the 7th Ward on St. Roch when she'd died
a few years earlier. I hadn't grown up in New Orleans, but Mom and Dad loved sending me down
here to stay with Mee Maw for a month or so every summer. That was where I learned how to do
hair and make-up, hanging out in The Beauty Spot
and sweeping up hair and cleaning. I loved all the
stylists who worked for Mee Maw, and it was quite
an education for a young gay boy. I learned to love
The Young and the Restless and *General Hospital*, that
gossip was fun so long as it wasn't mean-spirited,
and by the time I was a teenager I was washing and
setting hair, too. Mom and Dad were a little disappointed I'd decided on cosmetology school instead
of college. Inheriting the house right after my boyfriend of five years dumped me for someone else

seemed like a sign I needed to make a fresh start in New Orleans.

The Prius pulled up in front of the big camel-back double shotgun at the corner of St. Roch and Villere. I thanked Trevor, wrestled the case out and rolled it up the cracked walk to the front steps. I dragged it up, unlocked the front door and stepped inside, rolling the case in behind me before shutting the door.

When the house had been rebuilt after Hurricane Katrina, Mee Maw had turned it from two side-by-side shotgun singles into one big house. She'd always kept it spic-and-span, too. Everything had a place and everything in its place, she used to say. The ceiling fans and shelves didn't have a layer of dirt on them when Mee Maw was alive. I'd let the cleaning slide since I moved in.

My roommate Kyle was hanging from the pole he'd set up in the big front room. Kyle smiled at me and swung gracefully around the pole one more time before dismounting. All he was wearing was a very tight pair of Daisy Duke shorts, and his lean, muscular body was slick with sweat. "There you are," he said, wiping his hands on his shorts. "Did Lee Ann Vidrine call your cell?"

"Lee Ann Vidrine?" She was an occasional client. "No, she didn't."

"She's called the land line at least three times in the last hour," he nodded over to where our landline was sitting on a small round table. It was an old school Princess phone that plugged into the wall; Mee Maw had had it forever and never replaced it. Her old school answering machine was still attached to it, and the message light was blinking a red 3 at me. Lee Ann had been a client I'd inherited from Mee Maw, so she always called the land line. "And no, she didn't say what she wanted. Just for you to call as soon as you get home." He wiped sweat off his forehead. "I'm going to get in the shower. You want to go out tonight?"

"I don't know." I frowned, pulling out my phone and pulling up Lee Ann's number. It went straight to voicemail, so I left a message for her to call me back on my cell and slowly read off the number twice. "Tradd's ghosting me, too."

"I told you to forget him," Kyle called back over his shoulder as he headed to the back stairs, which led to our bedroom suites in the camelback part of the house. "And don't tell me you don't want to go out in case we run into him. That's why we SHOULD go out."

"Okay, okay," I waved, plopping down onto my couch as my phone started making shattering glass sounds—which meant it was a client, and sure enough, when I looked at the screen, it was Lee Ann calling me back.

"Darling please tell me you're free tomorrow night?" she said as soon as I said hello.

"Free for what?" I replied, getting a sinking feel-ing. Lee Ann was a friend of Marigny Orloff's—I'd gotten the gig for her show last year through Lee Ann.

"Marigny needs you for her show tomorrow night, she'll pay double—"

"No."

"Jem, please, she's desperate." Lee Ann pleaded. "And I'll guarantee you get paid."

"Double?" I replied, knowing I was going to say yes and hating myself for it, "But I want to be paid, in cash, before I arrive. The full amount."

"You are amazing!" Lee Ann almost shouted in my ear. "You'll need to be at Designs by Marigny around six—I'll email you all the details." She hung up.

I put my phone down.

Well, I thought, that made up my mind. I need-ed to drink tonight if I was working for that witch tomorrow night.

CHAPTER TWO

The chorus of Taylor Swift's "You Need To Calm Down" broke into my deep sleep and I blearily opened an eye and winced. It was way too bright in my room. I exhaled and reached out a slightly trembling hand to pick up my phone. Shade, my black cat, curled up on the pillow next to mine, gave me side eye, groaned, and closed his eyes again. My own eyes swam into focus and read LEE ANN VIDRINE written across the screen. The time in the upper left-hand corner read 9:47. It was far too early for anyone to be calling a gay man in his twenties on Saturday morning, and one would think Lee Ann would know that by now. Lee Ann was unmarried and always surrounded by gay men. I was tempted to hit decline, but some self-preservation instinct within my foggy brain remembered the gig at Designs by Marigny I'd agreed to last night. I took a deep breath, hit accept, and took the call on speaker. "Lee Ann," I rasped, a little surprised that my voice sounded about the way I felt. "Why are you calling me so early on a Saturday morning? I'm pretty sure this is a violation of the Geneva Convention protocols."

Making a joke was a mistake. Lee Ann has a loud, raucous laugh that carries, and I winced, resisting the urge to turn the volume down. "Well, if you'd answered any of my emails I wouldn't have had to call, so you have no one to blame but yourself." Lee Ann was always able to transfer guilt effortlessly. "And you know how Marigny is, so I thought I'd better call you to make sure you got them, and yes, I already CashApped your fee for tonight, so you don't have to worry about getting paid."

I opened my CashApp and sure enough, it was there. I smiled. "You're pretty trusting to front the money for Marigny," I replied.

"Leave Marigny to me."

"Gladly." I sat up in the bed. My head throbbed and my mouth was dried out, but my stomach was fine. Did we hit a drive-through on the way home last night? I had a vague memory of hot French fries and a milkshake. But nothing was open in the neighborhood that late?

What time had we left Baby Jane's?

I shouldn't have let Kyle talk me into going out last night.

Baby Jane Hudson's was a newish gay bar on St. Claude Avenue, downtown from Elysian Fields. Baby Jane's had been open for less than a year in a space where several gay bars had opened and closed over the years. It wasn't easy luring the gays out of the Quarter, for one thing—there were so many there all in walking distance of each other that it was much more convenient to simply head down to what we locals called The Fruit Loop because you could get a change of vibe and scenery simply by walking a block to a different gay bar. The new owner was a queer actor who'd worked for years on Broadway and retired to New Orleans, buying the space from the former owners, renovating it into a camp paradise. The space's big selling point was the stage—its earlier incarnations had done everything from mud wrestling to burlesque to actual theater, to no avail. Baby Jane's now featured a burlesque show every Friday night—"boylesque," is what they called it—and Kyle had done pole numbers during the show, one to a remix of Rihanna's "Take a Bow" and the second to the remix of Whitney Houston's "My Love is Your Love." Both routines were new, and Kyle insisted that I had to be there because he trusted my honest opinion.

Wondering if I'd run into Tradd the Rat, I'd gotten cleaned up and picked out a nice pair of tight shorts and a sleeveless black T-shirt. The outfit worked. No one was going to be recruiting me to do porn any time soon, but I looked good enough. We'd smoked a joint before heading down there for the first show at eleven. My friend Leon was bartending and kept slipping me a shot with every bottle of Bud Lite he served me. I could remember Kyle's first number, but the second was a bit hazy. I didn't remember what time I'd gotten home, but Kyle's second number couldn't have been before one, could it? The eleven o'clock show had started half an hour late. Leon called it "drag time."

At least I woke up alone.

I glanced around my room. It was a mess. The clothes I'd worn last night had been tossed into a corner.

What a dump. The whole house needed a good cleaning.

Great.

Mee Maw would be horrified at the condition of the house.

I pushed that thought away and rubbed my eyes again. "Lee Ann, let me brush my teeth and have a cup of coffee first and call you back, okay?" I moaned. "You just woke me up and I can't think clearly yet."

"As long as you promise to look at my emails before you do."

"Promise." I disconnected the call and climbed out of bed. I plodded into the bathroom and turned on the water, looking at myself in the mirror. I looked like I'd been run through a blender. Stubble on my upper lip and chin and neck. The whites of my eyes were red and angry. My thick red lips were dry and gummy. I brushed my teeth, scrubbing fur off my teeth and tongue. I turned on the hot water and lathered up, scrubbing my face clean before using an exfoliating scrub—Mee Maw always said you should start taking care of your skin when you're young. "When you've already lost that dewy glow it's already too late," I could hear her like she was there in the room with me. I slipped on a pair of sweats and went downstairs, phone in hand.

While waiting for the Keurig to heat, I opened the mail app. I scrolled through the asks for money from politicians and non-profits, the free iPads or Wal-mart gift cards I'd won without entering anything, emails concerned with erectile dysfunction or asbestos class action suits, there among them were several emails from Lee Ann with the subject line URGENT with more exclamations marks than necessary. When the first one opened, I saw she had shared a Dropbox folder with me. I touched that link and the app opened. There was one shared folder, labelled the COLOR PALETTES AND MODELS.

I frowned as I start clicking on images and they started opening. The first shots were of dresses, hats, shoes, and other accessories. I groaned. The colors were fine—I had shelves and shelves of make-up in my work room so I wouldn't have to buy anything new, but I'd need to make sure I had plenty of everything I need, and clean brushes.

I'd have to do an inventory anyway and maybe make a run to a beauty supply shop.

Then I clicked on an image labeled Scarlett, and when the image finished loading my headache got much worse.

I didn't wait for my cup of coffee to stop brewing. When Lee Ann answered I burst out, "Drag queens? She's doing a runway show with drag queens?" I rubbed my temples and opened the bottle of Aleve I kept in the silverware drawer, dry swallowing two tablets. "I've not really done a lot of drag work, Lee Ann." I should have asked for more money.

"You won the Bourbon Street Awards on Fat Tuesday two years running," she pointed out.

"That's a costume contest, Lee Ann." Held on a stage set up at the corner of St. Ann and Bourbon every year on Mardi Gras, sure, one of the costume contests was for drag—but not *performance* drag. I'd won the non-drag costume event last year for my chandelier costume, which had taken me weeks to build. This past Mardi Gras I'd won for my *Kiss of the Spider Woman* costume, complete with an enormous spiderweb made from chicken wire and papier-maché. I'd done my face up to look like Sonia Braga in the movie and had whipped up a shiny black dress.

"Drag make-up is just extreme stage make-up anyway," Lee Ann went on. "And drag queens are super-hot right now."

"And controversial," I replied. There had been talk at Baby Jane's last night about a possible protest of the show, but it never materialized. There had already been several incidents all over the state. Drag Queen Story Hours at libraries had been disrupted by protesters claiming that having children's stories read to them by drag queens was somehow sexualizing and grooming children. The state legislature was debating legislation banning gender care for trans kids. It was disgusting—more of the old "oh no can't have queers around children!" crap Anita Bryant started fifty years ago all over again. *They can't reproduce so they have to recruit! Pedophiles! Groomers!*

Vile, disgusting, dehumanizing garbage.

Funny how they leave the Catholic Church alone, and child beauty pageants.

It's never really about the children.

Besides, baby—we were born this way.

"Marigny wouldn't mind getting into the drag business, making dresses for the queens," Lee Ann said with a slight laugh. "And with all the anti-drag anti-trans stuff going on now, Marigny wanted to show everyone that she supports the queer community—"

"Her son is gay, isn't he?"

"Her youngest, yes. They both thought it would be fun and inventive and original to use drag queens for the runway show, and then have some of the queens perform at the party immediately after." She paused. "And don't worry about the queens' make-up; they are doing their own hair and make-up. What Marigny wants is for you to help coordinate the looks and maybe do some matching face art on them all? That's why I sent the color palettes for the show—so you can figure out what colors to use on their faces."

"Face art?" That made it more interesting. I didn't believe Marigny was using queens to be supportive—she was doing it for attention. She was probably hoping protestors would show up.

She'd probably *invite* them.

"Lightning bolts, stars, you know, that sort of thing, coordinated with the dresses and their make-up."

Like it was just that easy. I'd have to pack as many color palettes as I could to be on the safe side, and it would be a scramble.

If only make-up was as easy as everyone thinks . . . .

"You just need to be there around six," Lee Ann was saying. "The show itself starts at nine, and there's a cocktail and *hors d'oeurves* party that starts around seven; but you know how that works, no one will show up before eight." Which meant the show wouldn't start at nine, either. Times were seen primarily as suggestions than realities in New Orleans. And with drag queens involved…we'd be lucky to send the first one down the runway by ten.

Punctuality was not prized in New Orleans.

"All right," I said, getting the cream cheese out of the refrigerator for my bagel. "Six it is." I disconnected the call, wondering again at my sanity. A fashion show with drag queens as models? What a nightmare! When I'd done Marigny's last show, the cisgender women models had worn me to a frazzle. Not one had shown up on time. Then we had to rush because Marigny refused to face reality and wanted to get the show started on schedule. I pointed out that I could have them throw on the dresses but their hair and make-up wouldn't be ready "and the longer I stand here arguing with you instead of getting them ready the worse it will look." She finally saw reason, but kept hovering around the dressing room, looking pointedly at her watch and insisting we go faster. By the time the final look went down the runway I was so frazzled I was ready to jump into the river.

And then her check had bounced.

But would this be so bad? Sure, the queens would be late, but they were doing their own hair and make-up. I didn't have to dress them or do anything more than just paint their faces. I looked through the dropbox folder. Marigny's primary color for her line was blue; all the dresses were in varying shades. Silver—I would use silver! Stars and lightning bolts, meteors, the moon . . . the more I thought about the more excited I was getting.

What was that RuPaul quote? We're all born naked and everything else is drag?

I'd just sat down at the table with my coffee and bagel when a shirtless Kyle breezed in the back door, air buds in his ears and his phone attached to his shorts. He was drenched in sweat and grabbed a paper towel to wipe off his face. He popped his ear buds out and put them back in their case, which he carefully placed in the Important Miscellaneous Stuff drawer next to the sink. I envied Kyle his commitment to being fit. His pole dancing was more than enough exercise to keep in shape, but Kyle also lifted weights at the gym three times a week and jogged a couple of miles every morning along the levee. He had the worst eating habits of any gay man I'd ever been around and yet never gained an ounce. He lived on bacon and cheeseburgers and fries and milk shakes and pretty much anything he could get his hands on. He burned off everything he ate, managing to keep that twenty-nine-inch waist and defined body honed.

Me? If I looked at a piece of cake for more than three seconds I could feel my butt getting bigger.

I was lucky if I made it to the gym three times a week, and Kyle usually wound up dragging me, kicking and screaming.

"Guess who's working Marigny Orloff's show tonight?" I asked glumly after swallowing a mouthful of bagel. "I got paid up front, though. And get this—she's using drag queens for models this year."

Kyle got a bottle of water from the refrigerator and gulped half of it down in one swig. "Good for getting paid up front," he said, gasping before finishing the bottle. "And smart. I bet she hired Mary to produce the show for her."

"Mary?"

Kyle grinned at me. His bleached teeth, straightened as a teenager, gleamed at me in the morning light. "You never listen to me," he teased, an old joke between the two of us from that brief period when we'd dated—we both claimed the other never listened. "I told you—remember? Mary Queen of THOTs?"

"Oh yes, of course." How does one forget a drag name like Mary Queen of THOTs?

I'd read about her on-line. *NOLA.com*, the web version of our newspaper, had done a great feature on her (him? them?) when she first moved to New Orleans the summer before last. Mary's real name was Ellis—the last name was lost to me. As Mary, Ellis had built an astonishingly successful career in drag. I'd heard of Mary before she moved to New Orleans. Mary wasn't RuPaul levels of famous but was still a big name in the drag world. Ellis was a triple threat—Mary could sing, dance *and* act. According to the story, Ellis had done a community theater production of *La Cage aux Folles* when he was in high school as one of the show bar's queens ("I had no lines," Ellis remembered in the article, "but I looked *fierce*.") He found a drag mother after moving to San Francisco and started getting bookings around the Bay Area. Soon enough, she was selling out performances all over the country, either headlining local shows or filling cabarets to capacity. She'd worked shows in Vegas, Tahoe, and Reno. She'd even done some television work. Long story short, she fell in love with New Orleans when performing here and decided to make it her home base rather than San Francisco.

She'd talked about opening a drag training school in the article.

"I still think you should go to her school," Kyle was saying. "I keep telling you, you'd kill at drag. You've got the skills, you can sew—"

"But I'd have to get on stage in front of people and perform," I replied. Yes, as a little gay boy I'd dreamed of becoming a star—Broadway, television, movies. I'd made Oscar acceptance speeches in the mirror holding a bottle of shampoo. I could read music, and I could sing some—but was hardly trained and didn't have much of a range. My freshmen year in high school I'd gotten a part in a school play—playing Prince John in *The Lion in Winter*—and it was a disaster. I was terrified, threw up before the curtain went up and again after it went down, and couldn't remember any of my lines. The second performance the next night was even worse.

After that, I gave up any ideas of performing and stuck to wardrobe and make-up ever since.

"The best way to get over stage fright is to face up to it," Kyle shook his head. "It gets easier the more you do it, believe me." He grinned. "And once you hear applause…there's no turning back."

"People would applaud if all you did was stand on stage in a thong," I retorted.

"True." He batted his eyes at me. "But promise me if Mary is producing this show tonight, you'll talk to her about enrolling." Kyle went on. "She does a lot of producing, too—you'd be sure to book gigs."

"All right, if Mary is producing tonight's show, I promise you I'll talk to her about her next workshop," I said, scrolling through the other images in Dropbox. I recognized some of the queens from the local clubs—Floretta Flynn, Desirée laDouché, Tamponia String—but I didn't see Mary's picture and I didn't recognize the others.

Talking wouldn't hurt, right? It didn't mean I committed to enrolling or performing.

"Swear to me you'll talk to her—and if she's not doing this show, that you'll call her." Kyle insisted. "Jem, your *Kiss of the Spider Woman* costume on Fat Tuesday—people are still talking about that. You can sing, you're funny, and you're not a bad dancer, either." He winked. "You just need more practice reading people for filth. But you don't have to be a comedy queen. But as a multi-threat?" He whistled. "You'd be the top queen in New Orleans in no time."

I waved my hand. My head was starting to clear, and the headache was going away. The bagel was settling my stomach and it looked like my Saturday was going to be a good day after all. I'd already gotten paid for tonight's work—thank you, Lee Ann, and good luck getting your old buddy Marigny to reimburse you but not my problem—and Lauralee's check last night would cover the monthly bills with some left over. I wouldn't have to worry about money for a little while, maybe could even get a little bit ahead.

I could check off another month without asking my parents for help.

They always would give me the money but the process I had to go through to get it—sometimes I wondered if it was worth it. It would always start with my mom lecturing me about my irresponsibility and telling me to get a regular paying job, no matter how soul-destroying it might be. As much as I loved doing hair and making people feel beautiful, it was hard to do in a chain salon where they booked people every half-hour, if not every fifteen minutes, didn't let you keep all your tips, charged you a ridiculous chair rental, and there was little to no room to be creative. It was a turn-style, on your feet for eight

41

hours or more, washing and cutting and combing and drying one after another like a production line, chatting and making small talk and having to listen to their gripes and complaints and problems, only to come home physically and emotionally exhausted, the tired running from your aching feet up your tightened calves to the throbbing of the lower back from hunching over all day.

No thanks.

Although sometimes I wondered, when listening to my mother harangue me and sob and weep about my failures as an adult human, if maybe that wasn't worth it to never have to go through this every single time I needed help?

You're going to be thirty before you know it and what do you have to show for it? I could hear my mother's voice ringing in my ears.

God help me if she saw how I'd let the house go.

I suppose I should be grateful. Plenty of parents disowned their children when they came out. Mine didn't approve—that wonderful old *we love you but we don't approve of your lifestyle* dodge they think will give them a Get Out of Hell Free card when they get to the pearly gates—and me leaving Dallas for New Orleans after Mee Maw left me her house had relieved a lot of the pressure on both them and me. I didn't see them very often, we texted or emailed most of the time, and hopefully I wouldn't need their help again. I'd managed to scrape up the money every month to pay everything and buy food for nearly a year…but Mom *had* sent me a check for a thousand dollars for my birthday in April.

Kyle went up the stairs to his master suite in the camelback and I heard water running through the pipes after a few moments.

Top Queen in New Orleans. I grinned at the idea. I think Kyle mainly wanted me to start doing drag so I could be in the boylesque shows at Baby Jane's with him. I shook my head. No, there wasn't any way I could make a living doing drag—at best, it would wind up being a side hustle that wouldn't be cheap. Sure, I could make my own gowns, but fabric wasn't free, and neither were sequins. I could get make-up and wigs and hair extensions at wholesale, sure, but I'd be going through a lot more make-up than I would doing glam. The nice thing about the Broadway roadshows was they provided the make-up for us and had also already defined the looks. Those were the easiest gigs, really—unless you got some diva actor or actress who complained about everything and treated you like something they'd stepped in.

There were far too many of those out there.

I finished my bagel and made one more cup of coffee while I scrolled through the images of the queens I'd be working on tonight. Lee Ann's email also explained the aesthetic Marigny was going for with the show, but from what Lee Ann was describing it didn't seem too difficult or intense, the problem was time. If I painted their faces, I'd have to monitor for touch-ups every time they changed. I probably was undercharging, the more I thought about it, and remembering what a pain in the butt Marigny was to work with that last time. She was unfiltered, to put it nicely, which meant there had been a lot of hurt feelings and indignation not only from her models but from the entire crew working backstage. I'd found myself sneaking out to the bar for a belt of gin far too often to stay as sober as I should have been, but she was so nasty and mean-spirited I didn't care.

I rolled my eyes. I'd forgotten how awful she was to work with afterwards because I was so furious about that check bouncing.

But this was the last time I'd work for Marigny Orloff, no matter how much Lee Ann begged or was willing to pay me.

Because I doubted she'd changed much since the last show.

CHAPTER THREE

Designs by Marigny occupied an enormous lot on a corner of St. Charles Avenue and Nashville Street. It was an expensive address in New Orleans. The size of the lot pushed its value to over a million alone, not taking into consideration the mansion itself or the outbuildings. A brick fence about six feet tall covered in coral stucco plaster ran along the sidewalk, giving the surrounding yards privacy. The house was built sometime after the Civil War. It was an enormous three-story plantation style house with the obligatory round columns supporting the roofs of the wraparound galleries on each floor. The railing on the first floor gallery was covered with ivy, and at the front right corner bougainvillea cascaded over the railing and dropped down behind the rose bushes. I could spy the roof of an enormous tent set up behind the house. Her shows were always in the backyard. The runway went down the steps from the rear gallery and always along and through the gardens in the backyard, with chairs set up discreetly in seating areas between the flower beds and trees.

I paused when I reached the corner of the building. There was some traffic coming up and down Nashville, and the street was lined on both sides with parked cars. I remembered there was a beautifully laid out garden and gravel parking area in the back near the carriage house—she also rented the yard out for weddings, and part of her business was designing wedding gowns. I suppressed a grin, remembering how ugly the gown she'd closed the show last fall with had been. The model was beautiful, slender, with a nice shape to her. The wedding dress had not fit properly, but I couldn't imagine any female shape that could possibly be flattered by that strange silhouette.

Or maybe, I just didn't like her designs because I didn't like her. I could be petty like that.

The tent covered the entire back yard. It had been anchored to the brick fence and brackets attached it to the second floor gallery. Uniformed personnel were setting up strategically located bars, while others were setting out white folding chairs in neat rows throughout the garden. Just like the last show, the runway—a red carpet, of course— descended the back stairs and then wove in and around the garden, with more seating in corners where the models could stop, twirl, and show off their dresses. More people in uniforms were carrying covered heating dishes for food into the carriage house, which ran the length of the backyard at the back property line.

"Jem! There you are." Marigny Orloff descended the back steps from the gallery with a strained look on her face.

Like always, her long, carefully colored blonde hair was tied back into a braid dropping down her back. Someone, well into her cups at the last show, had told me rather nastily that Marigny wore it that way because she believed the weight of the braid would pull the skin on her face tighter and eliminate those pesky lines on her face. "An Uptown facelift," the woman had added with a cruel laugh. As for what she was wearing…

I always found it interesting that New Orleans' only serious, independent fashion designer didn't know how to dress her own body to look its best. I wouldn't trust someone who couldn't make a flattering dress for herself to make one for me, but clearly, society women in New Orleans didn't have the same scruples. Her long dress was made of some bright, shiny blue material that gave her pale skin a bluish tint. It was in an Empire style, with the pushed-up and squished together breasts created by the square neckline with the rest of the dress falling away from the high waist cinched together just below the breasts. She barely made five three in her heels, and while the Empire style was perfect with women with short torsos and large breasts, Marigny was low waisted, making it a fashion *faux pas*. From the looks of her make-up, she'd taken none of my freely given advice and caked on much more than was necessary. The point of make-up was to enhance and conceal—done properly most people wouldn't notice you were wearing any, particularly given the soft, flattering lighting mounted inside the tent.

Marigny was wearing so much make-up a myopic bat could see it in candlelight.

Her eyebrows had been penciled on, a look I don't care for, and she had a triangular, cat-like face with prominent cheekbones sharp and hard enough to cut diamonds, and she must have had filler put into her lips. Beneath her make-up she looked shiny and waxy, and there was a tell-tale line from the corners of her lips up into her cheeks which was a tale-tell sign of fillers and Botox. I wasn't sure how old Marigny was—I just knew her youngest son was in his mid-thirties, so she had to be in her upper fifties at the least. But she did look good for her age, even with the garish make-up and bad dress.

"Nice dress," I commented politely as she approached.

"Thank you for stepping in at the last minute," she replied, brushing off my compliment, because compliments from the help don't matter to women like Marigny Orloff. "Everything is set up in the show room—dressing tables, mirrors, everything you could want. Ellis is already here—"

"Ellis?"

"Ellis, Mary, whatever you want to call her," she waved me off, "Just ask her where she wants you and what she wants you to do." She strode off down the walkway past the bubbling fountain—which seemed to be a bronze of three muscular nude male youths toasting each other, the water bubbling out from their goblets. She shouted something at one of the caterers, and I took that chance to roll my case up the walk, drag it up the back stairs, and let myself in the back door.

Designs by Marigny had originally been built as a single-family residence for a wealthy high society family. If I wasn't mistaken, it had been designed by Henry Howard, one of the city's most noted architects of the nineteenth century and whose surviving work usually was registered as a historic landmark. Marigny's grandfather had bought it sometime after World War I. The rumor was the Orloffs got rich bootlegging during Prohibition, but that money had mostly dried up in the decades since Prohibition was repealed. Marigny was the last of the family, holding onto the house with an iron grip. When she'd set up

49

shop as a designer, she'd redone the downstairs to turn it into a showroom, with a work room set up for alterations, trying on clothes, and getting them fitted properly in the back.

That was the room I entered when I opened the French doors. Tables and mirrors had been set up everywhere, and a good-looking man was sitting in a wingback chair, his iPhone pressed to his ear. He nodded at me when I walked in. He was wearing very tight form-fitting black jeans, which outlined beautifully shaped legs. His tight black T-shirt had *I don't think we're in Kansas anymore* written in a gorgeous flowing gold script across the chest. His feet were in leather sandals, and his toenails were alternately painted gold and purple. His head was shaved, and his eyebrows had been plucked to thin arched lines over his big gray eyes. He had great bone structure, with strong cheekbones over hollow cheeks, a cupid's bow of a mouth, and a cleft in his chin.

"Uh huh, uh huh, uh huh," he was saying in a lilting soothing tone into the phone. "So, yes, darling, don't let him get the best of you. You come on down here and you do the runway proud, show that little jerk he can't hurt you, and forget him. Oh, you're welcome, darling, any time, what are friends for? See you soon," and he made kissing noises before disconnecting the call and rolling his eyes at me as he stood up. He was nearly five ten, which put him at around four or five inches taller than me.

His arms were tanned and muscular and completely smooth. His plain fingernails were cut short. "You must be my back-up, Jem." He said with a warm smile, holding out his hand to shake mine. "I'm Ellis Ikehorn, better known as Mary Queen of THOTs when I perform, and I'm producing this nightmare and wonder what horrible thing I must have done in a previous life to deserve this?" He rolled his eyes "Whatever it was, it must have been *bad*."

"Ellis, lovely to meet you, yes I'm Jem Richard." I said, laughing and shaking his hand.

"You're Kyle's roommate, aren't you?" He beamed at me. One of his front teeth was chipped and there was a crooked incisor on his lower row of teeth. "Kyle keeps telling me you need to register for my school." He looked closely at me, narrowing his eyes for a few moments before snapping his fingers. "You were *Kiss of the Spider*-woman on Fat Tuesday, weren't you?"

I nodded, pleased. "I was."

"You looked *fantastic*!" He gushed. "And you don't do drag regularly?"

"I only do drag for costumes," I replied. "And I have to admit I don't have a lot of experience doing drag queens' faces. But I was told—"

"No worries on that score, they're doing their own faces, you're only here to help me pull them together into a cohesive look." He led me over to a table. "Why don't we just set you up here, and the queens can come over to you when they're ready?" He scowled. "They all should be here already, but when has a drag queen ever been on time?" He rolled his eyes. "Honestly, I swear sometimes the only reason I was successful was because I was *prompt* and a professional. Some of these girls…" he shook his head again. "Lee Ann said she was sending you the aesthetic we're going for? Stars over the right eye and lightning bolts over the left?"

She hadn't said that, but it was fine. "Yes, but—"

"Perfect!" He threw his arms around me and gave me a tight squeeze before squealing in my ear, "Floretta! Nefertiti!" He abandoned me to run greet two men who'd just walked in from the backyard. "You girls are late!"

"Huh. You should be grateful we showed up at all for this," one of them said with a sneer. "She never did pay us for that bridal shower we performed at."

"I told you Lee Ann and I would make sure you got paid," Ellis lowered his voice, and I turned back to getting my station set up, trying to make it look like I wasn't listening. *So, I wasn't the only one Marigny Orloff tried to screw out of paying,* I thought as I lined up my brushes and got out my blush palettes. Based on the gowns in Lee Ann's dropbox, the stars and lightning bolts made little artistic sense to me, but I wasn't a designer of Marigny's caliber, either. I had to give the woman props for keeping her doors open and her business going, especially since I thought she had little actual designing talent. I hated her clothes, would never send any of my clients to her door to buy a dress. Her clothes weren't cut to flatter the female body—I wasn't even sure if she had a genuine artistic vision.

If she did, I hadn't been able to figure it out.

I slipped out as Floretta and Nefertiti got undressed and started working on pulling themselves together. I grabbed a bottle of water from a tub filled with ice on the back gallery deck As the natural light of the sun continued fading, the lights set up beneath the tent sky gave everything a soft, gentle glow. Maybe Marigny knew what she was doing, after all, I mused. The shadows and gentle light gave the garden an almost romantic air, and I pictured drag queens strutting down the paths in Marigny's ugly dresses—yes, now the colors made sense, as well as the stars and lightning bolts in the colors and glitter requested. The low light would make sequins and glitter sparkle and bring the clothes to life.

Stronger light would have made the queens' make-up garish. This? This would make them look beautiful.

The slick bottle slipped out of my hands and rolled back behind the bar. Swearing under my breath, I walked around the tub and looked for the bottle. It had bounced under the bar, back where I couldn't reach it without getting on my hands and knees and crawling under there. It was going to be that kind of night, I thought, irritated, as I crept underneath the bar. I had just put my hand on the bottle when I heard Marigny's voice. "I told you I can't talk now," she said in a very low voice. "I don't care if it's inconvenient for you! Your convenience isn't my problem." There was a moment of silence, and I realized she was talking on her cell phone.

Awkward.

I was about to make my presence known when she spoke again. "You know the deal." Her voice was still low, but now had taken on a threatening tone to it. "I told you what would happen if you don't come up with the money. I don't care about my reputation, but you care about yours—do you really think you could hold your head up in this town in public ever again if everyone knew? So you'd better get me that money or you'll be very sorry."

I heard the crunch of her shoes against the runner and peered out from under the cloth, seeing her walk towards the back steps of the house.

If I didn't know better, I'd say she was blackmailing someone.

Well, it wasn't any of my business. I crawled out from under the bar with my bottle of water and followed the path to the house, going slowly so I wouldn't risk running into Marigny. But just when I reached the steps the door opened and a man in a tux stepped out, talking a mile a minute on his cell phone. He smiled at me and winked as we passed each other on the steps.

Jackson Orloff was Marigny's youngest son (of three), and her business partner in Designs by Marigny. Jackson was one of the first people I'd met when I moved here three years ago—we met at happy hour at Good Friends, started chatting, and had become friendly. Jackson wasn't my type—but he was nice looking in an Irish setter kind of way. He had strawberry blonde hair, cornflower blue eyes, and was a little on the stocky side. He was smart and funny, making me laugh without seeming to try. We were bar friends—we didn't share phone numbers, but we always said hello and had a genial chat whenever we ran into each other. I liked him, but didn't think we'd ever progress to anything closer than being acquaintances. He was a bit of a snob, for one thing—I didn't care if his mother was designing clothes for some movie or television star; I didn't care about Mardi Gras krewes or royalty or New Orleans society—which Jackson made clear was important to him.

Me? I just wanted to do my job, get paid and enjoy my life. I didn't see how dedication to that sort of thing made anyone's life better, but hey, to each their own, you know?

There were supposed to be ten queens total—Ellis was producing the show, so he wasn't walking—but as the clock kept creeping closer to eight, we were still two queens short. I was kept too busy to notice anything else—helping queens into their corsets, their pads, their gowns—while painting images on their faces when it was time for them to sit in my chair.

"How tall are you?" I heard Ellis ask from behind me as Tamponia String left my chair.

"I'm five six," I replied, wiping the table clean with a sanitary wipe. "Why?"

"Please tell me you wear a men's size eight shoe."

"I do," I replied cautiously. "Why are you asking?"

"Turn around." I did, to see Ellis looking me up and down thoughtfully. "You are almost exactly the same size as Trailor Swift."

Uh oh. "And?"

"Trailor just called," Ellis gave me a rueful smile. "She broke her ankle, so can't make it, so we're a model short—"

"Oh, no, no." I waved my hand. "Sorry, Ellis, but—"

"Three hundred dollars? And you get to save the show?" He winked at me. "Trailor was going to wear the wedding gown at the end. Haven't you always wanted to be a bride?"

"I don't think I ever want to get married," I retorted. "Seriously, Ellis, can't you get someone else? You *have* to know someone you can get at short notice?"

"They'd never get here on time, and we'd have to start late—Marigny would lose her mind! No one needs to see that," Ellis said grimly. "Look, you *killed* on Fat Tuesday, I know you can do this."

"But I don't have padding or boobs or a wig—"

Ellis clapped his hands. "Queens, may I have your attention please?" Silence descended. "Trailor broke her ankle and can't make it, but the show must go on." He gestured at me. "Jem here is the right size to fit into her gowns, but we need to get her made up and her hair done and she doesn't have any wigs—"

Every eye in the room turned to me.

There was dead silence. I was about to decline the opportunity again when Floretta snapped her fingers, "Come on girls, we've got to turn this boy into a Queen!"

And they fell upon me.

CHAPTER FOUR

"Close your eyes," Ellis commanded, and I obliged. I heard the hiss of an aerosol can and felt something being sprayed onto my face. "Open."

I opened my eyes to see Ellis' big brown eyes narrowed as he examined my face. He place a hand under my chin and tilted my head back, then turned it from one side to the other. "How do I look?" I asked hesitantly. I'd been making people up for years now, but this was the first time I'd let someone else do my face. I was wearing hip padding borrowed from one of the other queens—"don't worry about it," she'd said, waving away my thanks—and one of Ellis' enormous, country star red bouffant wigs.

In answer, he just smiled and spun my chair around until I was facing a mirror surrounded by light bulbs. My jaw dropped and my eyes widened.

I looked…*beautiful.*

He'd sprayed my face with red glitter spray, which wasn't noticeable until it caught a light and flashed red fire. My eyes had been outlined like an Egyptian queen, with the upper and lower lines extending out into a single line about a quarter inch outside the corners of my eyes. The foundation he'd used blended into my natural skin tone on my neck, and he'd painted my lips bright red, extending them a bit above and below to make them look thicker. Some of the other queens had come over while he was quickly making me up—he was much faster than I was—making suggestions and sometimes helping. Floretta had drawn the lightning bolt over my left eye and the star on the right in an electric blue, with glitter mixed into the paint so the symbols sparkled and shone when catching the light. My thick nose had been narrowed and blush painted upwards on my cheeks to give me the illusion of cheekbones.

"You really look gorgeous," Floretta called over as she touched up her lips.

"I do," I said softly, smiling at myself in the mirror. "But—"

"But what?" Ellis replied.

"I—I don't know if I can go through with this." I could feel the terror starting to clutch at my stomach, the goosebumps coming up on my arms, and the fear creeping into my brain. "I'm sorry, Ellis, but—"

"It's normal to have jitters before you go out on stage," Ellis reassured me, putting a hand on each of my shoulders and leaning down so his face was next to mine in the mirror. "I've been doing this since I was seventeen and I still have to talk myself into going out on the stage."

"But—"

"Remember," he whispered in my ear, "Jem might be afraid to walk the runway, but you're not Jem anymore."

"I'm not?" I glanced at his reassuring smile.

"You're—" He made a face. "We need a name for her, girls! We can't just send her down the runway without a name!" He winked at me in the mirror. "Do you have any ideas?"

Sometimes Kyle and I would drink wine and smoke weed and come up with hilarious drag names. I usually could literally rattle off ten names to Kyle without even giving it a second thought.

So, of course, now that I needed a name, I was drawing a blank.

"Here," Ellis pressed a plastic cup into my hand with a clear goldish-yellow liquid in it. "Drink this—liquid courage, and remember, you're going to be fine." He glanced around again. "A name? Anyone? Come on, I know you girls are more creative than this!"

I sniffed the cup. Tequila. My stomach was twisting into nervous knots and the smell of the liquid didn't help. *Get a grip,* I told myself, grabbing onto the arms of my chair with both hands. I was sweating beneath the enormous red wig I was wearing, and I could feel the tickle of a drop of sweat running down the center of my back. I took another good look. I looked stunning— as pretty and feminine as any of the other girls in the dressing room. My slight build helped, of course. I liked the way the star and lightning bolts over my eyes looked. The tight red-sequined dress clung to the padding on my hips and the deep neckline of the dress exposed a lot of the rubber breast plate I'd borrowed from one of the others. Ellis had taped the fake boobs together to make the cleavage was even deeper before spraying red glitter in there. The red pumps were pinching my toes, and I was nervous about the heels. I'd worn heels before for my Fat Tuesday costumes, but they were always a challenge.

"Come on girls, she needs a name," Floretta called from over by the door to the back gallery. The queens were lining up, ready for Ellis to send them walking down the runway. They had all practiced earlier that morning, but I had to wing it.

Which didn't help settle my nerves at all.

These pumps had lower heels than my *Kiss of the Spider Woman* outfit, so I should be fine.

Don't think about stumbling, I reminded myself.

But yes, even I had to admit I looked prettier than I would have thought. Ellis was a master of drag make-up. Usually when I did drag as a costume, the look of the costume and its effect were more important than looking pretty. I had made any number of women over the years look and feel beautiful…but had never done it for me. And red was most definitely my color when it came to wigs, dresses and lip gloss.

I looked pretty.

I also doubted that I could recreate this look by myself.

I pulled out my phone and took a quick selfie to text to Kyle, typing *I feel pretty and witty and gay* before sending it. I took a deep breath and downed the tequila. It was good tequila—it didn't burn yet still had all the flavor and went down smooth. I felt heat spreading out into my bloodstream and the knot in my stomach started to untangle. *I can do this*, I reminded myself again, *it's not like I've got to sing or dance or remember lines. I just must not trip or stumble. And need to have an attitude as I walk.*

"Can you think of a name?" Ellis whispered, taking the empty plastic cup and tossing it into the trash. "Just something temporary, it doesn't have to be your official drag name. We need a name before I can start sending people down the runway."

"*Official* drag name?"

Ellis barked out a laugh. "You look good in

drag, honey. If you want to start booking gigs and performing, you're going to need a name…but we just need something now to introduce you as you walk out onto the runway."

"You really think so?"

He reached down and grabbed my free hand and squeezed it with both of his. "I really think so, Jem."

I believed him.

I stood up, putting my hands on the table for balance in case the heels got away from me. The heels were more of a wedge than a stiletto—I couldn't have handled a stiletto—but when I let go of the table, I was steady on my feet. I took a few steps. Piece of cake. I smiled at Ellis. *Just don't trip when you're out there*, I reminded myself.

"Who's your favorite movie star?" Ellis asked, futzing with the back of my dress.

"Movie star?" My mind went completely blank. "Channing Tatum?"

"No, no, no, a woman. You have a favorite singer? TV star? Character from a movie? Book? Anything." He straightened my wig a bit. Ellis stepped back and looked at his handiwork, smiling in pleasure.

"Marie LaHeaux?" I blurted out.

"Not bad, but no. It's clever, but—" He shook his head. "I mean, it's a good one, but I don't know if I'd risk bad juju like that, you know? When it comes to voodoo and spooky stuff, I think it's better to leave it alone. Oh my God!" He snapped his fingers. "I've got it. Joan Crawfish." I must have made a face, because Ellis quickly added, "Oh, not for a permanent name, honey, just for tonight." His eyes lit up. "And when you go out in that gold and kind of metallic looking dress I'll call you Joan the Maid of New Orleans!"

I started giggling and hiccupped. The tequila had gone straight to my head, which was probably not a good thing. "That's fine." *Thash fine* was how it sounded to me.

Not a good sign. No more shots for me.

"You're not going to be stuck with it, we can come up with something better and more permanent later if you'd rather," Ellis directed me to the back of the line of queens waiting to be introduced and sent down the runway. I heard my phone chime—a text, probably Kyle replying to my drag face—and took some deep breaths as Ellis opened the door. I heard an announcer calling out the name of each queen as she went through the door to applause from the crowd in the yard.

Was I really doing this? My palms got damper as I got closer to the French doors. And then Ivana Getlaidt was going out through the door, sashaying and swaying her over-emphasized hips as she waved to the applause.

My stomach clenched.

It was my turn.

Ellis whispered in my ear, "Slay, queen, slay!" as he put his hand in the small of my back and propelled me out onto the back gallery just as Ivana reached the bottom of the stairs, posed in one direction before turning and posing in the other as her name came out of the loudspeakers discreetly set up in the garden. She turned sharply, walked out to where the path branched and turned to the right.

The lights were shining right into my eyes as I made my way down the stairs carefully—the wedge heel was a godsend, a stiletto would have sent me sprawling—and when I reached the bottom, whomever had the microphone announced, "And making her New Orleans debut is Miss Joan Crawfish!"

There were cheers and some applause, punctuated by flashes of camera lights as I posed from one side before turning to the other, doing the royal wave with my right hand while placing the left one on my hip. I realized, turning from one side to the other, where Ellis had gotten the name from—the color of my dress was red as boiled crawfish. I took a deep breath and started walking. I'd watched enough *Project Runway* and *America's Next Top Model* to know how the sashay runway walk went—lift the knees high, cross a foot in front of the other with every step so your hips would swing—and remembered to stop and pose every time I reached a turn in the path. I couldn't make out the faces of anyone in the chairs because the lights were focused on the makeshift runway. *You can do this you can do this you can do this* I kept repeating to myself while walking, aware people were taking pictures of me with cameras and with cell phones.

So, this is how it felt like to walk a red carpet, I thought. I kind of liked it.

When I reached the bend in the path closest to the gate leading outside, I became aware of noises and some commotion coming from the other side of the fence. I kept my smile plastered on my face—my cheeks were starting to ache a little—but tried glancing over to the gate surreptitiously. I could see the headlights of cars and the red glow of taillights going past in either direction on Nashville through the gate at the end of the gravel area. Other than that, I couldn't see much of anything that might be going on out there. I kept walking, ignoring the sounds from the other side of the fence, and finally somehow made it back up the back steps as the first queen, Floretta Flynn, came out the door in her next dress—we were all scheduled to wear three before a break, and then three more to finish. She winked at me as we passed each other at the doorway, and inside the dressing area was a quick-change madhouse. Ellis unzipped me and I let the dress fall, stepping out of it and carefully rehanging it as I got down my next dress—a surprisingly lovely seafoam green dress with dozens of sparking crystals sewn into it—and stepped into it, working it up over the hip pads and over the breast plate. I zipped up Ivana, and she returned the favor before I checked her make-up and mine to make sure everything was still perfect, no touch-ups needed.

Marigny's clothes looked bad on women, but were perfect for drag.

"What's going on outside?" I whispered to her as we lined back up to go back out for our second run.

"More protesters." Ivana made a face. "Because, you know, *drag queens* are the biggest threat to public safety." She waved a hand. "Someone really needs to check with the straights to make sure they're okay." She scowled. "I *wish* I had the power to make people gay. I sure wouldn't be doing drag shows for spare change, I'll tell you that."

"I bet Marigny decided to use drag queens tonight because she *hoped* protesters would show up," the queen in front of her, Tequila Sunrise, said over her shoulder. "More publicity for her, you know, and her show." She rolled her eyes. "And she gets to claim to be an ally for the queer community. Everyone wins." She mimed sticking a finger down her throat and throwing up.

I frowned.

Were we safe here?

I remembered the cops at the front gate. Neither had made me feel safe.

Could we trust the cops to protect drag queens?

What I'd gathered from reading on-line was that the attacks on drag queens—turning them into some existential threat to all that was good and decent in the world, grooming and sexualizing children—was an off-shoot of transphobia. To the ignorant, transwomen and drag queens were the same thing, which wasn't true. Yes, some drag queens were trans and some transwomen started the process of transitioning by doing drag. But a Venn diagram of transwomen and drag queens didn't form a perfect circle. But haters who don't understand and refuse to learn always dismiss transwomen as men in dresses, hence drag queens. They started targeting Drag Queen Story Hours and "family friendly" drag shows under the guise of "protecting" children.

Yet you never see them protesting in front of Catholic churches or schools—or anywhere child abuse regularly does occur. You know, it's usually youth pastors, priests, coaches, Scout leaders, and camp counselors.

I didn't like Marigny, but if she had decided to use drag queens as models to draw protesters to get publicity, that was . . . well, hadn't she put us all in danger?

Just because no one's shot up a drag show yet doesn't mean they never will.

But before I could ask anything else it was my turn to go back out through the door and down the steps again. Then I was walking through the garden again and back up the stairs. I put on the gold dress so Ivana could zip me up, and Ellis was pressing another plastic cup of tequila into my hand. "You're doing great," he whispered as I downed the second shot. I coughed this time, but it went down smooth. I made a note to ask Ellis what brand it was—I was always up for a new tequila. And then somehow, I was going back down the stairs, my mind fuzzier from the second shot, but I managed to somehow make it all the way around without stumbling or making a fool of myself.

"All right, ladies, we have a half-hour before the last three walks," Ellis clapped his hands, silencing the buzz of conversation. "This is the time to grab a smoke or use the bathroom."

I did have to go to the bathroom, so after taking the Maid of New Orleans dress off and carefully hanging it up again, I slipped on a white terrycloth robe with make-up smeared all over the collar and slipped out into the hallway. Peeling off the hose and the hip pads wasn't as easy as you'd think. As I struggled in the bathroom, I thanked God that I wasn't a woman.

Then again, a woman wouldn't be wearing the hip padding.

I opened the door after drying my hands and heard voices, but not from the direction of the dressing room. As I shut the bathroom door behind me, I heard a male voice say distinctly, "If you do this, Marigny, I will ruin you."

"You don't scare me," she replied scornfully. "What do you think you can do to me? I'll tell you what—nothing. There's *nothing* you can do to me, and I am through being afraid of you. You can't stop me from telling the truth—no one can."

I heard footsteps, then the side door to the gallery slammed shut.

Who had she been talking to? Should I be nosy and stick my head out into the showroom? While I was deciding I heard another door open and shut. Now curious, I walked out of the hallway into the dimly lit showroom, which made up two-thirds of the first floor. Marigny wasn't planning on the party moving indoors at any time during the evening, apparently. I hadn't noticed the disarray in the showroom because I'd come in the back. But it was hard to miss it. Mannequins were scattered about, some completely bare, others in a stage of half-dress; like it had been time to change the clothes showcased on them but they hadn't been able to finish before the party started. I walked quickly across to the front door and opened it. There was no sign of the man Marigny had been talking to, but I could see the tops of protest signs over the top of the fence, with the off-duty cop still standing in front of the gate.

Of all things to protest—a fashion show?

I turned around and gasped as I bumped into someone.

"I'm sorry, excuse me." I stepped back, feeling the blood rushing up into my face as I looked up into an almost impossibly perfect male face.

He was wearing a camel hair suit jacket over tan slacks, with pale blue Oxfords on his feet. His shoulders were wide and broad, his silk dress shirt pulled tightly across his chest—the buttons were straining over the deep cleavage. His waist was small, and his arms looked powerful inside the jacket. He was taller than me—almost all men are—but he was about five nine, maybe five ten. His face was ridiculously handsome, his skin that olive color that tans so beautifully, and his cheeks and chin looked smudged from the slight bluish-black shadow that had grown in since he had last shaved. His eyes were the green of the sea where it was shallow, with golden flecks that danced in the dim light. His lips were thick and sensual, his nose perfectly sculpted and centered between two strong, determined cheekbones. His lashes were long and dewy. He couldn't have been much older than thirty.

He grabbed onto my arms with both big, strong, calloused hands and balanced me carefully. "Sorry, didn't mean to sneak up on you like that." He smiled pleasantly. "You're Joan, aren't you?"

I felt myself blushing even harder. "Well, just for tonight. I'm usually just the glam squad, but someone dropped out last minute and I could fit into her dresses so…here I am." *Girl, THIS is why you're sin-*

gle—you turn into a blithering idiot every time you're around a hot guy. No wonder Tradd ghosted you.

"First time?" He put his hand under my chin and tilted it up, looking at both side of my face intently. "You'd never guess. And you owned the runway." He winked at me. "All right, I'll let you get back to your show."

As he closed the front door behind him, I realized he was the man I'd just heard arguing with Marigny.

I resisted the urge to go running after him, get his number, give him mine, throw myself in front of the wheels of his car, something, anything to get him to stay.

But as I walked slowly back to the dressing room, I realized he must be straight. I'd have noticed a man that good-looking from five hundred paces, so if I'd never seen him before he probably didn't frequent gay bars—or hook up apps, for that matter—because there was no way I could forget him. Those eyes, those shoulders, the strength in those hands . . . I shivered in delight as I opened the door to the madness that was the dressing room. Ivana and Ellis descended upon me like seagulls on a French fry with my first dress for the second round.

Ellis kept pushing tequila shots into my hand and I downed them without even thinking about it as the rest of the night sped past in a blur—well, the blur also probably had something to do with the tequila shots—but before we knew it, it was time for all of us to take a triumphant stroll around the makeshift runway last time. I could barely see through the wedding veil and had to carry the train so I didn't step on it. Marigny herself walked behind me, clapping for the audience as she reveled in their approving applause. I didn't get it myself—the dresses I'd worn were pretty but neither functional nor flattering, and the silhouettes would only work with a certain body type—hence the corset Ellis had strapped me into like a straitjacket.

But I wasn't one of her customers, either.

I also couldn't help thinking I could construct the clothes better than the ones I'd been wearing, at least. But they'd been fitted to another figure, and I wasn't precisely the same size and shape as the queen I'd replaced, Trailor Swift.

Back in the dressing room, Ivana unzipped me one last time and I returned the favor. She unlaced my corset, and I took my first deep, decent breath in hours. As I used cold cream to clean the make-up off my face after placing the wig on a holder, Ellis pulled up a chair and sat down next to me. "You've never done drag before tonight?"

"Only for costumes and even then, not often." I admitted as I wiped my face clean. My skin almost sighed in relief once the paint came off. "I only did *Kiss of the Spider Woman* on Fat Tuesday because I liked the idea more than me doing drag."

"You're a natural," Ellis said, taking a tissue and wiping at my forehead. "You've already got the walk down and mastering heels are half the battle." He pressed a business card into my hand. "If you want to come to my next drag school, it starts in two weeks." He glanced around, and leaned into me, "I'll only charge you half-price because I think you have what it takes to be a star."

"Thanks," I replied, slipping his card into my make-up case, thinking how excited Kyle would be when I told him I'd gotten the Mary Queen of THOTs stamp of approval.

Ellis kissed my forehead. "Think about it, seriously. You're a natural."

CHAPTER FIVE

"Are you staying for the party?" Ivana asked me as she zipped her wig case closed. Without make-up or padding or her larger-than-life persona, "Ivana" was a freckle-faced ginger boy somewhere in his late twenties. His hair was that shade of red that's closer to a yellowish-orange, like a match flame—I always think of it as Archie Andrews hair—and he was cute with his snub nose and round chin and ears that stuck out a bit. Without his make-up on he looked like a child. He was thin and shorter than me by a few inches. I could count both his ribs and his abs as he pulled on a collared pullover over his head. But he had strong, thick thigh and calves. "I don't know if I want to try to get a Lyft with those protestors out there and carrying my stuff? Might as well paint a target on me and be done with it, girl." He clucked his tongue and grinned at me. "My real name is Tommy." He said as he turned back to his mirror. He also had a bit of a parish accent, what New Orleanians refer to as "yat"—"zink" instead of "sink," "warsh" instead of "wash," that sort of thing.

The story is they're called yats because they say *where y'at* instead of *how are you?*

"The protestors are still out there?"

"Mmm-hmmm." He was brushing out his curls, liberally applying gel to flatten them out. "You'd think they'd have better things to do on a Friday night—oh, wait." He dropped his voice on the final two words for dramatic effect, a hand gracefully rising to his throat. "I guess that's why Marigny canceled the performance."

"Performance?" I rubbed cold cream on my face and started wiping off the thick make-up. I was going to have to use an astringent when I got home to clean my pores. Maybe a cucumber mud mask?

"Yes, some of the girls were going to perform for the party, too." He dropped his hairbrush into his bag and turned to smile at me. I hadn't noticed his clear braces before. "Marigny paid them, but she thought it was better to cancel the performances, thinking maybe the protestors would clear out before her guests started to leave." He shrugged. "At least that's what Ellis said."

Some of the other queens had already changed and left, rolling their suitcases behind them like flight attendants fighting their way through an airport. Ellis was still around somewhere, just not in the dressing room, and other than Ivana, only Floretta—*Jeff*—and "Kym Karkrashian," whose real name was also Kim ("It just makes things easier") remained behind in the dressing room with us.

"If you're not sticking around for the party, you should come with us to Baby Jane's," Tommy said. "Some of the girls performing tonight were in the same class at Ellis's school as me, I like to show up and be supportive of my sisters."

"Oh, you went to Ellis's drag school?" He had my attention now. "I was thinking about that."

"You're a natural," Tommy enthused. "I couldn't believe it when Ellis said this was your first time in drag. No one would have guessed!" Then he laughed. "It's a lot of fun, and of course the class does a live performance for graduation."

"I don't know," I replied, thinking, *if everyone thinks you should do this, maybe you should?* "I mean, I have a pretty good gig already—"

"You don't have to make a career out of it." Tommy turned back to his mirror. "Just do it as a hobby." He made a face at himself in the mirror. "A very expensive hobby, sure, but still a hobby."

"I think we should all stick around for the party until the protesters leave," Kim called over as he pulled up a tight pair of ratty blue jeans. "It may not be safe out there for us."

I was wearing a pair of baggy jean shorts covered in paint spatters and with holes fraying in too many places to even try blending in with Marigny's guests. The green Tulane tank top I was wearing wasn't much help, either. "Isn't everyone like super-dressed up out there?"

"Darling, it's New Orleans," Kim laughed as he buttoned up the fly of his jeans. "No one cares—and besides, they'll know we were the models. We may have fans out there waiting for us!" With an expressive movement of his hands, Kim got to his feet and headed for the French doors. When he opened them, I could hear voices talking, ice tinkling in glasses, and cars going past on Nashville. There was jazz music playing in the background—probably the WWOZ broadcast—and a woman standing there with her hand raised, ready to knock. "Well, hello, darlin'," Kim cooed as he walked past her, "go on in—everyone's decent—at least when it come to their clothes, anyway." He turned back with a wink, and then disappeared down the stairs.

"Rachel?" I asked, standing up with a delighted smile on my face. "Is that you?"

"Jem!" Rachel Delesdernier Sheehan grinned and threw her arms around me in a tight hug. "You're doing drag now?" She held me at arm's length and laughed. "You looked amazing!"

"Someone cancelled, and I could fit into her dresses, so I got roped into filling in," I replied.

Rachel was one of my clients, not as regular as Lauralee, but regular enough. Rachel was one of the New Orleans Delesdernier family, meaning she was political royalty in New Orleans. There were several mayors, governors, and senators in the branches of her family tree, and she'd married into yet another Louisiana political dynasty, the Sheehans. She only needed glam a couple of times a year—certain things she had to make an appearance at, which she laughingly called "royal audiences." She was also publisher of *Crescent City* magazine, a popular monthly glossy covering the city in more depth than the daily or weekly papers could. She knew everyone in New Orleans who mattered, knew all the best gossip while it was still fresh, and was also a good source of referrals for me.

"I mean, a fashion show, Rachel? This is the last place in the world I'd expect to run into you!"

Being New Orleans royalty, Rachel could get away with things lesser members of society would never dare to try. Her clothing aesthetic was "comfort above everything." She was capable of the gown and glove and stiletto look—I'd helped her with that several times—but she'd been a tomboy and still preferred sneakers and sweat suits to anything else.

She was pretty, with expressive blue eyes and dark hair with a hint of auburn in it. She was in her early forties or so, but still looked like she was in her late twenties. She kept herself fit biking and jogging and taking yoga. She also had a wicked sense of humor that I enjoyed.

She rolled her eyes. "We're doing a cover story on Marigny and her business—the only couture designer in New Orleans, you know, the usual puff piece nonsense where she talks about her inspirations and blah blah blah." Rachel sat down in the chair next to me. "So, I've got a photographer here and I've already spent several hours interviewing her this week." She added, in a low voice only I could hear, "And that's three hours of my life I'll never get back." She sighed before continuing, "I mean, I get it, yes, she is the only New Orleans-based fashion designer, and she's been running Designs by Marigny for decades, so that's the kind of local success story we should celebrate in the magazine." She said the last in a wooden monotone, making it sound like giving Marigny a cover story hadn't been her idea.

"Did she promise to buy ads?"

"What?" Mockingly she slapped my shoulder. "Are you implying that the journalistic integrity of *Crescent City* magazine can be bought?" She laughed. "Advertising dollars talk in my business, and yes, she's agreed to two full page ads per issue through February. And so, here I am on a Friday night with my husband out of town on business, looking for someone to hang out with." She beamed at me. "Promise me?" She winked. "If it sweetens the pot at all, I drove so can give you a ride home if you want."

"How long do you think you're going to stay?" I asked. I pulled out my phone and looked at it. No new messages from Tradd or anyone. *Stop it and give up on Tradd already. He ghosted you. And you can do better. Have some self-esteem.* "Well, Kyle's performing at Baby Jane's tonight and he wanted me to come, and Tommy is heading over there to catch the show, too." I looked at my phone and was a little startled to see how early it still was, "But I hate the thought of waiting for a Lyft with those protestors outside." I shuddered. You never get used to having slurs screamed at you.

I learned in junior high school not to react.

Externally, anyway.

Emotionally? Yeah, it still sucked.

"Oh, they're already gone," Rachel replied with a cynical laugh. "I was out there watching, thinking maybe I should talk to one of them as background, you know, for the Marigny story?"

"Did she tell you why she used drag queens instead of models?"

"Well, her story is she wanted to do something creative and different and original, and if she could show support for the queer community, why not?" She rolled her eyes dramatically again. "I think she did it for publicity, if you want my opinion. Designs by Marigny will be on the front page of the *Times-Picayune* tomorrow, and every news show tonight will have at least a one or two minute story on the protests." She whistled. "And that was all the protestors cared about, too—publicity. The most dangerous place in this city is between Graham Steuben and a television camera. Once the television news crews got their footage and left, they were out of here in less than ten minutes, tops." She made a face. "Disgusting trolls." Rachel, I remembered, had a younger brother who was gay and lived in the lower Garden District with his husband, which was why *Crescent City* was always relentlessly pro-queer. "I hate giving them oxygen, but they are news. Steuben is such a monster. I swear, he looks like someone who has bodies buried in his basement. Boys, at that." She made a face. "Culture war bullshit, really."

"Yeah, I bet if someone started digging into Steuben, they'd find a lot." I finished putting the rest of my make-up and brushes away in my case—everything has a place and everything in its place is my motto—and snapped it closed. I held up my hand as she opened her mouth.

"Check out our next issue, dropping on Monday," she replied smugly. "We did a cover story on them—I don't need to add that it wasn't positive coverage, do I? I had one of my reporters do it—I didn't think I could get that close to one of them without slapping the snot out of them. Come on out to the party and have a drink with me, please?"

I looked at my phone one last time before slipping it into my shorts pocket. She was right. I'd been in the show and hadn't expected to stay for the party, and if anyone had an issue with the way I was dressed—well, who cared?

Floretta—*Jeff*—floated over to the doors and opened them wide. "Come on, ladies, let's go meet our fans!" He said with a grand gesture.

"I need to run to the bathroom again," I said, standing up. "I'll meet you at the back bar in a few, okay, Rachel?"

She looked at her watch pointedly. "I'm timing you." She leaned in closer. "Please don't leave me alone with all of those awful friends and clients of Marigny's."

I laughed and shooed them out through the doors, which I closed behind them. I started to put the latch on, but...how would we get back in? *Everything in here is probably safe*, I thought, *and besides, who wants to steal my make-up?*

I walked down the short hallway to the bathroom again and locked the door behind me. My calves hurt and so did my feet—the clog heels were easier on my legs than stilettos would have been, but my legs weren't used to any kind of heel. I stretched my calves, undid the fly of my shorts and took care of business. I washed my face and hands, dried them on a guest towel that needed laundering last week, and had my hand on the doorknob when I heard a voice clearly from outside the door.

"There you are!" a male voice said from inside the dressing room, and I heard the French doors close again. "I know you're avoiding me, Marigny, but you can't hide forever."

"I'm not avoiding you," she replied unconvincingly. I didn't know her well and I didn't know who she was talking to, but she was lying, and badly. "Besides, there's nothing you can do or say to change my mind."

"You can't, Marigny, you know you can't. I don't even care for my sake, but—"

"The truth is the truth, and it always comes out," she said a little primly.

He barked out a laugh. "But whose truth is the real truth? You've always been a liar, Marigny, and everyone knows it. Go ahead, do your worst. You're already a pariah in this town, go ahead and make it worse for yourself."

Heavy footsteps crossed the dressing room floor, the French doors opened and a few seconds later slammed shut. Awkward, I thought, wondering if I should wait for Marigny to leave so she wouldn't know I'd overheard. I didn't want to talk to her, either. I didn't like entitled women like Marigny, who think they either shouldn't have to pay for services—and make you hunt them down and threaten with legal action to cough up what they owe.

Freelancers like me depend on getting paid when we provide a service—if you can't pay for it, don't book me. Your finances aren't my problem, they're yours.

I walked back into the dressing room and saw Marigny bending over my make-up case. "Can I help you with something?" I asked in my frostily polite voice.

She jumped away from my case and had the decency to blush.

"Oh, I-uh, um—Jem." She'd lost weight since I'd worked on her face last spring—her chin looked sharper, her cheekbones more prominent—and I could see the bones of her shoulders pushing out against her skin. Yes, she'd lost about ten to fifteen pounds in the year since I'd last seen her—fifteen pounds she couldn't spare. She looked gaunt and tired. Her make-up was sloppy. She'd lost a false eyelash at some point. The circles under her eyes were so dark and purple even the most powerful concealer wouldn't have worked. Her forehead also had that peculiar rigid, waxy look so many upper class women get from their dermatologist. Her lips looked fuller, too. "It's, um, nice to see you again. And thank you for filling in on such short notice." She laughed humorlessly. "I thought maybe using drag queens might be easier than models...

85

such nightmares those anorexic little witches can be...I always assumed they were so nasty because they were starving themselves, but who knew drag queens would be just as bad as models? With all their performance experience, I thought they'd be more professional."

"Anyone who's ever watched *RuPaul's Drag Race* could have told you queens enjoy drama," I replied evenly. "Drag queens are all about the drama, dear, don't ever think they aren't. And they're also artists—drag is an art, and aren't all artists temperamental?" I was an artist, but I wasn't temperamental...was I?

Well, maybe I was temperamental, but only about getting paid on time.

I can put up with a lot, but not messing with my coin.

She gave me a rictus grin that made me flinch involuntarily. "Well, they did the trick," she replied with a bit of smugness. "We'll be all over the news tomorrow."

Confirmation. Tommy was right.

Yes, she had hired drag queens for her runway to stir up controversy and get attention for herself and her business. Much as I hated to admit it, it was a smart business move.

Ethically, it was vile to use homophobia and transphobia to get attention and make money, but her conscience and ethics were things she could talk to God about when she reached the pearly gates.

You really can't expect ethics and morality from someone as flippant as Marigny.

"Well, it was nice talking to you," I said, heading for the back doors. "I'm going to get a drink."

She grabbed my arm, digging her talon-like nails into my arm. "Where do you think you're going?" she sneered. "You can't go into my party dressed like that. There's a dress code, Jem. I can't have you mixing with the level of people on my guest list looking like...a cheap hooker."

My palm itched to slap her. But she was the kind of person who would be more than happy to have her off-duty police officers escort me off the property.

And press charges.

"One thing you definitely know about me, Marigny, is that I'm not cheap." I paused with my hand on the door, looking down at her hand where she was holding on to me. "I suggest you remove your claws from my arm." I looked her straight in the eye. "I wasn't planning on staying long, just having a drink with a friend—but if you don't want me at your party dressed like this—" I gestured up and down my body, "—I get it, it's not really what you're going for with this party. Would you mind doing me a favor, though, and telling my friend I'm not allowed in? She's waiting for me at the back bar."

Her entire body seemed to relax. "I would be happy to, and thanks for understanding. Your friend's name is—?"

"Rachel Sheehan." I walked back away from the door and back to my make-up case. I grabbed the handle and tilted it to roll. "And please let her know I'll call her later."

It was petty and small, but it was Marigny Orloff.

If anyone deserved petty smallness, she did.

I started rolling the case towards the hallway.

"Wait—" she stopped me, forcing another fake grin on her cadaverous face. "Maybe we could work something out? You've got to admit you're not dressed properly, Jem."

There was a pleading note in her voice that I'm a bit ashamed to admit I enjoyed hearing. She wasn't wrong, but I wasn't about to give her any props. Ordinarily, I would have never let Rachel talk me into having a drink at a party where I was this badly underdressed. After all, I had clients at this party, or potential future ones. Making a bad impression by going to a formal party in paint-spattered cut off jeans and a Tulane tank top was not in my professional best interest.

But she had tried to cheat me once before, and now was saying I wasn't good enough for her party.

Fine. Let her twist in the wind a bit.

She was wringing her hands, clearly torn. The last thing she wanted was for Rachel, the reporter doing a cover story on her business, finding out Marigny had been terrible to one of her friends. That could easily change the tone of the piece. But at the same time, she couldn't let me out into the backyard because it *would* look bad to her wealthy society clientele.

The doors opened again before she could figure out what to say, and a tall, slender woman stood there. It was the woman who'd let me in at the gate. Like Marigny, she clearly believed that you could never be too thin—which was so not true in her case. She'd changed into a simple black silk strap dress that reached about mid-thigh, and slingback pumps. She had no breasts to speak of, and she was reaching that dangerous age where her skin was starting to not quite have the firmness of youth anymore? She would start sticking to sleeves soon. She had white-blonde hair cut in a shoulder-length bob, and a long, thin face with lips so thin they looked like an angry red scar cut into her lower face. Her face was heart-shaped, with high prominent cheekbones and a sharply pointed chin. Her make-up was a mistake. She needed to soften the angles, not make them look sharper. "Marigny, you need to come speak to the caterer," the woman said in a nasal tone. "He wants his check now."

Marigny's eyes darted back and forth between us before she finally said, "I'll be right there—you"—she pointed at me, "—wait for me here and we'll figure out something."

She breezed out the doors, leaving them open, but rather than following her, the woman closed them behind her and sank down into the chair Floretta had used. When I started rolling the case again the woman bestirred.

"Marigny wanted you to wait," she said.

"Marigny can learn to live with disappointment," I replied. "Can you do me a favor? Do you know Rachel Sheehan?"

She nodded.

"Give her my apologies and tell her I'll call her tomorrow," I said over my shoulder as I started rolling my case down the hallway.

"And Marigny?"

"I don't care what you tell her." I kept going until I reached the front door. I went down the front steps and headed for the front gate. I opened it and stood out on the sidewalk of St. Charles Avenue and took a deep breath. The cops were looking at their phones. I could hear jazz playing softly in the distance and the murmur of people talking in the backyard. The air felt damp and heavy, which meant rain was coming—hopefully I could get home before the skies opened. I put the handle back down and sat down on the case.

Well, it had been a night. I'd gotten paid very well—I wished Lee Ann luck in getting repaid, and I'd done drag for the first time. My calves and feet still ached a bit, but that was okay. I had Ellis' card in my wallet.

Why *not* go to drag school?

I did like dancing, and I loved to sing—even though, Kyle's kindness aside, I was often flat and off-key more than I wasn't—and maybe performing would be fun. Sure, I always got stage fright whenever I did plays in high school—I still didn't enjoy getting up in front of room full of people and talking—but this would be different. I had kind of felt *powerful* as I walked the runway, to applause and whistles and flashing camera light. If I could channel that—and I could already do hair and make-up, *and* I can sew . . . I could make some amazing outfits. I closed my eyes and imagined myself on stage at Oz, performing something by Taylor Swift—something vintage, like "Red" or "Blank Space," maybe.

I could even make that red sequined dress she'd worn in the video for "Red"—and the choreography she used had been simple.

But as I was opening my Lyft app to summon a ride, someone called my name from behind the gate.

"Don't go," Ellis said, opening the gate. "Stay and have a drink." He grinned wickedly at me.

He was very good-looking.

"Okay, one." I said, putting my phone back in my pocket, thinking as I rolled my case back towards the gate, *I hope I don't regret this.*

CHAPTER SIX

I rolled over in bed and woke up.

I felt terrible.

I was sweating and my room was very bright. I opened my eyes a slit and reached for the chord for the blinds, twisting them closed. Pressing a hand to my clammy forehead and scooting up to a sitting position, I tried peeling my eyes open. They were gummy and there was eye snot in the corners, which I wiped away. My head was pounding and I felt sick to my stomach.

There needs to be a law against serving cheap wine at a party, I thought, moaning softly to myself. *But tequila shots were also involved, and did we do shots at Baby Jane's last night, too?*

I should have followed my instincts and taken

a Lyft home from Marigny's party like I'd planned. But no, I thought Ellis was cute and didn't want to miss out on any fun, so I'd been talked into staying at the party and then going along when the other queens moved it to Baby Jane's. I seemed to remember that some of the performers last night at the bar were former students of Ellis's?

How did I get home?

At least, I thought as I reached for my phone to lower the air conditioning, *I woke up alone.*

My head felt like someone was driving a nail between my eyes. *Grease, I need grease,* I thought. I heard the air conditioning kick on and threw the covers off me. I hadn't even turned on the ceiling fan before I poured myself into bed. Looking around as my eyes started to swim into focus, I saw my jeans and tank top from last night crumpled into a pile just inside my bedroom door. *I must have been super drunk if I hadn't remembered to close the blinds.* The sun in New Orleans can be brutal so I usually kept the blinds closed so the sun wouldn't wake me up in the morning. I'd opened them late yesterday afternoon while I was packing my make-up case and—

My make-up case. Where was my make-up case?

I had it with me when I left Designs by Marigny.

If I'd been too wasted to remember to close the blinds and turn the air up, would I have remembered to take the case when I got out of Ellis' car?

Assuming Ellis had brought me home.

I hate alcohol-induced amnesia.

I reached up and pulled the string to turn on the ceiling fan. With a slight creak, the blades started turning overhead.

I wouldn't be able to fall back asleep until I knew for sure whether that make-up case had made it home with me or not.

I swung my legs around slowly and put my feet on the floor. A wave of nausea washed over me and threatened to pull me under, but I took some deep breaths and it passed. Every muscle in my legs started screaming at me when I tried to stand. My lower back also ached, and it took me a couple of moments to remember oh yes, you did drag last night and wore heels. As I flexed and unflexed my feet, I could feel the angry tightness start to loosen a bit.

So at least that wasn't permanent, unlike the brain cells I'd murdered.

You need to stop drinking so much, I thought as I reached for my gray sweatpants, draped over a chair in the corner, and slipped my feet into my house slippers. Bravely, I tried to push myself up to a standing position. And stop going out so much. No wonder Mom is always on my case to grow up.

I could hear her voice in my aching brain, you're going to be THIRTY before you know it, and what do you have to show for yourself?

"Nothing." I said out loud in a croak.

It took me a try or two, but soon I was not only

upright but not swaying, either. That was good. I looked at my watch. It was almost noon. I fought the urge to get back in the bed and pull the covers up over my head.

It was Sunday. No clients, no appointments, no nothing. Just a whole day of possibilities ahead of me—if I survived this hangover.

I needed a bacon double cheeseburger.

I pressed my index fingers into my temples— Mee Maw had always sworn that helped with a headache. She'd believed in a lot of folk remedies and homeopathic medicines. Some of the stuff she'd been right about. Stinging nettles did help with sinus pressure and peppermint oil would cool you down—but she also believed the moon landing had been faked.

The fingers pressing into the temples did not work.

I needed aspirin. I slowly shuffled over to the bathroom, which was a disaster area. That's right, *clean your bathroom* was on my chores list for this weekend. Figuring it could wait until I felt better, I turned on the sink spigot and started splashing cold water into my face. I was afraid to look in the mirror.

Love your eye shadow, I heard someone saying to me over the din of the music and the crowd noise last night. I opened my eyes and glared at my reflection. Yes, there was still eye shadow and mascara on my eyes—well, the mascara had smeared around my eyes. That's right, I'd taken off all the make-up except for the eyes. I'd intended to go back and do my eyes before we left Marigny's . . . but then I'd drunk too much of Marigny's incredibly bad red wine. I vaguely remember Ellis and Tommy talking me into going with them to Baby Jane's. We'd gotten there in time for the midnight show, and Tommy had dashed off to the bar to get us shots.

But the rest of the night?

A blur.

I tried remembering more. Had I made a fool out of myself? Kyle enjoys it when I drink too much, but when I hear about my antics later, I usually resolve never to drink like that again.

Until the next time, of course.

The next time you want to go out remember how you feel right now.

I cleaned myself up a bit. Feeling almost human, I headed downstairs to forage for food. I could have some toast to settle my stomach down a bit.

My grandmother's house was a camelback double shotgun. The name came from the fact that the second story was only at the rear of the house—the camelback. When the house had been split into two singles, the master bedroom suites for each side were up on the second floor. When she'd turned the house into a single, tearing out walls and recreating rooms, she'd left the two master suites separated. Kyle slept on the other side, and our bathrooms shared the common wall—so if one of us had an overnight guest, the other couldn't hear.

Not that I had many overnight guests. Kyle was a lot more popular than me.

I looked down the long, steep narrow staircase that emerged into the workroom just off the laundry room/pantry on my side. I took a deep breath. To my aching, hurting brain the stairs looked endless, growing continuously while I stared down its length. *You can do this,* I reassured myself, grabbing the railing with my right hand and putting my left foot down gingerly on the first step. My calves screamed as I shifted to take another step.

Maybe there was some BenGay in the kitchen.

Each time I set a foot down, the jolt sent a lightning bolt of pain through my skull.

Whoever invents a pill you can take to either prevent or cure a hangover will win the Nobel Prize and my undying gratitude, I thought as I staggered my way down the long and steep staircase, my hand clutching the railing with a death grip. The steps were also a little slippery. My mouth had dried out again and I kept trying to summon up some spit as I winced and hobbled my way down to the first floor.

I also gave myself a good cussing out for drinking so much of that cheap red wine Marigny had been serving. *Wine before liquor you've never been sicker.* I should have stopped with the shots and whatever else I was drinking and switched to water when we got to

Baby Jane's. Why would Marigny serve such cheap wine to a crowd of people she was trying to impress? Outside of the help, the only people who'd been at that party were people who could afford one of those overpriced gowns, so why cut corners on the liquor?

There's no better way to turn off New Orleanians than by skimping on the liquor.

But maybe they knew better than to touch her wine? I'd learned my lesson—not that I would ever go to another one of her parties.

Why hadn't someone warned me?

Everyone knew the secret to a great party was good liquor. You could even serve inedible food— frozen and heated in the microwave— so long as the booze was top-shelf. But everyone had seemed to be having a good time. Rachel had introduced me to several women who'd asked for my card. I'd even gotten compliments on how good I'd looked on the runway. I laughed at myself. The compliments and potential new business had put me into a good mood, and the tequila shots Ellis had served me during the show had gone to my head. I'd have drunk grain alcohol at that party if someone had offered it to me. That was why I'd stayed longer. I'd gotten a plastic glass of the red wine, fully intending to have just that one drink—maybe a second—and get a Lyft home. Rachel introduced me to someone while I was on my first glass, and there were waiters walking around with bottles topping off people's glasses.

I don't think my glass had ever been empty. And then Ellis and Tommy started talking about going to the midnight show at Baby Jane's, I'd mentioned Kyle was performing and that was that.

And yes, I could now remember putting my make-up case in the trunk of Ellis's car.

I hobbled down the bottom two steps and did a quick glance around my workroom. The Gucci rolling case was right where I always left it, parked next to the cabinet where I kept all my extra supplies. The spot next to it, where the LV went, was empty.

"Oh, no," I sat down in my desk chair and covered my face with my hands. I loved that old Louis Vuitton case. It had been Mee Maw's favorite possession, the first expensive thing she'd ever bought for herself once the Beauty Shoppe had started taking off, and it was one of the things she'd specifically left to me. It wasn't in great shape—there were rips and tears, and the clasp caught sometimes.

But it had been Mee Maw's and she'd loved it. When Lauralee bought me the new Gucci case, at first it felt like a betrayal to use it. But it was bigger, carried more, and was easier to pack. I knew I shouldn't have taken it.

Mee Maw had also loved this house and look at what a mess it is.

I had Ellis's card somewhere. Probably in my wallet. Upstairs, in my shorts pocket.

It could wait until I felt more human.

I filled a glass using the filtered water spigot and washed down two aspirins. There was no BenGay in the medicine drawer, though. I put some bread in the toaster and started brewing a cup of coffee. At least I knew where it was. I bet Ellis forgot he had it, too. I glanced at the kitchen window. The thermometer outside the window read 87 degrees. There wasn't a cloud in sight and the sky was that vivid bright blue that meant heat.

Was there anything in the case that would melt and ruin in the heat?

If so, it was already too late to do anything about it.

As I spread peanut butter on my toast, I hoped I'd remained somewhat in control at Marigny's party. That wasn't the kind of party where my smart mouth would be an asset. As it is, I don't have much of a filter when I'm completely sober. Add alcohol to the equation and things can get ugly quickly. But I'd given out a lot of business cards—I may not remember a lot, but I don't think they would have asked if I had been slurring and insulting them, would they?

Kyle swears sometimes that when I drink, I act like I'm a contestant on a game show called *Who Can I Offend the Most?*

An exaggeration—but not by much.

"At least you're funny when you're reading people," he always added.

Maybe I was a natural born drag queen after all.

I sat down at the kitchen table and munched away at my peanut butter toast. Washing it down with my coffee, I was starting to feel a lot better. I smiled. *How had I gotten home? Kyle or Ellis?* Baby Jane's was walking distance, but I didn't feel comfortable walking home from there late at night by myself. Our neighborhood was starting to gentrify, but it was still a little on the sketchy side. There was still crime in the neighborhood—cars broken into or stolen, muggings, the occasional shooting—enough so that I wouldn't ever try the few blocks between our front door and Baby Jane's. It was probably okay, but why risk it?

I was waiting for a second cup of coffee to brew when the doorbell started ringing.

I wasn't expecting anyone. Maybe Kyle? I didn't hear any movement upstairs. Knowing Kyle, he'd sprung from bed like he'd just shot-gunned two Red Bulls and gone to the gym.

Which was why Kyle looked like he did. Dedication.

But maybe it was Ellis bringing my make-up case back!

I padded through the house to the front door as it rang again, a little more insistently this second time. "COMING!" I shouted, picking up the pace a bit and glad I'd had time to eat something to get my stomach under control. I peeked through the blinds—you never just open your front door in New Orleans. There was a man and a woman standing on my porch, and beyond them a black SUV was parked at the curb in front of my house. I didn't see Kyle's car. They were both in business attire, despite the heat, and they didn't look like Jehovah's Witnesses or Mormons...I unlocked the deadbolt but left the chain on. I opened it slightly. "Yes?" I said through the two-inch crack I'd left in the door.

Two badges were immediately held up to my face. "We're looking to speak to a James Richard?" The man asked. He was younger than the woman and looked vaguely familiar in that way everyone doesr in New Orleans—you know, like you've seen them somewhere before. Probably because you have. "I'm Detective Blake Dorgenois, and this is my partner, Latoya Picot." The woman, who was several inches taller and slender, inclined her head to me when he said her name. "We understand you were at a fashion show last night at Designs by Marigny?"

"I was." I replied, looking from one to the other, a little confused. "Is it a crime to go to a party?" I laughed. "The wine she was serving was a crime, but that's not why you're here?"

"Do you mind if we come inside to speak to you? We just have a few questions." Detective Dorgenois asked with a friendly smile. "Besides, it's awfully hot out here, and that cool air coming through your door is kind of irresistible."

"I don't need a lawyer, do I?" I was joking but felt a little unnerved when they exchanged a glance.

I undid the chain and opened the door, waving them into the big front room. "Come on in."

I smothered a laugh at the looks on their faces as they took in my grandmother's decorating style. She'd been what people might have called a hippie back in the day when she was young and had never really changed as she got older. She disproved the axiom that everyone gets more conservative the older they get. The walls of the enormous room were painted what she'd called "Mykonos blue"—it reminded her of the skies in the Aegean Islands, where she'd spent some time when backpacking through Europe one summer—but she'd also been a big supporter of local artists. Her interests decorated the walls, from the enormous framed and mounted black-and-white poster of Humphrey Bogart and Ingrid Bergman from Casablanca to some gorgeous swamp photography from a talented local photographer and Jazz Fest posters from the 1980s to just about anything you could think of that she might have thought, in her whimsical way, looked good. None of her furniture matched ("if I wanted to live in a boring suburb I'd move to one"), all collected from second hand shops and yard sales. I gestured for them to sit on the cream-colored couch whose seams were starting to fray just a little bit. I offered them coffee, which they declined. Then, remembering I wasn't wearing a shirt, I darted back to the laundry room and slipped on a dirty Saints sweatshirt before heading back to the living room.

But when I came back, I flushed as I realized what a mess the house was. Mee Maw would have died from embarrassment if she knew I was letting strangers see the house the way I'd been keeping it.

"So, you were at the fashion show at Designs by Marigny last night, and stayed for the after-party?" The handsome man spoke again, and I took a better look at him as I slipped into my La-Z-Boy chair.

He was criminally handsome. No man should be that beautiful. He had thick, curly bluish-black hair he wore short, with a strong masculine jawline, a cleft in his chin, and deep dimples in his tanned cheeks. He had the kind of skin that never burned, just got darker and prettier the more time he spent in the sun. He was wearing a white short-sleeved button-down shirt that hugged his big biceps tightly. His shirt— well, not to be catty, but he probably could have gone up a size and would have been fine—which meant he liked his shirts tight enough to show off the thickly muscled chest, the small waist and flat stomach, and there was a dusting of black hairs over his muscular forearms. His pants were also tight.

He was the kind of guy you looked at from across the bar and prayed you'd catch his eye.

His were deep blue. As blue as the Gulf of Mexico out where it gets deeper, so deep you could get lost in them forever . . .

I realized he was staring at me, waiting for me to answer him. "I'm sorry?"

"Did you notice anything unusual going on last night while you were there?" he repeated, uncapping a pen while balancing his notepad on his knee.

"Well, before the show, it was chaotic," I said, sipping my coffee. "I was too busy to really notice much of anything, really. I was helping some of the girls with their hair and make-up, and then of course one didn't show up—"

"We were told you helped out, stepped in?" A corner of the woman's mouth twitched like she wanted to smile but wouldn't let it out.

"Yes." I replied, smiling at them both. "I mean, I've never done drag before except as a costume—I won the Bourbon Street awards this past year—"

"You were *Kiss of the Spider Woman!*" Blake burst out, a big smile on his face. "I knew you looked familiar. That was an amazing costume."

"Thank you," I replied, genuinely both pleased and flattered, while ticking off the *probably gay box* in my head. Sure, the Bourbon Street Awards started drawing straight people down to the corner of Bourbon and St. Ann as the event got bigger and bigger every year—but it was still a safe bet than any man down there was probably gay—or at least a little open to giving it a try sometime.

Down, girl, I told myself. *He's a cop. And probably taken anyway. Guys who look like him are never single.*

"You had some kind of issue with Ms. Orloff?" This was Latoya, the woman, now. Her voice was smooth as silk, and her face was beautiful, classic— the kind that should be immortalized in marble.

I took a deep breath. "The last time I'd done some work for her, her check bounced and I practically had to threaten to file charges for her to make it good," I didn't bother keeping the bitterness out of my mouth. "It took months. MONTHS. I swore I'd never work for her again. And I wouldn't have, either, but Lee Ann Vidrine paid me up front so—" I shrugged. "Money is money."

"You didn't see or hear anything you might have thought strange?" Blake asked, scribbling on his little notepad.

I thought back and winced. "I'm sorry, but— well, I drank a lot at the party, and then went to see a show afterwards, and so, well, I'm a bit hungover this morning and there's a lot I don't remember about last night."

"Wasn't there an issue about her not wanting you to go to the party?"

"Oh, that." I waved my hand dismissively. "I wasn't dressed properly, and she did have a point. I was on my way out, when a friend came after me and talked me into going back to the party. Marigny spent most of the night ignoring me, which was fine with me, I don't like her and the less time I spend talking to her the better."

"But it was just because she bounced a check to you?" Latoya asked casually, crossing one long leg over the other. "There was nothing else going on between the two of you?"

"No. I mean, I know her son Jackson—he's gay—and he never has anything positive to say about his mom, but—" I shrugged. "I don't think I've ever heard anyone say anything positive about Marigny other than Lee Ann—and even Lee Ann had her limits with Marigny." I shook my head again. "I'm sorry, what is all this about? Did something happen at the party last night?"

Blake flipped his notebook closed and they exchanged a glance, both standing up at the same time. "We're just covering all the bases, Mr. Richard."

"Call me Jem, please. What bases?" They started walking to the front door. When I opened it, Blake handed me a business card.

"If you think about anything else from last night, or remember anything, give me a call, I'd appreciate it." He said as he walked out my front door.

"But what? What is going on?"

Blake folded his arms across his chest and it was a miracle none of the buttons popped when his chest swelled up. "Sometime after the party last night, someone shot and killed Marigny Orloff." He saluted me and winked. "If you remember anything, give me a call."

CHAPTER SEVEN

A chill went through my body as I stood there in the doorway, watching them get back into their SUV and drive off.

Wow.

It was a bit hard for me to wrap my mind around. It didn't seem real. I'd just seen her last night. I flashed back to the conversation we'd had about me going into her party. We hadn't even raised our voices. Surely, they didn't think that gave me a motive?

Like I would kill someone over a slight insult like that?

No, I thought as I closed the front door. I started to put the chain on, but—I pulled the door open again and looked up and down the street. No sign of Kyle's car, which was odd. Mee Maw's jade green

Mercury was sitting in the driveway. I didn't drive it much—it was so much easier to just take Lyfts, or ride with Kyle to the grocery store. I tripped the deadbolt but left the chain off for Kyle.

The chain had been on, though.

I needed more coffee.

I carried Blake's card with me back to the kitchen so I could make another cup of coffee. I dumped the cold remnants in my cup out into the sink and put another K-cup into the machine. Maybe I should have offered them coffee? I'd never had the police come to my door before to ask me questions. Was there etiquette for that? Probably, there was etiquette for everything.

I smiled. Detective Dorgenois had been hot. I put the card down on the counter and looked at it, wishing there was some reason I needed to call him and get him to come back. If real life was like a porn movie, the hot detective and I would already be going to town in the living room.

He'd looked familiar—but that didn't mean anything in New Orleans. Everyone here looks familiar. I'd probably seen him at the grocery store or at Wal-mart.

An image of him dancing shirtless, his jeans hanging low on his hips. sweat running down his muscular chest, popped into my head.

"In your dreams," I jeered at myself, but the image was persistent. Had I seen him dancing in one of the gay bars at some point? I focused on the image, closing my eyes, trying to remember. He was dancing, his arms up over his head while he wiggled his hips from side to side. The jeans kept slipping down as he danced. There was stubble on his torso, sweat glistening in his armpit hair, and—

That was a lot of detail for a daydream.

No, I must have seen him out dancing one night. Of course, someone who looked like him dancing shirtless would get my attention. And of course, I would have never even made eye contact with someone who looked that great.

Marigny Orloff was dead. Murdered.

No matter how hot I thought the detective was, that was still fact.

The reality hit me between the eyes.

I shuddered as goosebumps broke out all over my body. I'd just seen her last night. And now . . . gone. Poor thing. Her sons . . . they must be broken up.

Had anyone notified Lee Ann? They'd been friends since they'd been girls, Lee Ann had told me once, adding, "we both know where the bodies are buried."

I shivered. Maybe not the best choice of words, Lee Ann.

Someone had *killed* Marigny.

I took a few deep breaths. No one deserved to be murdered. Maybe the killer had been a guest at the party. Maybe it was someone I knew, someone I'd met, someone I'd talked to last night. The thought roiled my stomach and I shivered again.

Someone I knew had been murdered.

No, I hadn't liked her. I don't like anyone who tries to cheat me out of money. I'd probably wished horrible things would happen to her more times than I should have. But come on—she'd bounced a *large* check, which was a crime. She was lucky I hadn't sworn out an arrest warrant instead of just trying to get her to make her bad check good, but none of that had been serious. It was just frustration with the situation. I'd never wish harm on anyone. She didn't deserve to die because she'd tried to cheat me.

But writing a check knowing full well it was no good was a terrible thing to do to someone self-employed. I'd needed that money, too. I'd had to borrow money from Kyle for over a week before my next appointment with Lauralee.

I couldn't be the only person she'd tried to screw over. The fact she'd even try was proof she'd done it before and gotten away with it.

Wow. Poor Jackson! I didn't know him well but yikes. I couldn't imagine how I'd react if someone killed my mom.

My stomach clenched again.

How had she seemed to me last night? I didn't know her well enough to say. She didn't seem any different than when I'd worked her show last spring. She was calmer last night, but she'd also hired Ellis to produce last night's show. Her spring show was all her, and she'd been a frantic mess backstage, barking orders at people and looking frazzled and tired—but not too tired to be condescending and snobbish. I'd been very excited about booking the gig, too. Lee Ann referred Marigny to me, and I had to be interviewed. She'd seemed distant and cold, but her questions were professional, and she'd impressed me. I'd met with her a few more times to decide on the final make-up and hair for the models. It was fun. I'd never done a fashion show before, and I was hoping Marigny would turn out to be a good source for referrals. I really wanted to break into the wedding business—and she sold wedding dresses. So, I worked my butt off to make sure every model's look was perfect when she went down the runway. By the time the models and Marigny took their victory lap, I was exhausted. "Excellent work," she said when she handed me the envelope with the check in it. I felt great about everything...until I checked my bank balance and realized her check had bounced.

I was raised with such a strict sense of morality that it never occurs to me until too late that a lot of people in this world can't be trusted. I would never hire someone I couldn't pay, so why would I think anyone else would? I still can't wrap my mind around it.

Lee Ann of course had been mortified and offered to make the check good. I refused to let her because I wanted Marigny to pay me. It was *her* debt. *She* needed to pay.

I can be relentless, as Marigny found out.

But once the cashier's check I'd insisted on cleared—I took it to the bank it was drawn on, to be sure—I was done with Marigny. You only get one chance to screw me over. I'd only done the show last night because Lee Ann prepaid me...which meant she would never get her money back from Marigny.

Well, it wasn't my problem. My coffee brewed, I added sweetener and creamer and sat back down at the kitchen table.

I heard Kyle coming down the steps on his side of the house. Ah, so he was home. While my stairs opened into the bedroom converted into a combination pantry/work room for me, we'd converted the bedroom on his side into a workout room. There were mats and a weight bench and dumb bells, and some other accoutrements he used to teach cardio classes at our gym. His pole was usually set up in there, too—unless he was teaching a class or had a performance scheduled.

He walked into the kitchen half-asleep and only wearing his black Calvin Klein boxer briefs. Kyle wasn't shy of his body (I wouldn't be either if I looked like that) but since he usually pole-danced in either a bikini or a thong his underwear was more cover than he usually wore in public. He started a cup of coffee for himself, and then started digging through the refrigerator to find something to eat. I watched him root through the yogurt cups with a bit of amusement. Kyle would always buy a vast variety of yogurt flavors but only would eat the strawberry or blackberry flavors. It was fine—I would eat the others—but it always kind of amused me he'd buy flavors he wouldn't eat. As lean and muscular as Kyle was, he ate like a horse. I looked at a piece of cheesecake and could feel my pants getting tighter. Kyle could eat that entire cheesecake and lose three pounds.

Finally, he put his hands on the last strawberry banana cup, and stood back up, yawning and stretching at the same time. He smiled lazily at me as he grabbed a spoon from the silverware drawer and straddled a chair on the other side of the table. "How you feeling this morning?"

"Better than when I first woke up." I replied. "Where's your car?"

He raised his eyebrows at me. "You were wasted last night, weren't you?" He scratched his arm. "Don't you remember? Ellis dropped us both off."

"Do you remember me getting my make-up case out of his car?"

Kyle shook his head. "No, you didn't." he grinned. "You were a mess. I had to help you up to your room." He stared at me. "You don't remember any of this?"

"There's a lot I don't remember about last night." I replied. "Someone murdered Marigny Orloff. That's who was at the door earlier. Official police business," I replied.

"*What?*" I don't think I'd ever seen someone's jaw drop before. "Shut up. Are you serious?" He shook his head and scoffed, "I'm guessing someone finally put a stake through her heart? Was it Jackson?"

It was my turn to be confused. "You knew her?" I shouldn't have been surprised. Kyle grew up in New Orleans and he knew everyone.

He waved a hand. "I dated Jackson a long, long time ago. Very briefly. One or two dates, at most. Sweet guy, but he's a mess." He sighed. "Marigny wasn't thrilled. I had a little too much melanin for her liking. And the way she treated him? It's a wonder he didn't kill her years ago."

"She was racist?" It wasn't a surprise. Last night's models had all been white, and they had been when I worked her previous show, too. I couldn't remember any Black employees at Designs by Marigny, and all her guests at the party last night had been white.

"Oh, no more than most," Kyle replied with a roll of his eyes. "And she didn't over-compensate the way some white women do. No, it wasn't because I'm Black, she didn't like me because I wasn't high enough on the social ladder for her son." He sniffed. "It's not like Jackson was going to be Queen of Comus or something. And the Orloffs aren't exactly that high up on the ladder themselves. It was her grandfather that made all the money, you know. And Marigny's father blew most of it. I don't think she inherited much from him other than that house on St. Charles and a lot of debt." His brow furrowed. "The cops didn't come by because you're a suspect, did they?" He grinned. "Are you a suspect?"

"Probably. We'd exchanged some harsh words last night, when she didn't want me going to her party in jeans and a T-shirt, but nothing that would make me go back later and kill her. It's absurd."

"Well, a lot of people saw you getting hammered in Baby Jane's last night, so you might have a pretty good alibi if it comes to it." He winked at me. "I'd be happy to tell the cops you were clearly too drunk to leave the house after we got home."

"What time did we get home?"

"Around four."

"They didn't seem to suspect me, but I was there last night, and we did have a bit of a past. But nobody would kill someone over a bounced check, and besides, she made it good anyway." *After I'd practically had to threaten her with the district attorney.* "Ticking off boxes, I guess. They're probably going to talk to everyone who was there." Our large black cat, Shade, hopped on the table and started purring, making figure eights in between us.

Kyle started scratching Shade behind the ears, and Shade started headbutting him. Kyle collected strays. Shade had been one who'd shown up right after Kyle moved in, and of course, Kyle started feeding him . . . and now Shade was our indoor cat. There were about another five or six from the neighborhood we fed, but I drew the line at one indoor cat.

I pushed Detective Dorgenois' card across the table to him. "You know this cop?"

His eyes widened in surprise, and he whistled. "Next time he comes to our door you better wake me up," he said, taking a sip from his coffee. "He is way too good looking for his own good. Such a pretty, pretty man. And that body, too." Kyle whistled. "A snack for sure."

"You know him?" Maybe I hadn't fantasized seeing him on the dance floor.

That got me a look, complete with raised eyebrows and a head tilt. "Don't tell me you've never noticed him out," He replied. "He's totally your type."

"He's gay?" I asked, keeping my voice calm while my heart was doing jumping jacks inside my chest. "You're sure?"

"Well, if he's not, he sure spends a lot of time out on the dance floor every weekend with no shirt on," Kyle went on. "He was married to an older guy for a long time, but I think his husband died last year?" He frowned. "But he played around before . . . before he was widowed, I mean. I think maybe they had an open relationship? Blake likes to go out and dance, and he was always going home with someone. I missed my chance and have regretted it ever since. Never got a second one, either." He looked sad, and added dreamily, "We were on the dance floor and having the best time dancing together—" I've seen Kyle dancing with guys, and if he's interested it's obvious to anyone watching, "—but I went to the bathroom and to get a drink and when I came back, he was gone. I never had another shot at him, dang it, and now he's been in my house while I was sleeping? There is no God." He pouted, took a drink from his coffee, and shook his head. "Wait, he came to the door?" I could see the wheels turning in his head for a moment. "I'm sorry, I got distracted by the idea that Blake was in my house, and we let him go without taking advantage of this situation." He shook his head again. "If he ever comes by again— sorry, getting distracted again. I can't believe someone killed Marigny. Poor Jackson. Awful as she was to him, she was still his mother." He made a face. "Maybe I should call him to check? No, he's probably dealing with a lot, doesn't need me bothering him." He gave me a wicked look. "And here I was wanting to ask you about Ellis."

"Ellis?"

"You like him, don't you?" Kyle's grin was enormous. "You were flirting up a storm with him last night."

My heart sank. Great. "I didn't make a fool of myself, did I?"

"No more so than usual." He held up his hands when I glared at him. "No, it was cute, and he didn't seem to mind. He was flirting back. I was kind of surprised you didn't go home with him or invite him here."

"I'd have thrown up on him." I rubbed my eyes. "But I'll call him later about the case. You're sure I left it in his car?"

"Guess you'll have to call him and find out."

My cell phone started vibrating, which sent Shade flying off the table and out the kitchen door at light speed. I picked it up and looked at the screen. Rachel Sheehan's face smiled at me from the screen. I hit accept and held it up to my ear. "Hi, Rachel, what can I do for you?"

"Jem!" Rachel Sheehan managed to sound both friendly and professional at the same time. "Have you heard?" She went on, without giving me a chance to respond, "I'm sorry if I woke you up, but I had to call as soon as I heard the news."

"What news?"

"About Marigny." She took a deep breath. "She was *murdered* last night."

"Yes, I know," I replied. "The police were just here."

"They were?" Her excitement dripped from every word. "Did they tell you anything?"

"No, not really," I replied. "They didn't ask me a lot of questions—just if I saw or heard anything that seemed out of the ordinary."

She laughed. "Obviously, they'd never been to a fashion show at Designs by Marigny before. Nothing ordinary about any of them, let alone Marigny herself."

"Rachel."

"Oh, I know you're not supposed to say bad things about dead people, but she didn't miraculously turn into a saint by getting herself killed," Rachel sounded cross.

"You're covering the story, aren't you?" The lightbulb finally went on over my head.

"We'll cover it, of course, but we're not a daily," she demurred. "So, it's not like I'm going to be breaking scoops or anything. But did you see or hear anything last night that seemed off?"

"You're asking me to think this morning?" I replied. "My head hurts already."

"Oh, you were drinking the red wine, weren't you? Never drink wine at Marigny's. It's always something cheap and awful."

"You could have warned me last night." Ellis' tequila shots and whatever I'd had at Baby Jane's had helped create the hangover but I let the cheap wine take the blame. Kyle made himself another cup of coffee and signaled to me he was going upstairs, mouthing the words got a class. I nodded as he slipped out of the kitchen.

Rachel was still talking. "I know, I should have but I was a bit lit already myself and wasn't thinking, sorry. Listen, I need to run—but if you think of anything—"

"You'll be the first person I'll call," I replied. *Well, no offense, Rachel, but I would be calling handsome Detective Blake Dorgenois before you*, I thought as I disconnected her call.

I could hear water running through the pipes, signaling that Kyle was in the shower. I got up and made another cup of coffee.

I needed to find Ellis' card and find out when I could get my make-up case out of his car.

Grabbing my coffee, I climbed the steps to my bedroom. Poor Marigny, no matter how much I'd disliked her I wouldn't wish death on her—or anyone, for that matter.

Well, sometimes when someone made me angry, I'd blurt out "Oh, I could just kill him" but it wasn't serious.

What had the rest of the party been like?

My head had been in a weird space. The tequila shots—how many had we done? Two? Three? And the crash from the adrenaline high of doing the runway had left me feeling tired, drained, and sleepy. Rachel had dragged me over to the bar, but before I could order anything she'd been dragged away by someone. THAT was when the red wine debacle had begun. There had been a live band—a jazz trio—set up over by the carriage house, and some people were dancing on the paved parking area near where they were playing. The wine had tasted bad, but after the second sip I didn't mind too much. By the third it no longer tasted like mouth-wash and was going down easily.

Once I was mingling with Marigny's guests in my tank top and shorts, I saw it was exactly the kind of crowd I would expect to see at one of her shows—a lot of rich or well-known New Orleans women. I recognized some of them from other events or seeing their pictures on the local society pagewebsite. I said hello to a couple of clients, made small talk with them and their husbands before heading back to the bar for a refill of the bad wine. There was a lot of expensive jewelry on display—diamonds and rubies and emeralds and sapphires sparkling when they caught the light. I was surprised to see so many women wearing heels—despite the fact the party was in the back gardens of Designs by Marigny. The paved paths were too narrow for people to gather on, so most had moved off to the sides or onto the grass or the parking area. The fact none of the women took a header was an accomplishment.

I was glad I'd taken off those murderous heels and put my sneakers back on.

Smiling and nodding politely to any number of society queens and *nouveau riche* social climbers, I

maneuvered through the crowd and asked the tuxe-
doed bartender for more red wine. I turned and surveyed the party, taking in all the details I'd missed
while walking the runway. The massive live oaks
twinkled with little white Christmas tree lights. I
recognized a tall woman who was clutching the arm
of Marigny's gay son, Jackson—but it took me a
moment to place her as Reena Collins.

Reena Collins was kind of a celebrity. A former weather girl for one of the local news stations,
she'd left her job when she'd married into one of
the older society families with the bluest of bloods.
She'd shot her husband after seven years of marriage, claiming she'd mistaken him for a burglar
and of course, every New Orleans society lady
could hit a bull's eye blindfolded from a hundred
paces. The gossip had been flying—the marriage
hadn't been happy, there were rumors that Jimmy
Collins had been gay and had men on the side and
that Reena herself had any number of lovers—but
the inquest ruled accidental death and the case was
closed. About a year later Reena was once again
the hot topic around town when she'd married her
personal trainer, who was fifteen years younger
than she was. She'd thrown him out and filed for
divorce less than a year later, and again the gossip
flew: the second husband had helped her kill the
first, she'd married him out of gratitude (or had
been blackmailed into it, depending on who you

were talking to). The divorce had started out nasty, but to the disappointment of the gossips Reena and her second husband had eventually settled everything out of court. And now there she was, wearing an expensive white silk wrap dress and clutching Jackson's arm like she was trying to draw blood with her nails.

Jackson looked like a deer in headlights—and I was about to be merciful when he managed to pull free from her and headed for the bar. He said hello to me politely as he walked past me, his eyes going up and down over my clothes with an eyebrow going up and a slight tic at the corner of his mouth—but he didn't say anything.

I couldn't imagine what it must have been like to grow up with that woman as his mother.

But now that I was thinking about it, he did seem a bit preoccupied, maybe even a little angry or concerned?

He was the youngest of three sons, the only gay one, and the only one who'd gone into the family company. The older two had odd names, but I couldn't remember what they were other than ridiculous. I seemed to remember him telling me once that he wished his mother would retire—he chafed under her thumb, and she wouldn't even consider any of his ideas for expansion—but wasn't the business always on the brink of closing?

Anyway, their business was none of my business.

I rinsed out my coffee cup and placed it in the dishwasher. I picked up my phone and went upstairs to take a shower and get started on my to-do list for the day.

The first thing on the list was to find Ellis's card and locate my make-up case.

CHAPTER EIGHT

The hot water felt amazing, like it was scouring everything from the night before off my skin. Finally, pink from the heat and scrubbing, I reached for my towel.

My stomach growled. I needed food.

The sun streaming through my blinds was bright and hot. I turned on the ceiling fan to circulate some air. I fished my wallet out of last night's jeans before tossing them into the laundry basket. Ellis' battered, bruised card was there with some crumpled bills I'd forgotten about. I made sure everything else was there—driver's license, debit card, the credit cards I carry with me just in case. I picked up my phone and fired off a quick text: *this is Jem do you have my make-up case by any chance?*

I put my phone down and leaned back into the pillows. I was hungry. I'd been putting off a grocery run for a while now. I was making a list when my phone chirped. Hoping it was Ellis answering my text, I reached for the phone.

The text was from Rachel Sheehan.

Jackson was the one who found her.

I wasn't sure how to respond to that, so I didn't.

Poor Jackson. I wondered how Lee Ann was dealing with it. They'd been friends since childhood.

I thought about calling her but remembered she lived in the Quarter.

I could go have lunch down there and swing by her place to check on her, since I was in the neighborhood. And I can stop at Robert's on the way home for groceries. Win-win!

Today was one of those last gasps of summer—the sun was hot and the humidity thick as grits. I backed the Mercury out of the driveway and headed uptown. Trying to find a place to park on a September Saturday in the French Quarter wasn't worth the hassle, so found a spot a block off Esplanade down river from the Quarter. I walked down Bourbon Street to the Nelly Deli at the Ursulines corner. Once I had my bacon mushroom cheeseburger in hand and a sweating bottle of cold water, I walked up to Cabrini Park and ate in the shade of a large live oak while watching the Quarter dogs playing in the park.

Lee Ann lived on Dumaine, between Royal and Chartres, so I walked down to St. Philip and turned towards the river. I skirted a ghost tour of some sort and ducked into the CC's at the corner at Royal for an iced mocha.

There was a street band playing a few blocks further up the street. *You haven't spent much time in the Quarter in a while,* I thought as I reached the corner of Dumaine and Royal. Sure, the Quarter might always be packed full of tourists, but it was a charming neighborhood. When I turned the corner to walk down Dumaine, someone dressed entirely in black came out the front door of Lee Ann Vidrine's house. She fumbled in her purse and shakily lit a cigarette.

It took me a moment to realize it was the woman from last night at the gate with the guest list. What was her name? Isabelle?

Isabelle de Pew.

She was wearing a long black skirt, a black turtleneck sweater, and a pair of black ballet flats. Her hair was pulled back into a merciless ponytail. She put on an enormous pair of black sunglasses before blowing out a huge plume of smoke. She slung the strap of her purse over her shoulder, and walked down the steps.

She was tall but couldn't possibly have weighed more than ninety pounds. She wore no make-up other than plum lipstick, and her skin was almost translucent pale. She could have been any age from thirty to fifty. She slouched, her thin shoulders slumping down, and her bird-like head rested on top of a rather long, thin neck that wouldn't age well. She put her head down and hurried towards me.

I did a mock double take when she reached me. "Isabelle?" I turned as she walked past me. "That is you, isn't it?"

She stopped and turned back to look at me. She lifted the glasses. Her eyes were narrow, bloodshot, and green. "Do I know you?" she asked, her voice cold.

"Jem Richard." I stuck my hand out. "We met at Marigny's party last night. I helped with the make-up and hair for the show?" *And ended up walking in it?*

The stiff lines of her face relaxed. "Of course, I'm so sorry." She held out her right hand for me to shake.

It was cold and limp.

"You must be so upset." I shoehorned some sympathy into my voice and hoped my distaste for her wasn't written on my face.

Her eyes filled with tears. "Marigny was more than just a boss to me, she was like a second mother. I—I don't know what I'm going to do without her."

Look for another job? I thought, but said, "You were close?"

She sniffled and wiped at her eyes. "Yes, terribly close. She was mentoring me." She nodded. "I have a degree in Fashion Design from the University of

Missouri. I came to New Orleans specifically to work for Marigny."

My internal lie detector was going off. "Oh?"

She nodded again. "Marigny was very admired in the industry, you know. The necklines and sleeves, the amazing silhouettes she would come up with… as soon as I saw some of her designs, I knew I wanted to work for her, learn from her, soak up her knowledge and talent."

She was certainly laying it on thick.

"And her integrity in staying in New Orleans rather than going to New York!" Her eyes flashed, and two spots of red appeared in her pale sunken cheeks. "You have to admire that, don't you?"

Your paycheck must have never bounced, I thought. "It's just so awful," I replied, shivering. "It must have been a burglar, don't you think? I mean, I can't imagine anyone wanting to kill her, can you?"

She stared at me. "One never knows."

"You wouldn't happen to know Jackson's number, would you?" I asked. I gave her a feeble smile. "I think I may have left my make-up case at the store last night."

"At Marigny's?"

When I nodded, she reached into her purse and fumbling around, finally coming up with an engraved silver business card holder. She flicked it open and pulled out a card. "I don't seem to have my phone but call me later and I'll get the number for you."

"Thank you." I took the card and watched her go, wondering why her business card case was engraved with the initials "MO".

I shook my head. Really, Jem, you always expect the worst of people. Marigny could have given it to her—and the MO might not even stand for Marigny Orloff in the first place.

I climbed up the cement steps to Lee Ann's front door. It was set back a bit, and on the left wall there was an intercom and a buzzer. Underneath the buzzer was a note to deliverymen to leave packages next door at the mask shop if there was no answer.

When I rang, I expected her to speak to me through the intercom, but instead the big front door swung open.

"I told you—" She stopped when she saw me, and her face relaxed. Her eyes were red and swollen, and she wasn't wearing any make-up. She was wearing a billowy, striped housedress. "Oh, Jem, I wasn't expecting you."

"Hello, Lee Ann." I gave her an ingratiating smile. "I'm sorry to come by unannounced like this, but when I heard the news, I couldn't help but think about you—"

She closed her eyes and took a deep breath. "Oh, how kind of you." She stood aside so I could step inside. "Do come in, won't you? It's just terrible what's happened, just terrible."

As she shut the door behind her and turned

the deadbolt. She motioned for me to follow her. "I must apologize for the mess—I wasn't expecting anyone." She shook her head. "My mother always said one should always keep the house clean because you never know when people will just stop by."

"No worries, you should see mine." I really needed to do something about my house. "I'm sorry—I know I should have called first." I followed her through a doorway on the left side of the hall into an enormous kitchen.

"It's all right, dear." She replied absently, crossing the room to the refrigerator. "You've never been here before, have you?" She shook her head.

"No." I hadn't. Lee Ann always came to me for glam.

I took in the room while she got down a glass from a cabinet. I'm not much of a cook, but this kitchen made me green with envy. An enormous wrought iron chandelier, with black crystals, hung from a gorgeous medallion in the center of the eighteen-foot-high ceiling. There was counter space along the wall facing the street and the wall opposite the hallway, with cabinets on the walls above. There was a massive double sink in the center of the counter on the street side, directly underneath dark curtains masking a window. A huge butcher-block island was centered in the middle of the room. There were black wrought iron sconces mounted on the other walls, holding black tapered candles. The walls were painted a dark maroon, which made the whole room seem gloomy rather than cozy and warm.

"Would you like something to drink?" She asked.

I held up my half-empty cup of iced mocha. "Nothing for me, thanks."

She poured herself a tall glass of V8 and added a healthy dollop of vodka before sticking a stalk of celery into it. I noticed her hands were shaking slightly. "Let's go into the living room, shall we?"

I followed her into a room that opened off the kitchen, decorated in a style that looked like it came out of a straight-to-streaming B-movie about Marie LaVeau.

Like the kitchen, the walls were painted dark and wrought iron sconces holding black candles were placed at strategic intervals. The identical twin of the kitchen chandelier hung from the ceiling. Lee Ann walked over to the windows and pulled the thick dark brocade curtains apart, tying them back on each side with black Mardi Gras beads. I could now see the walls were a different shade than the kitchen—these were more of an eggplant purple.

Dust motes floated in the bright sunbeams. There was what appeared to be primitive African-style art and masks on the walls between the enormous sconces. In the light, I could see that the frames were terribly dusty. Musty old books were piled on every available open surface, and on top of the stacks of books were skulls—including human and alligator. Massive ferns, brown at the edges, waved from enormous pots. There were two dark colored wingback chairs flanking a table, their backs to the windows.

Underneath the table was a stuffed eight-foot-long alligator, his shellacked scales covered with a thin layer of dust.

Lee Ann smiled as she sat down in one of the wingback chairs. She gestured for me to sit down facing her on the matching love seat. I couldn't help but notice there was a thick, round black candle sitting on top of a stack of books on the table next to her. It looked like a name had been carved into the side. She saw me looking and turned it around.

"Putting a curse on someone?" I asked. It was serious dark magic to carve someone's name into a candle. According to the superstition, the life of the person whose name is cut into the wax will burn out along with the candle.

I suppressed a shudder.

"Are you sure you don't want something?" she asked, taking a drink. Her hand was still trembling.

"No, I'm good, thank you." I tore my eyes away from the black candle. "Are you okay, Lee Ann? This must be such a shock to you."

"That's so kind of you." She blinked, the corners of her mouth turning up in what was supposed to pass for a reassuring smile. "Besides, it'll do me good to talk about her. Marigny was my best friend, you know." Her head bowed for a moment, and she added, "Ever since we were girls together at McGehee. I can hardly believe she's not going to be around you know?" Her voice broke, and she wiped at her eyes with a tissue.

"I can't imagine how you must feel," I replied.

"It doesn't seem real, somehow. I mean, I just saw her last night."

"Oh, you were at the show? I didn't see you."

"I stopped by after for the party. If you've seen one of Marigny's shows, you've seen all of them. Oh!" She clapped a hand over her mouth and her face reddened. A tear slid out of her left eye. She ignored it. "We had our ups and downs over the years, but she was my oldest friend. I can't...I can't imagine what I'm going to do without her." She wiped at her face again. "And the police coming by here, like I'd kill her. Insane."

"They stopped by to see me this morning," I replied.

"I suppose they have to talk to everyone who was there last night." She finished her drink. "Poor Jackson. I can't imagine how he must be feeling. Do you think I should call him? Maybe he doesn't want to be bothered."

"I'm sure he'd be happy to hear from you." I replied, my eyes creeping back over to the black candle. The letters that hadn't burned off yet looked like E-S-E.

"I see you've noticed my candle," She coughed. "I don't believe in that sort of thing, of course. It was more—symbolic than anything else." She waved a hand. "It made me feel better."

Yeah, so then what was the deal with the rest of the bizarre decorating choices? "Symbolic?" I asked.

"Does it really matter?" She dismissed the whole subject with a sweep of her hands.

"I guess not." I crossed my legs and took a drink. "I also wanted to thank you for getting the gig last night—"

"And making sure you got paid?" she gave me a half-smile. A long-haired white cat leaped into her lap. Lee Ann twisted her lips. "Marigny was always bad with money." She shook her head. "Just as bad as she was with men. She was married five times, you know." She closed her eyes and took a deep breath. "She wasn't good with people either. I used to warn her—" she cut herself off. "For all the good it did."

"You knew her most of your life, didn't you?"

She nodded. "We went to school together, you know." The cat started purring in her lap. I bit my lower lip to keep from smiling. With the cat in her lap, Lee Ann looked like a 'take over the world' villain from a James Bond movie. "It seems like we've always been friends—I really can't remember a time when Marigny wasn't there, you know?" She pushed the cat off her lap and brushed away cat hair. "We had our ups and downs but we always forgave each

other in the end. She wasn't perfect, you know—
even if she thought she was." She smiled. "But when
someone is your friend…you overlook all kinds of
things. You make excuses for them, and because you
let them get away with little things without saying
anything, then they start with the big things. But
the thing with Marigny was it was never personal,
you know. She just didn't think how her behavior
would affect other people…she didn't like hurting people and was always sorry. She cared about
me, loved me in her way. We were like sisters. No
matter what happened with the men in our lives,
we always had each other." She pursed her lips. "At
school the other girls always made sure she never
forgot that they didn't think she belonged there. The
Orloff money was too new." She barked out a laugh.
"Marigny never forgot it, either. She told me once
if it took her the rest of her life, she would get even
with those mean girls."

"And did she?"

She looked at me, her head cocked to one side,
her eyes narrowed. "You could say that. Marigny
might have been considered white trash by those
rich society snobs, but she was a very beautiful young
woman." She gestured to herself. "I was a beautiful
young woman, too. And I felt bad for her. I thought
she behaved the way she did because of the way she'd
been treated growing up. There's no worse feeling
than wanting to fit in and being mocked, is there?"

But people get over it when they grow up, I thought, remembering my own horrendous high school experience. Aloud, I replied, "No, no there isn't. And how did she get even with them?"

"She was a beautiful young woman. You do the math." She gave me a brittle smile. "It was all so long ago. And it's not really who she was anymore. After she got back from Paris—she didn't care so much about that anymore." She laughed again. "The girls who treated her like crap when we were in school were her clients—she designed their wedding dresses, their ball gowns…"

"Did she always want to be a designer, work in fashion?"

"She could always sew, I'll give her that. But she used to have to make her own dresses, you know, for Mardi Gras balls and school dances. They made fun of her for that, too—but bless her heart, she always said she preferred to make her own because then she could have exactly what she wanted. She used to make dresses for me, too—she had a flair for it. But no, she never talked about going into fashion when she was a girl. She just wanted to get married, have kids, live in the Garden District in a big house and be queen of a ball. But she wasn't Queen of Rex…"

"Patroclus?"

"It disbanded years ago. I doubt anyone even remembers it anymore." She raised her eyebrows. "She was proud to be Queen of a ball, though. Her family

138

might not have had much money . . . but her mother made sure she went to the right schools."

"And she worked at Chanel in Paris?"

"That's what she said," She laughed. "She never liked to talk much about Paris—which I thought was odd." She shrugged.

"And five husbands?"

"To be fair, she went through the first three in no time at all." She wiped at her eyes. "But considering she didn't get started until she was in her late twenties, though—she certainly made up for lost time. Before she left for Paris, she was only interested in men that were already taken."

"Married men?"

She nodded. "Or engaged." Her eyes sparkled maliciously. "Preferably men engaged to girls we met at McGehee."

The cat, purring, was rubbing against my legs. I reached down and scratched between its ears. "And you?"

"No, that was never my style." She scratched her arm and looked away. "She always laughed at me, said it was my bourgeois upbringing. I just didn't see the point in getting involved with men that I had no future with. But for Marigny, it was all about revenge." She laughed bitterly. "Marigny was always about revenge. That's why she was writing that book."

"She was writing a book?"

"Wrote a book. It was finished. A memoir." She finished her drink and stood up. "Are you sure you don't want anything? I'm going to have another."

"A memoir?"

She nodded wearily. "She thought her life was fascinating. But she wasn't fooling me. She was using that book to get even with people, spilling secrets and dishing dirt. I told her she was crazy."

"Did Marigny get along with her ex-husbands?" I gestured toward the black candle. "Did she have any black candles in her house?"

"She was friendly with most of them, I think, except the last. Tony—she really hated him."

"But why did her children use Orloff as their last name? I figured they wouldn't do that if…"

"Marigny did that." She cut me off. "After the marriages failed, Marigny legally changed their names. She felt that if she was going to be raising them they should have her name."

"Were their fathers okay with that?"

"They didn't stop her, did they?" She made a face. "Marigny was married to her business more than anything else. The husbands always took second place to Designs by Marigny, and men don't like that." She waved her hand wearily.

"But you said she hated her last husband—"

"Tony was a leech," she interrupted me angrily. "A complete leech. But Marigny was crazy about him, wouldn't hear anything against him." Her eyes flashed. "That was her vanity talking, of course." She clicked her tongue against her teeth a couple of times. "She was past sixty—well past sixty—and she refused to even consider the idea that a man in his mid-thirties would only be after her money." She shook her head. "What else would a thirty-five-year-old man want from a woman almost seventy, besides her money?"

"What was his last name?"

"Castiglione." She waved a hand, her face twisted. "He was a yat—a good-looking one, I'll give you that—but I told her he was a mistake. She wouldn't listen to me, of course—called me a snob." She wiped at her eyes with her hands. "We had a terrible fight about that—both said some things we shouldn't have—things that could be forgiven but never forgotten."

I nodded, a little surprised. I'd always gotten the impression that Marigny was rather grand and liked to put on airs. I couldn't picture her dating a yat, let alone marrying one.

Snobbery is alive and well and living in New Orleans.

"Apparently she'd always resented me, for my family." She turned her head and looked away from me. "All those years, that resentment about my family was brewing just below the surface. She called me a snob! Me!" She looked back at me, and polished off her second drink with a big gulp. "I've

141

always thought the New Orleans caste system was horrible and unfair. Who cares how many people your ancestors enslaved, or whether you're French? But when Marigny got angry, there was no reasoning with her. She was convinced he was in love with her, and that was that."

"And she married him?"

She nodded. "They lasted a little over a year. Her previous marriage lasted the longest—I guess her fourth? She was married to Jack for about eight years. None of the others lasted more than two— just long enough for her to have a kid and then poof, it was over. But Tony Castiglione was by far the worst. He destroyed her, broke her heart. And she was obsessed with him. She couldn't let him go." She barked out a harsh little laugh. "He had a mistress, you know. Marigny found pictures of them together—in Marigny's bed."

"Oh my God." I blurted out involuntarily. "That must have hurt."

"She was devastated—and then she got mad. And like I said, when Marigny was angry there was no talking to her, no reasoning with her. She wanted to get even."

"Did she?"

She nodded. "She hired private eyes to follow him and find out who the girl was. She never told me who she was, mind you—and I didn't ask. Marigny would confide in me from time to time, but she also kept a lot of stuff private. She'd agreed to co-sign a loan for him at the bank, so he could open his own training facility, and of course she backed out of that. He created quite a scene at the store—he threw a chair through one of the front windows and screamed at her—Jackson had to call the cops and have him taken away."

Sounds like a motive for murder to me, I thought. "So, there's a police report on file?"

"I would assume." She narrowed her eyes. 'But that was over two years ago—why would he wait till now . . ." her voice trailed off. "Come to think of it, she did tell me she'd seen him the other day."

"Where?"

"She didn't give me any details, just that she'd seen him and hoped it would be the last time she ever did." Her voice shook. "I guess she got her wish, didn't she?" She buried her face in her hands. "Do you mind going? I think—I think I'd like to be alone."

I gave her a hug, told her to call me if she needed anything, and let myself out the front door.

CHAPTER NINE

My first thought as my mind slowly emerged from darkness was *where am I? What happened?*

That was followed by a painful throbbing in my head.

Ouch.

I moaned and opened my eyes—well, tried. There was something cloth tied around my eyes.

That can't be good.

I tried moving and couldn't.

I was sitting up in a chair.

My hands and ankles were tied tight.

Something was tied around my mouth, too. I moved my tongue over it.

I was so thirsty. *Unnhh unnnhhh unnhhh,* was all that came out when I tried to talk.

I was bound, gagged, and blindfolded.

No, this was definitely not good.

And I had no idea where I was.

I tried to move again but all I managed to do was make my head throb even more. Because of the gag I had to breathe through my nose, and as panic started rising inside of me I inhaled deeply and held it. I exhaled and took in another deep breath. Okay, I was calming down. Panicking wouldn't do me any good. *Relax, Jem, think this through.* Control your breathing to stay calm, was what the therapist I'd seen as a teenager used to tell me as a non-pharmaceutical method of fighting panic attacks.

Easier said than done

Focus, Jem.

I was aware of noises nearby—crashes, things breaking, someone swearing in a low voice—and it started coming back to me.

I'd been to Lee Ann's to see how she was doing but wound up only more confused than ever. Lee Ann had seemed upset, but more preoccupied than anything else. I'd walked back through the lower Quarter to where I'd parked in the Marigny. It was a beautiful afternoon, sunny and warm. I'd always liked Lee Ann. She'd been one of Mee Maw's favorite clients, and even after she officially "retired" and sold the Beauty Shoppe, she'd still done Lee Ann's hair. I'd met Lee Ann a few times when I summered in New Orleans, and she was at Mee Maw's funeral.

We'd talked, and I told her I was moving to New Orleans to live in Mee Maw's house, and that was how I started doing Lee Ann's hair. Lee Ann had referred other clients to me, as well, and as my reputation spread among the more-moneyed ladies of the city, my business began taking off. I'd even started thinking of her as more of a friend than a client. We'd even had lunch or met for drinks a few times.

But today she'd seemed different, not the Lee Ann I knew. I know everyone grieves differently, but she'd seemed…off somehow. I would have expected her to be in hysterics, unable to stop crying. Her best and oldest friend in the world had just been murdered! Maybe she was in shock? And what had Isabelle DePew been doing there?

Yeah, something had been off.

I drove home and parked in my driveway like always, walked up to the front door, put the key in the deadbolt—

And that's where my mind drew a blank.

What happened after I unlocked the front door?

How had I wound up like this?

Think, Jem, think—think and remember.

I felt my phone vibrating in my pocket and tried reaching for it—stopped again by whatever restrained my hands. I tried moving both hands again. Yes, I was tied to a chair. I tried moving my feet, too, but my ankles were bound even tighter than my hands.

Think!

Okay. I had turned left on St. Claude after driving out of the Marigny. I'd turned right at St. Roch, circled around on Claiborne to my side of the street, and pulled into the driveway.

Had Kyle's car been out there? I couldn't remember.

I turned off the car, grabbed the keys, clicked the fob to lock it, and went around the front of the house. I opened the gate and went up the front steps, got my key ready—

And now I remembered. Just as I was turning the key in the deadbolt I heard someone coming up behind me before everything went dark.

A home invasion!

I'd never taken the warnings about crime in New Orleans seriously.

The newspaper and news station websites and the comment sections on city pages in social media always talked about the "crime problem" in New Orleans. Yes, we had carjackings and rapes and shootings and robberies—so does everywhere else. I didn't take any of this talk very seriously because I can remember hearing those exact same conversations happening at the Beauty Shoppe those summers I was growing up here. It was always white women clucking their tongues and whispering about car-jackings and break-ins, always accompanied by "oh, New Orleans has changed so much." Mee Maw always told me later that was racist code.

"Even the most progressive white people here aren't really over desegregation and the end of Jim Crow," she told me once grimly while we watched *In a Lonely Place* with Humphrey Bogart and Gloria Grahame on TCM one night. There had been a rigorous conversation in the salon because a woman had been carjacked in the Garden District the day before. I'd noticed the comments on any article on *NOLA.com* about crime in the city were just more of the same. The mayor was often the one blamed, but there had been any number of mayors who faced the same problems. Those comments always looked back to a time when New Orleans was safe.

"When I was a kid I used to sleep on my grandmother's back porch and no one ever worried...we never used to lock our doors . . . I never worried about walking anywhere after dark . . . it's so dangerous there now! . . . it used to be such a great place to raise kids . . . such a shame how bad things have gotten in New Orleans."

The safe New Orleans of the past they referred to had never existed. New Orleans was born as a port city, and there has never been a port city in the history of mankind that wasn't a hotbed of vice and sin. Even Mark Twain wrote about the crime in New Orleans in the nineteenth century.

So when exactly was this period when New Orleans had been crime-free?

"It's no more dangerous here than anywhere else. You just always have to be vigilant," Mee Maw told me, "Like you would in any big city. Don't listen to those racists at the shop."

Our neighborhood was often mentioned on real estate websites as "in transition," which was realtor lingo for "probably more dangerous than you'd like." Once the gentrification of the Marigny and Bywater neighborhoods was underway, they'd moved across St. Claude to our neighborhood. Most old-timers called our neighborhood "St. Roch" or "the 7th Ward," despite the rebranding attempts by developers. St. Roch was an interesting mix of blighted houses, decaying inhabited houses that needed work, and ones that had already been, or were in the process of renovation. I sometimes checked the real estate websites to see what the property values were, rolling my eyes at what realtors called "fixer-uppers needing a bit of work." If you scrolled through the pictures of the property, you could see what they meant by "fixer-upper" was "gut completely and start over." And the prices! *Almost three thousand dollars for a blighted property that would need at least another couple of hundred grand put into it? Were they crazy?*

But most break-ins in our neighborhood were usually limited to cars—broken windows and the glovebox gone through. Mine was so old most kids left it alone, and it was usually parked in the driveway. Kyle's car had been broken into on the street several times. And sure, there was an occasional shooting in the neighborhood, but it usually it was either some kind of domestic situation or drug related.

I learned where the drug sites were in the neighborhood so I could avoid them.

You let your guard down because it was daylight. Stupid, stupid, stupid.

Outside of the headache, I wasn't in any other pain. Well, whatever they'd bound me with was cutting into my wrists and ankles—but other than that, I thought I was okay. It didn't hurt to breathe so my lungs were okay.

I need to get out of here!
Calm down, stay calm. Be logical, not hysterical. Think.

Okay, they'd come up behind me while I was at the front door and knocked me out—that was the headache. I didn't think anything else was injured. My hands and feet were securely tied. I was gagged. But I was also in my house. And as alarming as it was to be tied up, it seemed like a good sign to me. If they were going to kill me they wouldn't have bothered to tie me up, right? Yeah, we were being robbed—and I hoped Kyle didn't come home in the middle of this— but once they got whatever they wanted, they'd leave.

And Kyle would come home eventually.

I just had to be patient.

Unfortunately, patience isn't one of my virtues.

I wondered what time it was.

Kyle taught a pole class at Bywater Fitness every Sunday at one. He usually stayed and lifted weights afterward, sat in the hot tub for a while. He would also sit in the sauna for a while and use the steam room. Sunday was the day for what he called his "beauty regimen" at the gym. He wouldn't be back for hours. He also had another show tonight at Baby Jane's, and was currently single. What time had it been when I got back home? I hadn't looked at my phone when I unplugged it from the car jack.

Oh God please don't let Kyle come back early and walk in on this, I prayed.

I heard footsteps approaching. A voice whispered in my ear, "I'm going to take the gag off you right now." He pressed something circular and cold against my temple. "I'm holding a gun to your head right now, you understand? If you scream I will shoot you. Nod if you understand?"

Oh God, I thought as a chill went down my spine. I nodded quickly.

Someone began fiddling with the gag at the back of my head. I gulped in air through my mouth once the cloth went lax and dropped away. I resisted the urge to scream as loudly as I could because it wouldn't do any good. He'd just shoot me before any curious neighbor came by to see what was going on. My mouth was so dry, and my lips felt like they were cracking. "Water," I croaked out, "please can someone get me some water?"

The voice was right in my ear and the hair on my arms rose. "If you're good maybe."

"Please, get me some water and I'll tell you anything you want to know."

"Where is the case?" the voice whispered in my ear. "Tell me where it is and I'll give you some water."

"The case?" I asked, confused.

"The case, the case, the one you had with you last night," the voice said impatiently. "Tell me where it is, and I'll go."

"You mean my make-up case?" I gagged again and coughed a few time for good measure. I heard the footsteps walking away again. I heard the sink in the bathroom running, and after what seemed like an eternity, the footsteps approached again and something hard was pressed against my lips. Cold water started trickling into my mouth, and I gulped down swallow after swallow. The cold water felt amazing in my mouth. Finally, he pulled the glass away from my lips. "It isn't here."

"What do you mean it isn't here? Where is it?" You never think about how menacing a whisper can sound until you're bound and gagged and someone who has complete control over whether you live or die starts whispering to you. Just because he hadn't killed me already didn't mean he wouldn't if I didn't give him what he wanted.

"I don't know for sure," I replied. I flinched away from the direction the whispering was coming from, because I was expecting a blow for not knowing. I took it as a good sign that a blow never came. "I left it somewhere last night. I think I may have left it at Designs by Marigny—I was going to call Jackson to see if I could go look for it but I don't even know if I can get in because it's a crime scene you know someone killed his mother last night." I took a deep breath. "I drank too much at the party. I don't even remember leaving that party—" I hoped he'd believe that lie, "—and I've been trying to find it this morning. I don't want to have to replace everything." That was not a lie. "It belonged to my grandmother. It means a lot to me." Not a lie.

But there was no way I was going to send these thugs after Ellis.

I heard the burglar swear under his breath, and then there was another flash of pain.

Everything went dark.

I started coming to with someone tugging at whatever was binding my ankles. "Who's there?" I said, worried. My head ached even more than it had before.

"Oh, thank God, Jem! Are you okay?"

It was Kyle, his voice shaking.

Thank God.

"Can you take this blindfold off?" I asked, wincing from the sudden light as he pulled whatever had been tied around my head free. I blinked, water running out of my eyes, and I took in Kyle's frantic face, his eyes widened. He was holding what looked like a knotted tube sock in his right hand. In his left was the butcher knife from the kitchen. I was sitting in the old wooden chair I used for sewing, and both hands were duct taped to the arms. Both ankles were duct-taped to the legs.

Duct tape? I was lucky they didn't use that on my mouth!

"The cops are on their way," he said calmly, kneeling back down and sawing at the tape on my right ankle. "When I pulled up in front of the house the front door was wide open, and with your car in the driveway—I knew you'd never leave the front door open like that so freaked out immediately. I called the cops. When I looked inside I saw you and went into the kitchen to get something to cut you free . . . are you okay? You look terrible. What happened?"

"My head hurts." I said, moving my right ankle as it was cut free. He cut the tape off my other ankle, taking bits of skin and hair with. "Have you looked to see if anything is missing?"

My head was aching bad, but I doubted anything was taken.

They'd wanted my make-up case. Why?

"You've got a nasty lump on the right temple and a bruise, too." Kyle said as he went to work freeing my right wrist. "and I can see another one on the back of your head. Baby, you might have a concussion, so take it easy, okay? After the cops leave we're taking you to the emergency room. Go lie down on the couch when I get you free."

I nodded and closed my eyes. He was finishing freeing my left hand when the two uniformed police officers came to the door. After that, everything just happened in a blur. Paramedics arrived and started checking me out while the cops checked out the rest of the house. Guys arrived in protective gear, the biohazard version of a full body condom, to start taking pictures and dust for fingerprints while another cop began taking my statement. I wasn't much help. I hadn't seen anyone, hadn't recognized the whispering voice, couldn't say anything that might help identify the burglars.

It was frustrating.

Whoever had tied me up had torn the house apart. Chairs were turned over, couch cushions tossed everywhere, drawers opened and emptied in every room. I didn't want to see what they'd done to my work room. I eased myself down on the couch.

"I don't think you have a concussion," the female paramedic said after checking my pupils with one of those annoying pencil lights. "But I think you should go have your head X-rayed as a precaution."

"No, no, I'm fine," I said, not wanting to admit that I didn't have health insurance—one of the great joys of working freelance—and there was no way I was wiping out my meager savings account with a trip to the hospital and X-rays.

"If you start seeing double or the headaches get worse—"

"I'll go to the hospital or call 911," I replied wearily. "Thank you."

When I opened my eyes, I saw Blake Dorgenois standing in front of me. If there could be a bright side to a home invasion, seeing Blake a second time in the same day was it.

So of course the hottest guy I've met in months keeps seeing me at my worst.

"Can't let you out of my sight for a minute, can I?" He was dressed more casually than earlier. A tight pink collared Polo shirt, tight jeans, white sneakers.

"Yes, well, I may be desperate but I'm not that desperate yet," I replied. "Maybe in ten years, but not now."

He pulled up a footrest and sat down on it next to me. "What happened?"

I could see Latoya Picot talking to Kyle on the other side of the room while I told the story again.

"Specifically, the burglar asked about your make-up case?"

I nodded, wincing from the sudden pain in my head. "I didn't tell him where I think it may be," I said. "But why of all things is he looking for my make-up case?"

Blake shrugged his massive shoulders. "Your case was in the dressing room all last night, right?"

"During the show," I replied. "After the show was over, Marigny didn't like how I was dressed and told me I couldn't come to the party."

He raised an eyebrow. "You didn't mention that earlier."

"It didn't seem important." I started to shake my head again but stopped myself. "After I changed out of the wedding dress and back into my clothes, Marigny told me I wasn't dressed appropriately for her party and I needed to leave. I was leaving when Ellis came after me, insisting I stay for the party and offering to give me a ride home. One of the guests at the party was Rachel Sheehan, who's also a client of mine. She wanted me to come have a drink with her."

"And Marigny didn't have a problem then?"

"I don't really remember seeing her again before leaving." I closed my eyes. "I swear I put my case in Ellis' car because he offered me a ride home..." I clapped my hand to my shorts pocket and felt my phone. I pulled it out, unlocked it and ... no response from Ellis. I frowned. Maybe I'd have to call ...

"Ellis is Ellis Ikehorn, who produced the show last night?"

"Yes. I texted him this morning about it, but he hasn't answered."

"Can you think of any reason why anyone would be interested in your make-up case?"

"It was Louis Vuitton, but it's old. There are rips and tears in it. It belonged to my grandmother, so I've held on to it. I have a bigger, newer one I usually use, but I didn't need everything so I took the smaller case. All that was in it is my make-up stuff—brushes, mirrors, you know, the usual stuff a make-up artist takes everywhere with him."

"You're sure?" Blake asked again, fixing those beautiful eyes on me again.

"Positive."

"Marigny's body was found in the dressing room," Blake said slowly, closing his notepad and slipping it back into the shirt pocket so tantalizingly stretched out over his left pectoral muscle, "and the room had been torn to pieces. Like the killer was looking for something. And didn't find it." He nodded at the mess that had been my cute living room. "I think whatever the killer was looking for, he thinks is in your make-up case now."

I stared at him. "Then you need to find Ellis Ikehorn and warn him," I replied. "Because he's the one who has it. And if they're willing to do a home invasion to try to get whatever it is—then he's probably in danger, too."

"You still have my card?"

"I do."

"Call me if you think of anything."

Blake and Latoya left while they were still processing the house—that nasty black fingerprint dust everywhere—and they took Kyle's and my fingerprints, too—to eliminate us—and the paramedics gave Kyle some instructions of what to watch for with me. I took some extra strength Tylenol and held an ice pack to the lump on my forehead.

Finally, the last of them left and Kyle shut the front door and locked it, putting on the security chain, too. He leaned back against the door. "Can I not leave you alone for a minute?" he teased.

I forced a very weak smile on my face. "Apparently not."

"Girl, if you're trying to get that handsome cop's attention, you're doing a good job, but there has to be an easier way than getting attacked and our house wrecked." He put his hands on his hips and surveyed the damage. "It's going to take forever to get this place back in order."

"Yeah, well." I watched as he grabbed a broom and started sweeping up wreckage. I'd been so wrapped up in my narrow escape that I'd not really paid much attention how badly they'd trashed the place. But the smashed bits of porcelain he was sweeping up was all that was left of Mee Maw's collection of porcelain bisque dolls that she'd always sworn was going to be worth a fortune someday. There were fragments of broken and shattered glass everywhere—glass from framed posters and photographs, some of which were also scattered all over the floor. I felt a little sick to my stomach. Was it necessary to destroy Mee Maw's things, which were all I had left of her?

I stood up, a little wobbly, and started picking up things off the floor slowly. Oh, there were her snow globes. One was cracked, but the other three seemed okay. I sighed and tossed the cracked one—a scene of Jackson Square, which always seemed odd to shake so it snowed in the Quarter—into the garbage. She'd thought those would be worth something someday, too. She'd been a bit of a dreamer, collecting things she liked that might be worth something someday—she'd haunted flea markets, second hand stores, and antique shops on her days off, looking for treasures, so the house had been filled with all kinds of ancient knick knacks, stuff I'd always thought was junk but hadn't gotten rid of because it had all been hers, and that was all that was left other than pictures and memories.

And even those only went back so far. She'd lost a lot in the flood that followed Hurricane Katrina—which had made the things that had survived even more precious to her.

This house had been her everything.

And you let it turn into a pigsty, like a place where straight college boys lived. How could you do that to her house?

I looked around and gritted my teeth. Sure, the burglars had trashed the place . . . but it had already been trashed.

I was reaching down to pick up one of her Jazz Fest posters—it had been sliced when the glass shattered—when my phone vibrated.

Ellis. *Text me your address and I'll drop it off.*

CHAPTER TEN

"You don't have to help," I said, taking the broom away from Kyle and wondering if I should text Ellis back, warn him. "This is my mess."

Kyle put a fist on one hip and blinked at me. "I live here, too, darlin'. Do you think they went through our bedrooms?"

I hadn't even thought about that. My heart sank and my stomach turned. I leaned against the counter and rubbed my eyes. "You always think you're safe in your own house..." and my voice broke and I could feel tears coming. Kyle pulled me in for a tight hug—he really is the best hugger—and held me for a few moments. "Do you think we should get a burglar alarm?"

He gave me another look. "Your grandmother

161

lived in this house when this neighborhood was high crime without a problem, and now you're thinking we need a burglar alarm?" He shook his head. "And what good would it do? No one pays attention when a car alarm goes off. And even it the alarm company alerts the cops, it's not like they are quick to respond anyway. But if it makes you feel any better—"

"You're right, it won't make any difference." I took a deep breath. "Why don't you go look around upstairs and see if the crooks went up there? And if they dusted for prints?" It was bad enough we had to wipe down every surface downstairs, but if we had to do it up there, too? I looked around at the mess on the floor, at the black dust all over my kitchen counters and the table. I reached under the sink for my Clorox wipes and went over the kitchen counter. It worked. One wipe was enough for the entire counter on either side of the sink. I heard Kyle going up the stair to my room and could hear him moving around as I finished wiping down the kitchen. I grabbed the broom and started sweeping up the pieces of glasses and porcelain and whatever else was on the floor. I'd gotten it all up and dumped it into the garbage can when Kyle came galloping down the stairs.

"I can't tell if the crooks searched your room or not," he said with a crooked grin. "But they didn't dust up there."

"I know where everything is in my room," I replied without looking at him.

"You got this kitchen cleaned up pretty quick." He said. "I'll start picking things up in the living room."

I followed him out into the big room and sighed. What a mess.

I kept reminding myself they're just things as Kyle and I cleaned it all up.

That was what Mee Maw said when we all came down here after Katrina to clean out her house. I wasn't very old then, but I remember my dad being a lot more upset about the damage to his childhood home than Mee Maw was. Mom and Dad both thought she should take the insurance money, sell the lot, and move to Dallas and live with us.

She just gave them a withering stare until they changed the subject.

Mee Maw was my paternal grandmother. My paternal grandfather was someone we never talked about; he ran off when Dad was just a baby and she'd never remarried. She worked hard and opened the Beauty Shoppe, becoming something of an institution over on Magazine Street. She was also the only person in the family who'd never treated me like I had two heads or something. My parents didn't know what to make of me. My older brothers were jocks, playing three sports and excelling at them. I had no natural athletic ability

163

and school was boring for me. I got decent grades but never studied very hard. I'm not sure why they started sending me to spend the summers with her in New Orleans, but those summers were the best times of my life. Her house in New Orleans was a safe space for me. She didn't care that I didn't want to play baseball and preferred watching old movies with her on TCM. Knowing I was going to New Orleans for the summer made the school years a little more bearable.

Whenever the bullies came for me and made fun of my lisp (cured by a speech therapist Mee Maw paid for the summer before my freshman year of high school—"if that's the problem and why the little monsters are picking on you, let's just get it taken care of") instead of getting hurt or crying, I just had to remember *only a few more months before I get to go home to New Orleans.* I barely remembered those summers immediately after Hurricane Katrina—I remember the construction work being done on the house the summer after, but the following summer it was all finished. Mee Maw loved that I was interested in the same things she was—hair, make-up, movie stars. She indulged me the way my parents never did. Mee Maw embraced my difference. She was the first person I came out to, when I was thirteen. She'd just smiled and said, "Some of the best people I know are gay men." She didn't care that I didn't want to play football like my dad and my older brothers or go to college. Neither of my brothers had the slightest idea of what they wanted to do with their lives when they went to college, not deciding on majors until they had no choice. My oldest brother Ashe now worked as a realtor in Dallas and Luke was a regional manager for a fast food company in Albuquerque.

I always knew I wanted to do what Mee Maw did—hair and make-up—but the idea of me going to cosmetology school had horrified my parents. Mom was a little more receptive to my sexuality, but Dad? Dad never got over not having a third son who accomplished the dream of a college football scholarship and an NFL career.

It wasn't my fault I was small and gay. My genes came from them.

If anything, it was *their* fault.

Mee Maw was the one who paid for me to go to cosmetology school.

I should have moved here after graduation. But she'd already sold the Beauty Shoppe and retired, so I just stayed in Dallas.

Her death four years ago had been wrenching for me. I moved to New Orleans so I could take care of her those last few months. Living in her house and being around her new things had always made me feel closer to her even though she was gone.

Sweeping up the shattered remains of her

things and putting them in the trash felt like losing her all over again.

They're just things, nothing that can't be replaced, she'd said cheerfully as she dumped moldy photo albums and Dad's ruined high school yearbooks into the dumpster.

Even after four years, thinking about her made me sad.

I kept pushing those thoughts out of my head while I cleaned, trying to focus on making the place look like home again. Mee Maw had been a stickler for cleaning. She used to joke that she made Joan Crawford look like a slob. Everything has a place, and everything in its place was her motto.

Don't make a mess you don't have time to clean up immediately was another.

I smothered a hysterical laugh. I'd been making a mess in this house for four years.

Not really a surprise that I was still single now that I thought about it.

I looked around and put my hands on my hips. No wonder Tradd ghosted you, I thought. He's seen your house. Tradd's house was immaculate. He also had a full-time job, as a social worker at the Odyssey House. I didn't have a full-time job, either. What had Tradd seen when he looked at me?

A mess. A mess with a filthy house who didn't work most of the time, always worried about money, and was just spinning his wheels, going nowhere.

Yeah, who wouldn't want a relationship with that?

Kyle was blaring dance music through the stereo speakers as he cleaned, dancing with the broom as he reached it under furniture to get stray shards of glass and crockery, shaking his backside as he wiped that awful black fingerprint dust off surfaces, missing spots I could see from the other side of the room

The worst of it was the invaders had swept all the family pictures off the mantel onto the floor. All the glass in the frames had shattered, and some of the frames were bent. Glass had sliced through some of the pictures. I picked the pictures carefully out from the bent frames without slicing myself with the glass, threw the wreckage into a trash bag that I took out and shoved into the bin.

The pictures weren't ruined, but some were damaged. Maybe I could scan them and repair them on my computer?

Yes, definitely need to scan them, I thought, remembering the moldy photo albums Mee Maw tossed away after the flood. Those pictures, those pieces of family history were gone forever.

I needed to save what's left digitally.

I wiped down ledges and counter tops, souvenirs and the bric-a-brac that somehow had managed to survive the rampage. I found a little porcelain mermaid she'd gotten from Weeki Wachi in

Florida on a trip we'd taken one summer to Sanibel Island. The fingerprint dust had ruined a couple of cream-colored pillows a dry cleaner might be able to save. We worked in silence, Kyle sometimes humming along with the music. I focused on the chore, trying not to remember Mee Maw's joy in her things, trying to not feel like somehow I'd failed her by letting her house go, that if she'd left everything to one of my brothers or cousins none of this would be in ruins today.

It didn't help that it was true.

Mee Maw would say they're just things. And she'd be right.

I noticed shadows were getting longer, which meant it was getting later. Kyle's show was at nine. I could get the downstairs finished and do my bedroom tomorrow. This house was going to be a showplace from now on. I owed that to Mee Maw.

And I'd get my own act together. I would. I'd stop drifting and figure out what I want to do with the rest of my life.

I was so deep in thought I nearly jumped out of my skin when the doorbell rang.

Kyle bounded across the room and checked through the blinds before unlatching the door. "Ellis!" Kyle threw his arms around him and air-kissed both cheeks. "Come on in. Make yourself at home—" he gestured around, "well, comfortable, anyway."

"Wow." Ellis said, rolling my make-up case in behind him. "What happened here?"

"Thank you so much," I said. "I couldn't remember where I left it."

"Sorry." He made a face. "I would have been here sooner but I was tied up—"

"So was Jem." Kyle closed and locked the door, putting on the chain. "Home invasion." he added grimly. "Tied up poor Jem and God only knows what they might have done to him."

Ellis's face drained of color. "Oh my God." He dropped down onto the couch. "What did they do to you, Jem?" He touched my swollen forehead and I winced. "That's a helluva knot and bruise on your forehead."

"I'm shaken up, but okay." I started shivering uncontrollably and reached out a hand to the wall to steady myself. "Bit of a headache, but nothing Tylenol won't handle." I gave my new friend a weak smile. "It's just a shock, you know? You never think something like that will happen to you—it's something that happens to other people."

"It's been a hell of a twenty-four hours, that's for sure." Ellis shook his head. "I'm sorry it took me so long to get over here. It never even crossed my mind last night that your case was in my trunk until I got home last night myself and got mine out of the trunk.' He laughed. "And I had a gig on the north shore this afternoon—a drag birthday party—so I

169

just took your stuff along with mine and figured I'd try to reach out on my way back to the city."

"A drag birthday party?" I stared at him. "That's a thing?"

"Yes, Jem. You can make good money these days doing drag—if you're a pro," Ellis replied. "Birthday parties, bachelorette parties, gender reveals, brunches...you can pretty much do it full time now. And drag queens aren't nearly as scary as clowns—no matter what the fundies are saying—and kids love us. I have a brunch booked for tomorrow that'll be good for almost a grand in tips, and then I'm doing a bachelorette party in Pass Christian that'll pay my bills next month." He waved a hand, and I noticed the nails were trimmed down and neat. "You're a natural, Jem. You really should take my next workshop. I'll give you a discount."

"I'll think about it." It wasn't a bad idea. Another source of income would be welcome, especially during those slow months when there wasn't a lot of glam work. Now that the summer was over things should start picking up—once the weather cooled wedding season kicked into high gear—but if I could make an extra grand every month doing drag...I already had the make-up. All I needed was wigs and costumes—and I could make the costumes. I could even start a sewing business making costumes for other queens...Mee

Maw used to make the costumes every year for the King and Queen of Ramses, one of the older Carnival krewes, hand-sewing sequins and crystals into their robes and royal clothing.

Maybe…maybe I could even afford to get health insurance?

I pinched myself to wake up from the dream.

I opened the top lid of my rolling case, and everything was right where I had left it the night before. I closed it and frowned at Ellis. "What time did you leave for the north shore this morning?"

He yawned. "About ten. The party was for the afternoon, but I needed to get ready and I wasn't about to drive an hour in full drag."

"And you haven't been home yet?"

He looked at me, puzzled. "No, I haven't. Why?"

I gestured at the still-messy living room. "This wasn't a random home invasion," I said. "They were looking for my make-up case. Which was at Marigny's, on the same night she was murdered."

"How do you know they were looking for your case?"

"They asked." I shook my head. "Nope, none of this is a coincidence."

"It's never a coincidence on *Law and Order*," Kyle said gravely.

I gave him a withering look. "You haven't been home since this morning?"

Ellis shook his head. "You think someone may

171

have broken into my place?" Ellis frowned, pinching his lower lip. "Do you think it's safe to even go home?"

My head was starting to hurt again. "I'm probably overreacting," I added, rubbing my eyes. "It's been a rough twenty-four hours, so it should be expected, I guess. The shock of having the police show up at my front door and then this…"

"It sounds like you're giving up," Kyle leaned against the wall, folding his arms. "That's no way to impress Blake Dorgenois."

"I'm not trying—"

"Blake? What does Blake have to do with anything?" Ellis interrupted me.

"You know him?" I asked.

Ellis blushed a deep purple. "Blake and I dated a bit earlier this year is all. He's in charge of the investigation?" He turned to me. "Are you interested in him? He's not looking for another relationship, you know, since his partner died year before last. He's just looking for a good time—not to discourage you or anything, I just wouldn't get my hopes up."

I exhaled, "My hopes aren't up. Blake is good looking, sure, but anything else Kyle is making up in his head." I waved my index finger at him. "Knock it off, Kyle."

He sniffed. "You can't blame me for trying, now, can you?"

"I can." I retorted. "Ellis, is there someone you can

call to meet you at your place? Maybe it's overkill but I'm not sure how I feel about you going home alone."

Kyle's eyebrows went up and I could have strangled him on the spot. Ellis was attractive, sure, but that wasn't why I was worried about him heading home alone.

Ellis stood up. "I'm sure it'll be fine. I live over in Holy Cross." Holy Cross was the last neighborhood within the city limits on the way to St. Bernard Parish, just on the other side of the Industrial Canal. That entire historic neighborhood had flooded terribly during Katrina when a barge left in the canal had crashed through the levee. The area also took on water that came in through Lake Borgne into St. Bernard Parish. The Holy Cross school campus that gave the neighborhood its name had been abandoned ever since.

It would wind up as luxury condos was my guess. That's what everything was being repurposed into—churches, fire houses, schools, and hospitals turned into luxury condos too expensive for working class people in New Orleans to afford.

I could never afford to buy Mee Maw's house in today's market. She'd paid practically nothing for it when she bought it, but houses in the neighborhood that needed gutting were going for hundreds of thousands of dollars. Mee Maw's didn't need gutting, so it was worth more than the blighted wrecks.

Kyle's rent paid the property taxes.

And if this "new Marigny" rebranding of the neighborhood realtors were trying to make happen ever took off, it would be worth even more.

"I think we should come with you." I replied. "I don't like the idea of you going home by yourself."

"No, there's no need." Ellis said. "Besides, you have a mess here to clean up." He glanced at his watch. "Some of my graduates are performing at Oz tonight, and I really should get going if I want to eat and catch their show. You boys should come."

"I'm performing at Baby Jane's again tonight," Kyle said.

"I think I'm going to stay in tonight,' I replied. I was tired. "Call me once you're home and safely inside," I replied, giving him a hug and locking the door behind him. I watched through the blinds as he got into his car and drove away.

I rolled the case into my workroom—and then put the latch on the back door. Sure, it was locked, and the latch wouldn't be much of a deterrent to someone who wanted in, but it made me feel better.

I opened the lid and checked everything again. Everything was there, in its proper place. I needed to wash my brushes again, but that could wait until tomorrow. I opened the first drawer, the slim one, to check on my fake nails and polishes—

And there was something there that didn't belong,

I picked it up. It was about a half inch thick, silver on either flat surface and white on the sides. A silver G was on one side.

It was a hard drive.

I whistled. Was this what they'd been looking for? I'd never seen this thing before and had no idea how it had wound up in my make-up case. Then I remembered going to the bathroom at the party and coming back to the dressing room to overhear Marigny arguing with that man. She'd been standing right by my make-up case.

Hadn't I caught her by my case?

Had Marigny put this in my case? Or had someone else?

I carried it over to my computer. I opened my top desk drawer and removed a cord, plugging one end into the hard drive and the other into my computer, which woke up. A little box appeared on my desktop: MEMOIR.

That's right—Lee Ann said Marigny was writing a memoir.

I moved the mouse so the cursor was on the icon and clicked twice. A window opened. The device was password protected, of course.

I took a chance and typed Marigny's name into the password box, but the box jumped a couple of times to let me know the password was incorrect.

I dragged the icon to the trash and disconnected it from my computer.

I reached for my phone and was typing Blake's number into it when I stopped myself.

I tapped my forefinger on the hard drive.

It wasn't mine, and I had no idea how it got into my make-up case. The case had just been sitting in the dressing room all night long at Marigny's. Any one of the models could have put this in my case. Marigny could have done it, too, or the man she'd been talking to, or any of the guests at the party, really. The dressing room hadn't been locked from either door, and any one of the guests could have easily walked into the house and then into the dressing room.

But why my case?

The right thing to do would be to turn this over to Blake and Latoya and wash my hands of this entire mess.

On the other hand, I was kind of in this already up to my neck. My house had been broken into, I had been assaulted, and my grandmother's things destroyed, so it was kind of personal now.

Maybe I could hang on to it for just another day or so . . . but I'd need to secure it somewhere a burglar would never find if they broke in again.

I glanced around my workroom. There were lots of places to hide something the size of the drive, but if they were obvious to me, they'd be obvious to a burglar.

I walked over to the wooden bookcase and reached up to the top shelf, where Mee Maw's set of Gothic romances from the late 1970s rested. I pulled out a copy of Victoria Holt's *The Legend of the Seventh Virgin* and slipped the hard drive against the back of the bookcase.

Then I slid the book back in front of it.

No one would find it there.

CHAPTER ELEVEN

I woke up Monday morning to bright sun-
shine after a great night's sleep and sat up in bed. I
stretched and yawned and felt marvelous. I reached
up to scratch my head and winced when I touched
the lump.

And it all came rushing back.

Someone had broken into my house and clob-
bered me twice.

Marigny Orloff had been murdered.

And someone had hidden a hard drive in my
make-up case.

At least my head didn't hurt anymore.

I could hear the shower going on Kyle's side
of the house. I reached for my phone to check the
time—it was almost nine—and moaned. I held it up

to my face so the phone would do the facial recognition thing and it unlocked.

I had an awful lot of text messages for a Monday morning.

I touched the icon and the list opened. Apparently, everyone I knew in New Orleans texted me after I went to bed last night. Kyle had helped me clean until it was time for him to head to Baby Jane's for his Sunday night show. I'd kept cleaning, grimly, wiping and sweeping and mopping until the entire downstairs was spic and span. I'd been proud of myself when I looked around before going up to bed. Sure, some things were missing—but Mee Maw had so much stuff you really couldn't tell.

Although I'd been so tired as I finished, I'd probably have to redo some of it today.

I'd been so dead to the world I hadn't even heard Kyle come home.

I smiled when I saw that the most recent text was from Ellis: *Hey, wanted to see how you were feeling this morning. If you don't have any plans, why don't you come by my studio? I'm putting together a new show for brunch at the Country Club this weekend and you can see how the magic happens.*

There was a smiley face at the end.

It wouldn't *kill* me to go watch, would it? I wasn't committing to enroll in his school.

And it hit me. He wasn't flirting with me. He just was trying to recruit me for the drag school.

I started to bang my head against my headboard but remembered there was a lump on the back of my head, too.

Still, better to have realized it now before I made a fool out of myself.

You don't know that. Just because you've always had bad luck with men before doesn't mean every guy you meet is going to ghost you.

And as I was thinking that, my phone vibrated as another text from Ellis arrived.

Actually, I have to go by the Country Club to double-check some things about the space. Why don't you meet me there for lunch?

The Country Club wasn't an actual "country club." It was a popular hangout that served food and had a community pool—you could pay a monthly fee to use the pool or just pay an daily admission fee. It was in the last full block of Louisa Street before the levee in the Bywater. The building itself was an old center-hall style Caribbean plantation style house. The front rooms were the restaurant, and the back room was the bar. There was also a bar out by the pool, and sometimes they had a deejay spinning dance music out there. It used to be a queer space back before Katrina, but after a renovation and face lift they'd started welcoming straight people so the crowd was usually mixed. I'd heard stories from older gays about what used to go on there when it was a queer space. It had been clothing optional and the stories made it sound like it had been more of a private sex club. They'd eliminated the clothing optional rule after a young woman was sexually assaulted. The older gays would always sneer *straight people ruin everything*.

Was he asking me on a date?

I leaned back against my pillows, liking the idea. Ellis was handsome, had a great personality and sense of humor, had a good source of income, and seemed interested in me.

You'd thought Tradd was interested too until he wasn't.

I pushed that negativity right out of my head.

If it was a date . . . he'd texted me, so he wasn't looking for a hook-up; that's what the apps were for.

I started to answer but wondered if it would seem too thirsty to respond right away. So instead, I continued scrolling through the various texts from a variety of friends and acquaintances. It was also clear that they hadn't heard about the break-in or anything.

They'd seen pictures of me from Friday night somewhere—Instagram, the paper, social media—and were curious.

When did you start doing drag?

Girl, you looked amazing!

I couldn't believe that was you and still am not sure I do!

All of them were complimentary, though.

I touched the Instagram app open and the first

thing I saw was my face.

Well, Joan Crawfish's face, anyway.

It was Jackson Orloff's account. I glanced at the time it was posted. Friday night. He'd taken this during the show, and someone had reshared it, taking it to the top of my feed. There were lots of likes and hearts on my picture, and the long thread of comments was all complimentary.

Maybe I should consider this more seriously, I thought with a pleased smile. *Maybe Ellis isn't just trying to recruit me for the money, but because he really thinks I can make a go of this.*

But the stage fright issue...

I hadn't been nervous once I went down the backsteps of Marigny's mansion Friday night, had I? I'd started enjoying myself as I walked through the garden, along the runner between flower beds and fountains. My confidence had grown with every step, with each change of dress and wig, with every compliment.

But I will not be Joan Crawfish. I need a better name than that.

I pulled on my sweatpants and walked into the bathroom for my regular morning routine. Mee Maw had gotten *The Times-Picayune* daily, but I'd canceled that choosing to pay the less expensive monthly rate for web access to *NOLA.com*. As I headed downstairs to get coffee, I opened their app and went to the Society page from Sunday. Sure enough, there I was, in full drag, alongside two of the other queens and Jackson Orloff. It was a rather unfortunate shot of Jackson—the expression on his face made him look wasted. I didn't remember the names of the other two queens, so was grateful for the caption: Jackson Orloff poses with some of the 'models', Scarlett Sahara, Floretta Flynn, and Joan Crawfish.

Yeah, I was going to have to do better than Joan Crawfish.

I scrutinized the picture, making it larger with my fingers. It wasn't hard to tell that drag queen was me. But I don't think anyone who didn't know me could identify me from the picture. The enormous red lacquered wig added almost six inches to my height, and the heels were at least four inches.

All three of us towered over Jackson.

As I sipped my coffee, I thought, *that's what I should do with that hard drive—it had to have come from Designs by Marigny. Maybe I should just give it back to Jackson?*

As if on cue, Kyle walked into the kitchen dressed for work in a Crescent Care T-shirt and jeans "Where does Jackson Orloff live?" I asked.

He did a double-take. "Good morning to you, too." He blinked rapidly and smiled at me. "Everyone at Baby Jane's last night was all about you doing drag Friday. Even got your picture in the paper!"

"Really?" I felt my face turning red.

"You should go to Ellis's school." Kyle made himself a cup of coffee and leaned back against the counter. "We could do the same shows. Wouldn't that be fun?"

"Maybe? I don't know." I'd never considered drag as a creative outlet. But if I could make good money…more income streams were always welcome. It hadn't been terrible wearing pads and a dress.

"Why were you asking about Jackson Orloff?"

"I did find something in my make-up case that isn't mine." I said slowly. "I was going to see if maybe Jackson recognized it?"

"Are you high?" Kyle gave me his are you serious face. "Didn't you just tell God and the police that the men who broke in here and assaulted you were asking about your make-up case? And now you find something in it that doesn't belong?" He shook his head. "I'm thinking you should be giving it to the police." He shook his head. "You should have called them last night when Ellis brought it over. Don't you want to call Blake again?"

I felt my face turning red. "I don't want to look thirsty." I mumbled.

"You're not being desperate," Kyle rolled his eyes. "Calling the police is literally your civic duty. You need to turn whatever it is you found over to the cops, so we don't get broken into and attacked again."

There was no way I was calling Blake now. He

probably already thought I was an idiot. I wasn't going to be blowing up his phone.

I could see if Jackson recognized it first, and then give it to the police.

"You're crazy for not calling the cops." Kyle grinned wickedly as he started brewing his own coffee. "A perfectly acceptable reason to call Detective Blake and get his fine butt back over here. But Jackson lives on Prytania Street, near the theater. He lives in one of those old Spanish looking houses on the river side, just before the street makes that jog?"

The Prytania Theater was a beautiful old movie theater, one of the few of its kind still operating in New Orleans. It was uptown at the corner of Prytania and Soniat. "Text me his number?"

Kyle rolled his eyes but he pulled his phone out of the back pocket of his shorts and a few moments later my phone dinged. I touched the link and my phone dialed.

He answered on the second ring. "Hello?"

He sounded awful, but to be fair his mother had just been murdered. "Jackson, this is Jem Richard—"

"Oh Jem! You were one of the models Friday night!" he sounded cheerful for a moment, before remembering. "Is there something I can do for you?"

"First of all, I'm so sorry about your mother," I said as Kyle rolled his eyes. I scowled at him and continued, "But I found a hard drive in my make-up case this morning that isn't mine, and I have no idea where it came from. The only time my case wasn't here was Friday night at your mother's—"

"That's weird, how did it wind up in your case? But bring it by and I'll see if it's one of ours. But you're going to have to hurry—my brother is driving down from Memphis and will be here in about another hour—and then I'm going to be having to make funeral decisions."

"I'm on my way and I won't be long," I quickly hung up and texted Ellis—*raincheck*? And he replied within minutes, *Will call after lunch.*

Jackson's house was rather nondescript, on a slight rise from the street, in the Moroccan stucco style popular in the city between the world wars. When I pulled up in front, I remembered being here once before. Shortly after I moved into Mee Maw's house, a guy I was seeing brought me here. How had I forgotten that terrible party? Jackson and his live-in boyfriend of the time had a horrible blow-up sometime that day; by the time the guests started arriving, Jackson was rather nastily drunk, and the boyfriend was snorting coke in the kitchen.

I'd escaped as quickly as I could.

His beige Lexus was in the driveway, so I parked in front of the house and walked up the concrete stairs to the small porch.

I heard footsteps approaching from the other side of the door. The door swung open, and I didn't have time to say anything as Jackson sobbed out my name and swept me into a bear hug, putting his head down on my shoulder and shaking with sobs.

"Oh, Jem, I can't believe she's gone!" he blubbered into my shoulder.

For want of anything better to do, I started petting his head awkwardly. I didn't know what to say.

I'm not proud to admit that I'm terrible in these kinds of situations. Maybe it's because my mother's response to anything and everything was "Life's hard, kid" while pouring herself another glass of whatever liquor was on sale that week. It's not that I don't have the empathy gene—for God's sake, Disney movies make me bawl like a baby—but when someone needs comforting, I just freeze up. I don't know what to say. I don't know how to make someone feel better. I always try to look on the bright side, but when someone's distraught the last thing in the world they want to hear is "cheer up! It could be worse!" So, I tend to let other people do the comforting, and show my support silently. "I'm so sorry," I finally managed to say, feeling like a complete jackass.

He gave me another squeeze and let me go, wiping at his swollen and reddened eyes. He looked a wreck—*seriously, Jem, his mother was murdered and he found the fucking body, how do you expect him to look*—and his highlighted brown hair was sticking up in every direction. Jackson had always had a stocky build, but his broad shoulders helped him pull it off. He was a little taller than me, and his eyes were hazel. Even when he frowned, he looked cheerful—his round face always seemed to give the impression he'd get over whatever was annoying him in short order. He usually was in a good mood and he had a wicked sense of humor. He tended to drink a lot, and he always dressed well—despite the dirty-looking Tulane T-shirt he was currently wearing over a pair of paint-spattered shorts. He blinked at me, his lower lip shaking a bit. "I know, I look a total wreck, don't I?" He waved me inside. "Come on, come in." He shut the door behind me and switched on the overhead light. "You want a drink?" He barked out a harsh laugh. "I know I shouldn't be drinking, but Christ." He walked over to the wet bar in a corner of the living room, and refilled a tall glass with ice, gin, and tonic. He took a long pull, exhaled, and gave me a weak smile. "Thank God for liquor."

"Nothing for me," I said, moving some magazines out of the wingback chair and sitting down. Jackson clearly hadn't inherited his taste for décor from his mother. If the big house at Magazine and Nashville looked like "French Quarter whorehouse" on the inside, Jackson's could have been straight out of a design magazine. Jackson had gotten a degree in Interior Design from Auburn—one of the top design schools in the country—and had worked in a top firm in Atlanta after college before coming back to New Orleans to work for his mother.

The décor at his mother's house must have caused him physical pain.

He sat down on the couch and took another slug from his glass. "God, what a fucking day." His hand was shaking.

"I heard you found her," I said carefully, hoping I wasn't going to send him over the edge again. "I'm so sorry—that must have been awful. I can't imagine." It was true; I couldn't imagine how I would feel to find my mother's dead body.

"Whatever her faults she was my mother," Jackson's voice broke, and he visibly struggled to pull it back together. "I don't think I'll ever forget finding her." He covered his face in his hands again.

Get his mind off it, I ordered myself, *let him get himself together before you ask about the murder.* "Do the police have any ideas?" I asked, setting my backpack down on the floor.

"They spent so much time with me I was beginning to think I needed a lawyer." He replied, staring into his glass. "Lots of questions about the will and who's inheriting what and the business." He shook his head. "Yes, of course we're having financial trouble because Mom was horrible with money and treated the business account like a savings account she could pull from at anytime—didn't she bounce a check to you?"

I nodded, feeling a bit ashamed about talking smack about a dead woman. But he asked, and it was true. "I wouldn't have been here Friday night if Lee Ann hadn't paid me in advance," I replied. "You're going to need to pay her back," I added gently. It was the least I could do for Lee Ann.

"Yes, yes." He waved his hand again. "You said you found something that wasn't yours in your make-up case?"

I nodded, reaching down and unzipping the front pocket of my backpack. I grabbed the hard drive and pulled it out, holding it out to him. "This was in the second drawer of my case," I said. "It's not mine—I save everything in the cloud—and I don't know how it wound up in my case. Do you recognize it?"

He turned it over a few times in his hands. "I mean, I can see it's a back-up hard drive, and Mom always used them." He smiled sadly at me. "She didn't trust the cloud, you see, since it was invisible. She needed something tangible, so she had a lot of these, going back years. Did you try to see what's on it?"

"It was password protected." I replied defensively, adding when he raised his eyebrows, "I was trying to figure out who it belonged to."

He handed it back to me. "Well, it's not one of Mom's."

"How can you be so sure?"

"Mom wasn't smart about technology but one thing about her—she was organized." He got up and walked over to a desk in a corner of the room. He held up an identical hard drive to the one I was holding. "She numbered hers, and every file that was on them was noted in a spreadsheet." I could see the number "32" written in red Sharpie on the one he was holding. He laughed. "She always used the same password—she was so security conscious and afraid of the cloud but always used the same password—Jackson520, with an exclamation point. My name and birthday, you know."

I repeated it several times in my head so I wouldn't forget it.

If he didn't want the hard drive, that didn't mean I couldn't check out what was on it.

And then I could give it to Blake.

He went on, "And this insane idea she had to write a book . . ."

I nodded. "A book?"

"A book. She kept saying she was going to write a memoir."

Memoir? *That was the name of the folder on the hard drive.*

"I imagine her memoirs would be interesting," I said slowly. "The years in Paris working at Chanel alone!"

"Mom was a liar, Jem." He exhaled. "Always. She told so many lies so often she started believing them herself. She never worked for Chanel in Paris, you know—but she told that lie so many times she really believed it, I think, at the end. That's why the whole thing about the book—why would she write a memoir?" He bit his lower lip. "She wasn't very good at picking men—that was her whole story. Well, that and her delusions of grandeur."

I licked my upper lip. "Was there anything in the manuscript…" I let my voice trail off; I wasn't even sure myself how to put it.

"That would make someone want to kill her?" He raised one of his eyebrows. "Not kill. I didn't read it—she wouldn't let anyone else read it—she was saving that for her big launch party." He made air quotes with his fingers as he said the last three words. "So, who knows what was in there? I thought she should at least have a libel lawyer look it over before she published it."

"She had a publisher?"

"She was going to publish it herself—she told me the details but I didn't really pay any attention to it." He waved one of his hands tiredly. "The print book was going to be print on demand, and she was going to sell the ebook through Amazon, I guess. Like anyone would want to read it." He ran his hand through his hair, smoothing it down finally. "She really thought she was telling a great American success story—you know she also had convinced herself that her grandfather was a Romanov?"

"A Romanov?" I couldn't have heard that right. "As in the Nicholas and Alexandra Romanovs? Russian royalty?"

"She even went to St. Petersburg to prove we were royalty. That's where she was after Katrina—in Russia. Most people went to Houston and Atlanta—my mother went to Russia."

"Wow." I didn't know what else to say.

"I see by the look on your face that you think she was crazy," he rolled his eyes and finished his drink. "She was. My great-grandfather was a butcher in St. Petersburg, not the illegitimate son of the Czar who came here to make his fortune in the new world.

"Did she find anything?"

He shook his head. "She doesn't speak Russian, let alone read it. She paid a translator a small fortune trying to prove her delusions of grandeur, just to find out we come from a long line of bourgeois butchers."

"I'd heard that the business was in some trouble," I said cautiously.

"She was never very good with money," he went on, getting up and walking back over to the wet bar. "You sure you don't want a drink? No? Okay." He refilled his glass and sat back down again. "The only time she was ever careful with money is when there wasn't any—and she always had the craziest financial priorities. She was very much about keeping up appearances—I remember when I was a kid having to eat peanut butter sandwiches for about a month because she'd had to pay her dues for Iris." Iris was a ladies' Mardi Gras krewe. "She'd set the house on fire before she'd let anyone know she was broke. But she always managed to somehow land on her feet." He gave me a sly look. "I mean, you've seen the clothes she designed. Yet somehow she always managed to sell enough dresses, or get commissioned to design some, to keep the business and the house going."

I diplomatically avoided giving my opinion on his mother's hideous designs. "You can't think of anyone who'd want to kill your mother?"

"Look, I know she was abrasive and people didn't like her—but like I told the police, you don't kill someone because you don't like her. She was infuriating, yes, and she got on people's nerves—but to kill her? Hardly." He was starting to slur his words, but took another big drink from the glass.

"Sweetie, I think you should go lie down," I said, feeling guilty. Had I been taking advantage of him when he was drinking? "Are your brothers coming in?"

"Bonaparte's flying in tomorrow, and Aramis and family are driving down today." He looked at his watch before closing his eyes. They were closed so long I was starting to wonder if he'd passed out when they snapped open. "Yes, I think I'm going to go lie down. Can you let yourself out?"

"Of course." I stood up and patted him on the arm. "And of course, you'll call me if there's anything I can do?"

He nodded. "Thanks, Jem, I appreciate that." He walked me to the door. "Nice picture on *NOLA. com* today. I wasn't sure they'd run any pictures from Friday, given—" his face started to crumple again.

I slipped out the front door.

CHAPTER TWELVE

The weather turned while I was at Jackson's. The sky was covered with clouds in varying shades of gray and black, and the wind had picked up. I shivered as I dashed down his walk to my car, managing to get inside before the first fat drops splatted on my windshield. I started the car and turned on the heat to get the chill out of me as the rain started a steady drumbeat on the roof of my car. I plugged my phone into the car jack and let the warm air blow over me.

Marigny had been writing a memoir? What on earth about? The most interesting thing about her was her history working at Chanel in Paris, but Jackson said that wasn't true. He's also seemed pretty sure it hadn't been her hard drive, but I'd try his birthdate on it when I got home to make sure.

It was just difficult for me to believe that this mysterious hard drive didn't have something to do with the home invasion, but why? What could possibly be labeled MEMOIR that someone would commit a crime to get their hands on it?

I checked my mirrors and with the coast clear, made an illegal U-turn on Prytania Street to head back to Jefferson and up to Claiborne to drive home. I turned on the headlights because it was getting darker. My windshield wipers were working double-time but visibility was still poor. By the time I got to the corner the streets were already starting to fill with the rainwater. Lightning flashed nearby and the weather alert alarm on my phone went off. The light at Claiborne was red so I glanced at the message as cars sped past, throwing up sheets of water onto my car and windshield. *Heavy rain, high winds, possibility of street flooding.*

In other words, just another rainy day in New Orleans.

Traffic was slow because of the rain and my stomach growled as I drove behind a Leidenheimer's bread truck, closely watching the taillights through the gloom. I hadn't eaten anything since getting up. I pulled through a Raising Cane's drive-through. The smell of greasy fried chicken made my stomach almost hurt, so I grabbed a handful of hot crinkle fries while I waited to pull back onto Claiborne.

Maybe I should just call Blake and ask him if he wants me to give it over, I thought as cars splashed an almost steady spray of water onto my car, *which is a legitimate reason to call.*

But I thought better of it as I pulled back out onto Claiborne Avenue. It was probably nothing. There were any number of explanations for how this had wound up in my case that didn't involve the home invasion. I didn't want to look desperate or thirsty. Blake was so good-looking he was probably used to gay men (and straight women) hitting on him all the time. If I called with this crazy story about a hard drive, he'd probably think I was one of those people and even if Blake was way out of my league, I didn't want him to think that. Ellis seemed interested in me, and why not just see where that goes?

And if I was wrong about Ellis, it didn't matter.

Men who looked like Blake were never interested in guys like me.

Getting ahead of yourself, Jem, I reminded myself as I got on I-10 to bypass the Central Business District and the French Quarter, *Ellis just invited you to have lunch. He's probably pursuing you as a potential student for his drag school.*

I popped some more crinkle fries in my mouth as I drove past the Superdome onto I-10. Even the highway traffic was moving slow. My stomach growled again and I took a sip of my sweet tea as an 18-wheeler went past me at much more than the

speed limit, throwing up water all over my windshield and rocking my car with the backdraft. I
cursed at him and licked salt off my fingers.

I'd always dreamed of performing. I used to
practice my Oscar acceptance speech in the bathroom mirror while holding a bottle of shampoo
when I was a kid. But just thinking about going out
on-stage, with eyes staring at me and a spotlight on
me, made my stomach clench. That horrible stage
fright experience was burned into my brain.

But...maybe I'd just gotten too far into my
head? I'd only been a kid. Joan Crawfish had been
fine. Maybe if I just put myself into that headspace,
that I was Joan Crawfish and she feared nothing,
was a star with fans who loved and adored her and
cheered whenever she walked out on stage—

And I could walk in heels. I didn't have to wear
stilettos unless I wanted to, right? I was a licensed
cosmetologist so I already knew how to do hair and
make-up. And I can sew. I could make my own
gowns. I already had a workroom at the house. I
just needed to get a better handle on drag make-
up, which wasn't all that much different from stage
make-up. It was kind of a cross between glam and
stage, really. I just needed to get my own breast
plates and hip padding.

And I could have fun with the make-up and
outfits, couldn't I? My Bourbon Street Awards
costumes had been very complicated and had tak-

en weeks of work. I wouldn't need to do that to do shows or brunches—unless I wanted to. I could do specialty costumes based around holidays... my mind was whirling as I drove past the Orleans Street exit and took another drink from my tea.

It would also give me an excuse to call Ellis . . .

Stop it, girl you sound desperate and thirsty, I scolded myself as I shot down the Claiborne off-ramp. Before long I was turning into the tight driveway next to my house. The gutter was under water already and spray flew up as I went through it. I parked and sat there for a moment as the rain just kept coming down. More lightning and thunder. The rain didn't look like it was going to let up any time soon. I took a deep breath, shoved the Cane's bag into my backpack, picked up my sweet tea and opened my car door. The moment I got out I was completely soaked. I splashed along the driveway, my feet sinking down into the water up to my ankles. The current was flowing fast and hard down to the street. I splashed around to the front steps and climbed up, shivering as the cold wind blasted around me while I fumbled with shaking fingers to get the key into the deadbolt. Finally the door was open, and the cold air conditioning washed over me. My teeth started chattering as I pushed the door closed behind me and flipped the deadbolt. I kicked off my shoes, peeled off my wet socks, slid my feet into my slippers and dashed upstairs, stripping off

my wet clothes as I went. Toweling myself dry, I
pulled on sweats over my goose-bumpy skin.

I still felt cold as I went back downstairs, but I
could live with it.

I made short work of the chicken fingers and the
crinkle fries that were left, and I took my backpack
back to my workroom. I attached the hard drive to
my computer again and clicked on the little icon
that appeared on my desktop named MEMOIR.
Once again, the box asking for a password popped
up, and without hesitation I typed Jackson520!

My little rainbow wheel turned a couple of rota-
tions before a "finder" menu opened and I was in. I
smiled. *Wrong, Jackson, this IS your mother's hard drive.*
I looked over the file names. There were four folders all named "drafts" and numbered. A fifth folder
was named "pictures." I opened the most recent draft
folder (the one named four) and all the word docu-
ments inside had a chapter and a number. I grinned
to myself. It was indeed Marigny's memoir.

I hesitated for a moment. Whether this had
something to do with her murder or not, this was a
violation of Marigny's privacy. I had no right to look
at any of this.

Then my nosiness won out. She was dead, after
all, and she'd intended to publish it, right? So, what
was the harm if I looked around a bit?

And I'd found it in my make-up case. Possession was nine-tenths of the law, wasn't it?.

I clicked on the "pictures" folder. None of the images had been renamed. The file names were just IMG and a number afterwards, like when I uploaded pictures from my phone. I clicked on IMG_001. The file opened, showing what looked like a professionally done photo of Marigny's big house, the green and gold awning with DESIGNS BY MARIGNY written along the sides prominently centered. The next shot was Marigny herself, wearing one of her own creations. It was cut wrong for her body type, and the silhouette made her look even more cadaverous than usual. She smiled dutifully for the photographer, but it looked awkward and forced, like she wasn't used to smiling. Her hair was in its traditional long ropy braid, draped over her right shoulder and reaching down to her waist. The image was black and white—but showed telltale signs of Photoshop and/or filters. Her face hadn't been that line-free since the first Bush administration. The longer I looked the more certain I was that photoshop had been used to trim her already small size down even further. The next few shots were interiors shots of rooms filled with old, heavy looking furniture. The living quarters of Designs by Marigny, I wondered? I scrolled down the index and randomly and opened IMG_102 and recoiled back from the screen.

The photograph was of a nude woman reclining on what appeared to be a four poster bed. She was wearing an elaborate crown on her messy hair and held a scepter. Her face had been digitally blurred, but everything else from the neck down was on full display. What on earth? I wondered as I closed the picture. It wasn't Marigny, so who was she? Why did Marigny have naked pictures of her on her memoirs drive?

I raised an eyebrow. Was Marigny queer?

No question. I needed to turn this over to Blake. But first…

I copied everything from the drive to my Cloud and disconnected the drive, putting it back into my backpack.

I walked back to the living room with my bag in hand, found Blake's card and picked up my phone, ready to call…but stopped.

I didn't want to look like some thirsty, desperate fool trying to get his attention.

I wasn't going to be that gay man.

I put my phone back down. *Just give it back to Jackson*, I decided. *I can tell him her password opened it and he's the better person to deal with it than me. And if his mom was a lesbian or bi or something, better he find out himself than have the police tell him.*

And the sooner I get this thing out of my house the safer we'll be.

The home invasion couldn't have been related to the murder, much as I wanted the two to be connected. If the burglars were looking for this, they hadn't found it and they wouldn't be coming back. And much as I hated admitting it, burglaries and break-ins happened all the time in New Orleans. Most people wouldn't think twice about one happening in my neighborhood. The only reason Blake and Latoya had shown up here at all was because I was a peripheral witness in their homicide case—just covering all bases. It had been obvious neither thought the two things were related.

I sat back down on the sofa. I could smell the grease from my lunch and I was still a bit hungry. I grabbed the remote and turned on the television. The Saints game was on *Monday Night Football* but that didn't start until later. I wasn't the biggest football fan in the world, but still. You couldn't grow up in my football-addicted family and not be. My father had been a star in high school, starting three years and even playing at a junior college. He'd gotten offers from some smaller division schools but turned them all down to go to SMU in Dallas. My older brother Chad had played, so of course, my parents had expected me to play. I hadn't wanted to, but Mom had made it clear she wasn't about to let me disappoint Dad. First was flag football, and then came pee wee. Chad had also been small when he was younger, but once puberty arrived he'd grown tall and big. When puberty came for me, I grew to my whopping five feet six inches by my sophomore year and that was it. I'd quit football my junior year when it became apparent to me that I wasn't going to get bigger and beginning to worry about getting hurt. Dad hadn't been pleased. Dad already was disappointed that I wasn't his idea of masculine. He didn't like that I was interested in hair and make-up, or that I was friends with the cheerleaders instead of the players. He also blamed Mee Maw for my feminine side—I'd heard him say it to Mom enough times: "spending every summer hanging around my mother's salon isn't making him a man." I hadn't looked back once Mee Maw paid for me to go to cosmetology school, and once she left me the house—I spent as little time in Texas as I could. Dad was just as cold and distant, and Mom never stood up to him.

"I didn't raise him marry that kind of woman," Mee Maw muttered to me once after I'd complained that Mom always took Dad's side over mine.

Like a message from Mee Maw in heaven, one of her favorite movies was starting on TCM, *The Strange Love of Martha Ivers*. Barbara Stanwyck had been her favorite—we'd spent a long 4th of July weekend bingeing her old *The Big Valley* TV series—so I settled back into the couch to watch. Martha had just murdered her aunt when my phone started ringing. I reached for it and grinned to see it was Ellis. "Hey, thanks for calling. Sorry I had to miss lunch."

"I've learned to live with disappointment," Ellis replied in a teasing tone. "I thought I'd give you another chance, though. I have a show tonight in Biloxi at the casino—last minute call to fill in—and thought it might be fun if you came with? You could help me with my make-up and get a behind the scenes look at a Mary Queen of THOTs show, see if it's the kind of chaos you can handle, maybe get something to eat later? We'd get back late—the second show starts at eleven—but if you're not doing anything . . ."

"Oh." I replied. I didn't have anything planned. But did I want to spend the evening in Biloxi?

"We could even..." he lowered his voice to a husky whisper, "get a discounted room and stay the night?"

I felt my face coloring with delight. I didn't have any plans for tomorrow either, for that matter.

"If I didn't have my class on Tuesday night we could stay for a few days," Ellis went on, "I really think you should consider taking my next work-shop. It doesn't start until next month. This class graduates next week."

"I'm thinking about it," I replied. A night at a casino hotel was sounding good to me, but at the same time did I really want to go away for the night with someone I'd just met two days ago? What if we couldn't stand each other once we were alone? *Thanks for the offer, but* . . . how could I say it without looking like a total loser and turning him away permanently? I took a deep breath. "I do like you, Ellis, but I don't think I know you well enough yet? I'm sorry, " I rushed on, not giving him a chance to answer. "I'm a little gun-shy. The last guy I was seeing ghosted me."

I could have ripped out my tongue. I could hear Kyle saying in my head, *Girl, the last thing you ever tell your new man is anything about your ex-man.*

Ellis whistled into the phone. "He was an idiot, obviously. But yeah, I'm moving kind of fast, that's kind of how I operate." He laughed. "And maybe that's why I'm single and in my late forties."

Late forties? "You are NOT in your forties."

He laughed. "Oh, bless you, baby, but I am for-ty-seven. Three years till the half-century mark."

"I would have guessed thirties at most."

"Oh, you are a keeper." He flirted. "Are you sure I can't change your mind?"

"I'm sure. Call me when you get back." He said he would, and I ended the call. I put my phone back down on the table with a self-satisfied smirk. He was interested in me. So what if he was almost twenty years older than me? Maybe the problems I kept hav-ing with the guys I dated was about the immaturity of guys in their twenties, who just wanted to ho around instead of settling down and falling in love.

The first gay man I'd ever known had worked at the Beauty Shoppe for Mee Maw. Rodger had opened his own salon on the north shore, in Rouen. Rodger had been insanely tall—to the younger me he'd seemed almost like a giant—but was probably around six five and also bone-thin. He always had his hair done in some magnificent style and color, wore rings on every finger and had tattoos up and down both arms. He was the first person I'd come out to when I was thirteen—who better, I figured, to come out to than a gay man who was kind of a role model? He'd been great, and had helped me drum up the courage to come out to Mee Maw, who, as he'd reassured me, hadn't cared.

I hadn't officially come out to my parents or brothers yet, but they *weren't* stupid. They had to have figured it out by now.

Then again, maybe they hadn't. Every time I went to visit my family someone said something incredibly insensitive and homophobic in front of me. I'd like to think they wouldn't do that if they knew. Or maybe they suspected and said something homophobic to see how I'd react? Make me mad enough to lose my temper and admit it to them at last?

Yeah, no. My family wasn't that Machiavellian. If they knew, they'd say something.

Anyway, Rodger had told me to remember to always be patient when it came to falling in love. "If someone doesn't see how special you are right away, don't sit around hoping they will someday because they won't," he said to me when we sharing lunch at the salon. Well, I was eating a sandwich from the Subway down the block—Rodger never ate anything, as far as I could tell he lived on cigarettes and strong black coffee. "And age is just a number. Don't ever think all older man are just itching to get into your pants—trust me you need a lot of patience to break in the younger ones—and when you're older don't think all the younger ones are just looking for a sugar daddy. The rules that apply to the straights do not apply to us. We can reinvent love and what a relationship is—as long as everyone is upfront and honest. Straight people have been brainwashed and gaslit for years by movies and books and TV shows. Don't buy into it. And never ever forget you have just as much value as anyone."

Maybe it was time to start dating older men than guys in my own generation. Why keep repeating the same old patterns? Meet someone on an app or in a club, have sex that very first night, date a few more times, and then the ghosting. Lather, rinse, repeat.

I also needed to take Kyle's advice and stop falling in love with every guy I slept with.

"It's just sex," Kyle would say as he dried my tears whenever the last ghosting got to me. "Guys just want to get off, Jem, you gotta remember that. If they have a good time, they may want to give it another go or two. But it starts getting stale after the third or fourth time and they get ready to move on, and it's easier to ghost someone than to deal with the drama of an actual break-up."

Much as I hated to admit it, he had a point. The guys didn't know I wasn't the type to scream or yell or cry or make a scene.

Maybe I should start out that way, "Look, dude, if we get to the point where you're done and don't want to see me again, just tell me instead of ghosting me, okay? It's a small town and there are only so many gay bars, so you're going to run into me again and why make that awkward?"

It wouldn't make a difference. Gay men were pigs.

And that made up my mind.

I pulled out my wallet and dug out Blake's business card. He answered on the second ring. "Dorgenois."

"Hey Blake, this is Jem Richard, who had the break-in yesterday? I was at Marigny's party Friday night?"

"I know who you are, Jem," he said kindly. "What can I do for you?"

"Maybe it's nothing," I hesitated, "but I found something in my make-up case that I didn't put in it?" I quickly explained how I'd found the hard drive after getting my case back from Ellis, my attempt to see what was on it, and so on right up until I called him.

I left out the part about figuring out the password and copying the files to my computer.

"So maybe it's nothing and the break-in had nothing to do with the murder," I finished, feeling goofy for calling and hoping he wasn't thinking I just wanted to see him again. Of course I did—who wouldn't want to look at Blake?—but even if someone who looked like that was interested in me, I was better off seeing where things might go with Ellis.

"I'll be right over," Blake said, ending the call. I slipped my phone into my pocket.

Maybe I was reading more into Ellis, too.

Why does everything have to be so complicated?

I went back into the kitchen and got a ziplock bag to put the hard drive into. There was something about chain of custody I remembered vaguely from watching television and cop movies, but a computer expert would be able to tell when the disk has been made and when it was worked on. Any digital trace I'd left on it was still there—

There was a knock on the front door. That couldn't be Blake already, could it? Whistling, I headed for the front door and took off the chain. I swung open the door expecting to see sexy Blake the police detective . . . only to find myself looking at someone wearing a rubber Drew Brees mask . . . and holding a gun pointed right at my chest.

CHAPTER THIRTEEN

"You've got to be kidding me." I snapped, putting my hands on my hips. "Seriously?"

Admitted, maybe not the smartest approach to having a gun held on you. But come on. Twice in two days? What were the odds of that? I mean, I'd lived in the 7th Ward now for almost four years and nothing. Now, two days in a row?

The good news was he didn't shoot me in response, which I took to be a good sign. The guy could have killed me yesterday, too, but he hadn't. Assuming this was the same guy—again, what were the odds of two home invasions by different criminals two days in a row?

I guess I was too emotionally drained to react like a normal person.

He just stood there, framed in my doorway, the gun pointed at my chest. Cars were driving past on St. Roch but no one was paying attention to what was happening on my porch. The sun had come out and it was getting humid as the standing water evaporated. There wasn't a soul in sight across the street on any of the porches.

Well, at least the rain had stopped.

"I mean, seriously, dude," I went on, like it was a toy gun. "Halloween isn't until next month. Come back then and I'll have some candy for you. You can have the whole bowl, I promise."

Yes, mocking a person holding a gun on you might not be the smartest thing to do. It certainly wasn't what I'd learned when Kyle and I took that 'neighborhood self-defense' course last year after one of our neighbors had been mugged walking the three blocks home from the St. Roch Market. The instructor, a lean and well-muscled young man, had spent four hours teaching us how to react and behave if we wound up in a situation like this, so we could get out of it safely without injury or death.

But I was too overwhelmed with disgust and anger that it was happening to me again in less than forty-eight hours—I mean, come on.

I was fed up and had reached my last nerve.

Besides, he was *already* holding a gun on me.

If this was how I was destined to leave this world and move on to the next, I'd rather go out defiantly. I wouldn't grovel and beg for my life.

And if I didn't get out of this alive, I wanted "defiant to the end" put on my tombstone.

The gun gestured upwards. The self-defense instructor's voice popped into my head. *When someone is holding a gun on you, always cooperate but always watch for an opportunity to take the gun away or get away. Getting away is the better option, but if you can't escape, watch for that opening. Try to get them talking, to see you as a person. It's harder to kill someone once you've recognized their humanity.*

At the time I'd thought it was stupid and inwardly rolled my eyes.

With a gun pointed at me, it made a little more sense.

Following his instructions, I raised my hands into the air over my head while trying to memorize details about him to give the police if I made it out of this alive—when, not if, I reminded myself. *Always think positively. Keep your cool now—you can always freak out later when you're safe.*

The person holding the gun looked to have a masculine build—narrow hips and broad shoulders. He was top-heavy, with kind of that Humpty-Dumpty type build rural Southern men tend to gravitate to as they get older. The bare forearms sticking out from the short sleeves of a black and gold Drew Brees jersey were covered in thick black hair, and there was a tattoo on the inside of his left forearm. The rubber mask he was wearing was one of those knock-off Drew Brees masks sold in the French Market or the souvenir shops in the Quarter—yes, I was right. It was a Drew mask, because the unmistakable birthmark on the right cheek was there just below the eye hole. His eyes were brown and bloodshot. The jersey was torn at the left shoulder, and the jeans had to be skinny-cut stretch denim because they hugged his skinny legs like tin foil. He was wearing white New Balance sneakers. He vaguely smelled of cheap cologne, sweat and cigarette smoke.

"Just tell me what you want, and you can have it," I said, backing up further into the living room, keeping my hands up above my head. "But there's no money in the house, and you need to hurry because the cops are already on their way."

I'd hoped casually mentioning that the cops were on their way might make a difference. It didn't, or he didn't believe me.

Good, I thought, taking another step backward. *Too much to hope that Blake was already in the neighborhood, though.*

He gestured with the gun again. "Sit on the couch!" He ordered. His voice was slightly muffled by the mask. It also sounded like he was trying to disguise his voice by lowering it. It wasn't necessary—the mask muffled his voice so well I wouldn't have been able to recognize it later.

And then it hit me. Sure, he was holding a gun on me. *But he was afraid I could identify him later—* voice or face, hence the mask and the attempt to disguise his voice.

Which meant he wasn't planning on killing me.

Didn't mean that he wouldn't, of course. He still might, but now that I was certain killing me wasn't in his plans . . .

I was so relieved my knees buckled a bit as I walked over to the couch.

"I said on the couch!" He gestured again with the gun. "NOW!"

"I know you don't believe me but I'm not lying about the cops being on their way," I said as I sat down on the couch, keeping my hands up just in case. "I'd literally just gotten off the phone with them when you knocked. Detective Blake Dorgenois? The name ring any bells?"

Now that I'd calmed down a bit, I realized he hadn't kicked my door in. He'd rang the doorbell and waited for me to answer. He wasn't going to kill me—so long as I played along and did what he asked. And the longer I could stall, the more likely Blake would get here. "Just tell me what you want and its yours," I said, my voice shaking a little bit.

I guess I wasn't as calm as I thought. "You know what I want. Don't play stupid," he snapped.

"I'm not a mind reader," I retorted, folding my arms in front of me and sticking out my jaw. "And this is getting old, you know? Wasn't it bad enough you broke in here yesterday and tied me up and—" I pointed to the knot on my forehead, "—well, this lump better not be disfiguring."

"What are you talking about?" He sounded confused. "I wasn't here yesterday."

"Sure, you weren't," I sneered. "And why would I believe the person in a mask holding a gun on me after forcing his way into my home for the second time in two days?"

"I don't care what you believe or what you don't." I could hear the smug gloating in his voice. "If you just get me what I want, I'll be on my way, no one has to get hurt—"

"I've asked you now three times what you want and you still haven't told me," I didn't bother keeping the scorn out of my voice. "You're not very good at this."

"Do you want to die?"

"And you need to hurry if you want to get out of here before the cops get here."

"You're lying."

I was glad he didn't believe me that Blake was on his way over. I just wished there was some way I could alert Blake to what he was walking into. Just keep him talking and Blake will get here to save the day and arrest this joker.

As if on cue, I heard a car pull up in front of the house and its engine shut off.

"That must be the cops now," I smiled at him. "They won't let you pose for a mugshot with that mask on, you know."

Keeping the gun on me, he backed over to the enormous window next to the front door. I kept my eyes on him, waiting for a chance for him to turn his head away—if he was going to look out the window, that might give me a chance to run for the back of the house. Mee Maw's gun was locked in a box under the bed upstairs, but I'd never fired it so there was no point in going for it. I'd just wind up shooting myself. (*Note to self: learn how to use that gun.*)

But if I could maybe make it to the backyard, there were any number of directions for me to run—and there was a gate at the back of the yard.

Escape was possible.

And sure enough, once he got to the window, he turned his head to peer through the blinds—and I leaped off the couch and ran for the back of the house, bending down and keeping my head low.

I heard a muffled shout behind me as I ducked through the kitchen door. I dove to the left to get out of the doorway just as he fired a couple of shots. I dropped down to my hands and knees and crawled across the kitchen floor, noting crazily that it needed to be mopped and hoping that I lived long enough to do it. I made it to the door to my workroom. Panting and sweating, I leaped through the doorway. Wishing the door locked from the inside, I pulled it closed and looked around for something to jam it shut with. My mind was racing and I could feel sweat running down my sides. Nothing, I didn't see anything that would work. There was an aluminum baseball bat leaning against the wall that we used to scare off the occasional raccoon that turned up to root through our trash, but I could hardly swing at bullets.

"What the actual—"I heard from the living room.

Oh my God, it wasn't Blake—it was Kyle.

My heart sank. I couldn't just escape and leave Kyle to deal with this guy.

"Okay, okay, I'll put my hands up if you put that gun away," Kyle drawled easily and calmly. My heart was thumping in my chest.

The fear and shock I'd suppressed somehow took over.

No, not Kyle.

I leaned against the door and wiped sweat off my forehead. My legs almost buckled but I forced my knees to straighten.

Kyle, on the other hand, sounded like he was used to coming home to find someone with a gun in our living room, like it happened every day.

Two days in a row. I hoped this was the end of that streak.

"Come out Jem!" the muffled voice yelled. "You don't want me to shoot your friend, do you? I'll do it! I'll blow his brains out!"

"Please don't," Kyle said calmly.

I didn't think he would shoot Kyle, but I couldn't take the chance he was bluffing. If he wasn't I wouldn't be able to live with myself if I stood by and let him kill Kyle if there was something I could do to save him.

I wasn't that selfish.

Where are you, Blake? How long does it take you to get here? Hurry up or you'll just find two more bodies.

I took a deep breath and wiped my face down with my sweatshirt.

I opened the workroom door and put my hands up. Feeling like a lamb heading to the slaughter, I walked back out of the kitchen into the big open room. Kyle was standing just inside the front door, with his hands up in the air. His work T-shirt was glued to his torso with sweat. The backpack he took to work every day was hanging from one shoulder. He looked at me and opened his eyes wide while tilting his head to the left—Kyle shorthand for *what have you gotten us into now?* All I could do was give him a feeble smile and a slight shoulder shrug.

Faux Drew, with the barrel still pointed at Kyle, gestured with the gun. "Sit on the couch," he said. Kyle obliged, still holding his hands up in the air. Faux Drew turned the gun to me. "You. Tie him up."

"With what? You think I've got a rope in my back pocket or something?"

My front door was wide open still. Anyone walking or driving by could look in and see an actual robbery taking place in broad daylight. As I was speaking, I saw a black Mustang with red interior pull up behind Kyle's aged Kia. Blake got out on the driver's side and glanced inside, his smile fading as he caught sight of faux-Drew and his gun. I watched Blake remove his own gun from his shoulder holster and gesture at me to keep him talking.

Great, we're going to have a shoot-out and he wants me to keep him talking, I thought, keeping my face impassive. But faux-Drew was gesturing with the gun again. I was still pretty certain faux-Drew didn't want to shoot us, but that could change once Blake came through the door with his own gun drawn.

And there was always the chance of getting caught in crossfire, or bullets ricocheting—

Stop it, I thought, giving myself a mental slap across the face. I started walking over to the couch. I still didn't know what I was going to use to tie up Kyle, but as long as I could keep faux-Drew's eyes and gun on us...the better chance there was of Blake being able to catch him off-guard and disarm him. "I don't have anything to tie him—"

"FREEZE."

Blake was standing in the front doorway, his feet shoulder-width apart, one hand pointing his gun and the other holding it steady. There was a clatter as faux-Drew's gun hit the floor, and I grabbed it when Blake kicked it across the floor to me. My hands shaking, I put on the safety (*he hadn't had the safety on!*).

Spots danced in front of my eyes as the adrenaline rush wore off and the reality of just how close of a call this had been began sinking in.

I saw down on the couch, hard and took some deep breaths.

"You okay?" Kyle whispered. "I don't know if I am."

"I don't know." I kept taking deep breaths as my vision began to blur and go gray around the edges. I started hyperventilating but my cheek stung as Kyle gave me a light slap.

"Hey." I glared at him, but it worked. He blinked his eyes and gave me a big grin

Blake handcuffed faux-Drew's hands behind his back. He pushed him over to one of my wingback chairs, and faux-Drew sat down, hard. Blake hooked his fingers beneath the mask below the chin and yanked it off.

I was half-expecting faux-Drew to sneer *and I would have gotten away with it too if it weren't for these meddling kids!*

I swallowed the hysterical laugh starting in my diaphragm. My hands were still shaking and I was having trouble catching my breath. Kyle pushed my head down between my knees and said, "Breathe, Jem, it's all over. It's all okay now."

I closed my eyes, and took a few deep cleansing

breaths. Acid churned in my stomach. I needed to slow my racing heartbeat and get centered again.

Easier said than done. Ever since I agreed to do Marigny's show my life had been chaos. Marigny had been murdered. My house had been broken into, twice. I'd had a gun held on me. I'd been knocked out and tied up.

I opened my eyes and looked at faux-Drew.

"Do you have any ID?" Blake was asking. He was wearing jeans and a tight black T-shirt, obviously off-duty. His curly bluish-black hair was mussed, and I noticed his jeans were ripped at both knees and a hole had worn through the crotch just below the zipper. I could see red fabric underneath.

Even after having a gun held on me, I could still check out a hot guy.

Faux-Drew looked crestfallen. He was somewhere in his fifties, maybe, with thinning reddish-blonde hair he'd combed over to hide the bare pink sparts, watery looking bloodshot red eyes, and a weak chin. He looked vaguely familiar, but I couldn't place him. His entire body had slumped down in the chair, and he was staring at the floor. "Wallet's in my back pocket."

Blake reached around and Faux Drew lifted himself slightly so Blake could pluck out his wallet. He opened it and whistled. "Jack Jorgensen." Blake scratched his head and smiled. "You were Marigny's fourth husband? Or was it the third?"

"Fourth." He muttered, still looking down at his feet.

Blake turned to us on the couch and smiled. His teeth were white, even, perfectly shaped, as were his thick red sensual lips. He hadn't shaved that morning, and his razor stubble gave his olive skin a bluish tint that was insanely sexy. So were the dimples in his cheeks.

Down boy, I reminded myself.

"So, Jack, why did you pull a gun on Jem here?" When he didn't answer, Blake started ticking off his fingers. "Attempted murder, kidnapping, attempted robbery—"

"Wait a minute—I didn't try to kill anyone!" Jack looked up, his eyes wide and his reddish face considerably paler than it had been. "Or kidnapping! Who did I kidnap?"

"When you hold someone at gunpoint, it's kidnapping in the eyes of the law, Jack," Blake said, patting his shoulder almost kindly.

"You shot at me." I pointed out. "I have bullet holes in my walls. Someone has to pay to get them patched."

Jack Jorgensen looked like someone had just put his dog to sleep. He dropped his head so that it just hung there, muttering to himself. If he hadn't shot at me, I'd probably feel a little sorry for him, since he looked so pathetic and defeated now.

But he HAD shot at me.

"I wasn't trying to hit anyone," Jack said sullenly. "He was trying to get away and I just wanted to stop him, so I could talk to him."

"You came to my front door wearing a mask—a Drew Brees mask at that, you deserve to go to jail for that blasphemy alone—and with your gun out and pointed at me when I opened the front door. Was I supposed to invite you in for tea?"

To my surprise and horror, Jack burst into tears.

Is there anything sadder than a cis straight white guy sobbing in your living room like a kid?

Blake met my eyes and rolled his. He was entirely too good-looking for his own good. His T-shirt shirt hugged his chest and shoulders, the sleeves slightly rolled up to emphasize his startlingly large biceps. His jeans also fit snugly. He gestured for me to come closer, so I got up off the couch and walked over to him. "I'm going to call for a patrol car to take him," he whispered into my ear, which tickled a little and I had to repress a girlish giggle. *Get a grip, Jem,* I snapped at myself inside my head. *He's not Channing Tatum.*

Although I would love to see Blake on the Magic Mike tour.

"But you're going to need to come down and give a statement to the station—you and your roommate." He looked over at Kyle, and I felt a little surge of jealousy as his eyes lingered on Kyle's lean, defined and still sweaty torso. "And swear out a complaint."

Wouldn't be the first time someone picked Kyle over me. I couldn't even be mad—Kyle was a very good-looking young man. The pole dancing practice and hours at the gym had chiseled his body into something Renaissance sculpture-like and of course, he was charismatic and charming and pretty much anything a gay man could ever want.

Blake had lowered his voice, but Jack only wailed louder. Blake went back out onto the porch to call for back-up, and I turned my attention to Jack.

"What were you after?" I asked.

Snot was running out of his nose and tears were dripping off the side of his face. I held up a Kleenex to his nose because I am not a monster, and I wiped his face, too. "We've never even met," I said softly, sitting down on my haunches in front of him. "What were you thinking?"

He hiccuped, which I took as a sign he was finished crying, and then hung his head even further. "Marigny's memoir. I wanted to get ahold of Marigny's memoir and make sure no one ever saw it."

Kyle did a double take. "What?"

"Why?" I replied. *And how did you know I had the hard drive?*

"I was able to get it from her office on Friday night, but she almost caught me. I barely had time to slip it into your make-up case and get out without being seen." Jack went on. "Marigny was trying to—maybe I should keep my mouth shut?"

"We can't testify to anything because it would be hearsay." Kyle watched a lot of *CSI* and *Law and Order*.

Blake hadn't read him his rights either, so I wasn't sure how that worked?

He started talking slowly, but as he warmed up, the words came tumbling out of him.

His marriage to Marigny hadn't lasted long. They'd met at a party, and they'd hit it off. "She was a lot of fun," he insisted when I gave him a weird look. "How was I supposed to know she was a demon?" They'd gotten married in Vegas after a whirlwind three weeks together, impulsively flying up for the weekend and then back. Jack was a vice-president for Hibernia Bank, and the Jorgensen name had once meant something in the city. Apparently, Marigny thought it still did. He wasn't wealthy. "It didn't take long for me to realize she'd married me for the money, which was crazy. I don't know where she got the idea that I was rich, but she did, and when she found out I wasn't things turned ugly between us very fast." He swallowed. "I'm not excusing what I did, but . . . Marigny decided she wanted to get rid of me, and wanted to be sure I couldn't lay claim to anything of hers, so . . . she hired a prostitute and drugged me, and took pictures." He swallowed. "She told me a few weeks ago she was not only going to write about my 'affair' in her memoir, she was going to include pictures, unless I paid her a hundred thousand dollars. Which I didn't have. And I knew she would do it. She was that kind of person, you know. *A monster.* But I knew she didn't trust on-line back-ups, so she always had everything on a hard drive."

"But how did you know which one she was using?"

"It was still attached to her computer, and she always uses the same password for everything."

"But you didn't come by here yesterday and trash the place?" I asked.

"That wasn't me. I'm so sorry." He buried his face in his hands and started blubbering again.

Blake smiled at me. "And now I think it's time you give me the hard drive, Jem."

CHAPTER FOURTEEN

I couldn't resist watching Blake walk down the front steps and to his Mustang.

His jeans fit so well he could have been a print ad for them. And the way his back narrowed from his shoulders to his waist…I shook my head and turned the deadbolt. I also put the chain on. I turned around to see Kyle looking at me, one hand on hip and one eyebrow raised.

I swallowed. *"Now* I think maybe we need to get an alarm?"

I'd always resisted getting one. I'd always been defensive about our neighborhood. Nothing was more irritating than telling someone where you live, only to have them recoil from you and utter some insulting iteration of *how can you live in such a dan-*

gerous neighborhood?

Yes, because living in St. Roch is little better than living in the Wild West.

It was always so tempting to reply brightly, "I get so much exercise from dodging bullets I don't need to join a gym!"

But it wasn't so funny now that Kyle and I both could have been killed.

He'd shot at me!

My ears were still slightly ringing from the gunshots that left actual bullet holes in the wall between the living room and the kitchen.

My legs were wobbly as I walked back over to the couch. I managed to sit down before I started hyperventilating again and leaned forward, dropping my head between my knees and taking deep, cleansing, calming breaths.

"I don't know if we need an alarm," I heard Kyle saying. "But am I going to have to move, child? Am I going to have to worry about coming home from work every day to find someone with a gun in my house?"

I heard him walking towards me but kept my head down.

Focus on your breathing and calm down. You survived. Kyle survived.

Again.

We're both safe.

I took another deep breath and sat back up. I let

the sudden head rush clear and put a finger to my neck. My heart rate had slowed, and I was starting to feel . . . not numb anymore. The shock was going away, and so was the adrenaline. I felt very tired.

Kyle rubbed the center of my back.

"Having an alarm wouldn't have saved me either yesterday or today," I said, relieved he wasn't mad at me. "This didn't have anything to do with the neighborhood being dangerous or not. This is all connected to Marigny's murder. I knew I shouldn't have let Lee Ann talk me into doing that stupid show on Friday night. I knew Marigny was bad news."

"Maybe," Kyle said, still rubbing my back. "But you're self-employed, Jem. You can't beat yourself up for not turning down money." He shook his head and shivered. "Not the first time I've had a gun held on me, growing up in the East, but you don't ever get used to that."

"Well, at least the police have the hard drive." I replied, then froze. Jack Jorgenson denied being the person who'd knocked me out Sunday and trashed the place.

Just because he'd shot at me didn't mean he was lying about that.

I'd been shot at.

Everything started going dark on the periphery of my vision. I put my head down between my knees, closed my eyes and took some deep breaths.

Kyle and I both could have been killed.

It didn't matter whether Jorgenson would have gone through with it or not.

He'd shot at me. The only reason I wasn't on my way to the emergency room or the morgue was because he was a bad shot.

That wasn't reassuring.

"Breathe, baby," Kyle said, picking up his pole and putting his other hand on his hip, shaking his head. "The one good thing to come out of this was seeing Detective Blake in his tight street clothes." He gave me a wicked grin, and mimed tossing his hair. "But if this dude wasn't the guy who broke in here yesterday and tied you up, who did that?"

Something was nagging at me but I couldn't quite put my finger on what it was. Something was off, didn't make sense.

I laughed inwardly. *None* of this made sense.

"Well, now that Blake and the cops have Marigny's hard drive, I don't think we have anything else to worry about," I replied, reaching for the tin I kept my medical cannabis prescription inside. I flipped off the top and shook out one of the pre-rolled joints I'd picked up the last time I'd been to the dispensary. I grabbed a lighter and sparked the end. I took a big hit, and held it out to Kyle, who shook his head.

"Nah, I better keep my head clear," Kyle replied, standing up. "Don't let me stop you, though. I got a pole class to teach tonight." He rolled his eyes. He crossed the big room and I heard him going up the stairs.

At least he wasn't mad at me. Not that I could blame him if he was—he had every right to be mad.

I leaned back against the back of the couch and took another deep hit. I held the smoke in and felt the tingling slowly spreading through my body as everything started to relax. I could feel the stress and anxiety draining out of my brain.

The best thing about moving here, I thought as I pinched the joint out and put it back in its plastic tube, *is medical cannabis is legal, thank God.* As soon as the first dispensaries had opened, I'd gotten a medical card and never looked back. Mee Maw had smoked a little bit every night to help her unwind and sleep, but she never let me have any. "Your parents would never let you come back here," she said with a shake of her head. "And don't risk it when you're at home, either. You go to jail and your life is ruined. And in Texas? Promise me you'll wait till you turn eighteen to try it."

It was just as illegal for her to have it, but I never pointed that out to her. I lived for coming to New Orleans every summer and wasn't about to do anything that would jeopardize that.

It was nice to be able to buy it legally now. It was a little more expensive than the street rate but the sales benefitted either LSU or Southern University, so I was doing my part to support college education in Louisiana.

I kind of liked the idea that my indulgence served to better the overall community.

Possession had also been decriminalized . . . which was why the Quarter always reeked of weed at night now.

Now that I was relaxed and it was all over, I felt a little bit sorry for Jack Jorgensen. How desperate must he have been to propose to marry Marigny, and gone through with it? But she'd been married multiple times, so she must have had some kind of appeal for straight men. The rules of attraction were impossible to figure out, primarily because there were none. Mee Maw used to say, "there's someone for everyone and who are we to judge? So long as no one's getting hurt, more power to them."

You see it in the gay community, too. We always assume if a younger man is with an older one, it's money related. But twinks can be attracted to daddies and muscleboys like bears; straight people were no different. I've never been able to figure out what straight men are drawn to in the opposite sex. Just because I'm not attracted to women doesn't mean that I can't recognize when a woman is beautiful or has an amazing figure. Female beauty is my *business*, but my focus was on making my client feel beautiful.

If you feel beautiful, people will think you're beautiful.

It's about *confidence*. Women are drawn to confident men, and men are likewise drawn to confident women. It wasn't that different in my community, either. Kyle was gorgeous and was secure enough to be confident.

I looked in the mirror and wondered what anyone would ever see in me.

Which was why I was still single and hoping.

Marigny had never lacked for male company. There were obviously men who liked that gaunt, skeletal look.

What could she have written about Jack that would make him so desperate to make sure no one ever saw it?

And there it was—what had been bothering me earlier.

It popped into my head and was so obvious I couldn't believe I hadn't been able to make the connection.

Jack said he'd taken the hard drive out of Marigny's office and had hidden it in my make-up case, intending to get it later.

Why had he waited two days to retrieve it?

He said he wasn't the burglar from yesterday . . .

If I had hidden something in someone else's make-up kit, I wouldn't have waited two days to try to get it back. How did he know I wouldn't do exactly what I'd done—found it, turned it over to either Jackson or the cops?

The burglar from yesterday hadn't known my make-up case wasn't here. The burglar from yesterday didn't seem to even know what he was looking for—un-

less he just trashed the place to be a dick.

What had she written in her memoirs?

I'd copied Marigny's files to my computer before disconnecting the hard drive. For a fleeting moment I wondered if I'd broken the law somehow, like interfering with a police investigation. No, I'd turned it over to the police and hadn't deleted anything from it. I hadn't tampered with the evidence nor interfered with a police investigation.

I probably I watched too many crime shows and movies. And read too many crime novels.

But what would Benson and Stabler do? Or Miss Marple? Or V. I. Warshawski?

They'd read every file they'd copied, that's what they would do.

I grabbed the joint and a bottle of water from the refrigerator on my way to the workroom. First, I went out into the back yard to make sure the gate was locked. I jiggled it a bit—the lock held, but the gate itself was flimsy. Anyone who wanted in could just kick it down. I made a mental note to look into other ways to secure the gate and went back inside the house. I sat down at my desk and opened the water. I relit the joint. I took another deep hit, pinched it out, and woke up my computer.

The folder sat there on my desktop, next to my JEM folder, and I rolled the cursor over the folder and clicked it open. I went back to the "pictures" folder—it's easier to look at pictures than read, after all—and started working my way through them all. I yawned as I looked at old pictures of her parents, standing on the front steps to the house at Magazine and Nashville. There were some candid shots of them, casual and dressed up. There was a series of faded wedding shots. A few shots of the woman I assumed was Marigny's mother holding a baby that must be Marigny. Then came the pictures of her as a little girl. I went back to the directory and scrolled to the bottom—the last picture was labeled IMG_256.

There were 256 pictures on here? Maybe I'd be better off reading. I scrolled back to the top.

None of the pictures were labeled. I had no way of identifying any of the people in her pictures. Many were from so long ago it was unlikely anyone besides Marigny could identify any of the people. I was about to give up when I reached pictures from her teens. Ah, yes, here she was, in white gowns with gloves going to Carnival balls. There were shots from her high school years and her yearbook photos. I scrolled through her photos of Carnival krewe courts, not bothering to pick her out.

And then I came across one that made me do a double take.

I clicked on the magnifying glass, making it bigger until it pixelated. I played around with the sizing until it was as clear as it was going to be. It was a scan of an old photograph, whose colors had started fading and going sepia over the years. There was a white quarter inch border on every side, and on the bottom was the date *20 Aug 1978.*

Over forty years ago, but that wasn't the weird part.

The girl in the picture was clearly Marigny when she was a teenager. It was impossible to miss the eyes, that distinctive long nose with the bulb on the bottom, or that sharp chin. She'd been much prettier when she was young (Mee Maw used to say "everyone's pretty when they're young; when you get old your inside starts showing on the outside."), but she'd apparently always been little more than skin and bones. She was wearing what I assumed was a frilly pink dress, and a corsage on one of its straps. If I'd been styling her, I would have picked a different silhouette—this one wasn't doing her any favors.

So she never really knew how to dress herself, I thought.

If anything, the silhouette of her dress was incredibly unflattering and made her look like she didn't have a figure or curves of any kind.

But more interesting than that was the man she was with, his arm around her shoulders and a big smile on his face, looked just like Lauralee Dorgenois's husband Barry.

It couldn't be Barry, of course. The man in the picture was in his fifties, at the very least, so if he were still alive, he'd be close to a hundred years old now. But the resemblance was uncanny. The black tuxedo he was wearing was straight out of the 1970s, as was the frilly blue shirt underneath the wide lapel jacket. He was beaming at the camera, and the flash had whited out his forehead, like it reflected off beads of sweat. The smile looked insincere, forced—like he'd been having a serious conversation with Marigny before the person with a camera interrupted them. He'd smiled for the flash, but Marigny hadn't bothered pretending. Her expression was sour and angry and sullen.

I opened my browser and did an image search for Barry Dorgenois. Several came up, including one of Barry at the Endymion Ball a few years ago. He was wearing a black tuxedo, with a stiffly starched white shirt underneath. The lapels weren't as wide or out of style as in the other picture. I screen-capped the picture and then opened it up next to the picture from Marigny's file. On a hunch, I plugged Marigny's snapshot into the image search window. The rainbow wheel spun, and a couple of the same images that came up on the search for Barry did again—but there were others that clearly identified the man in Marigny's photo as Judge Harlan Dorgenois.

Judge Dorgenois had his own Wikipedia page, so of course I clicked through to it.

Harlan Dorgenois, it turned out, had not just been any judge, he'd been Chief Justice of the Louisiana Supreme Court, elected after ten years as a federal appellate judge. He had been known as the "civil rights judge," striking down Jim Crow laws that had institutionalized racism in Louisiana for generations. He'd been despised. Hate mail and death threats sent to the house, crosses were burned on the front lawn of the Dorgenois home on St. Charles Avenue further uptown. Harlan had gone to LSU and then onto Vanderbilt Law School. He had married Thérèse Sheehan (I wondered how she was related to Rachel's husband, it truly was insane how small of a town New Orleans was) and they'd had five children: Barry, Iris, Daphne, Tanner, and Blake—

I blinked twice.

Blake. I pulled out my wallet and got out the business card he'd given me. Detective Blake Dorgenois.

How had I missed his last name and not made the connection to Lauralee?

You're not crazy. Why would you ever think the hot police detective would be the younger brother of one of the richest men in Louisiana? Rich kids tend to not become cops when they grow up.

There was a story there. I picked up my phone, pulled up Rachel on my contacts and hit call.

"Jem!" she sounded a bit breathless when she answered my call. "Are you okay?"

"All things considered," I replied. How could she know what happened today already? Yet another reminder that New Orleans was a small town. "Now I'm just wondering which one of Marigny's ex-husbands is going to show up at my front door with a gun next."

"Wait, what?"

I couldn't help but laugh. "I was wondering how you already knew." I explained the events of the day, leaving out the part about copying Marigny's files first—if she were related to the Dorgenois, it would be better to be discreet.

She let out a low whistle. "Are you sure you're okay? Jack Jorgensen always had a few screws loose if you ask me."

"I'm fine, really. After yesterday's break-in—"

"That's what I was referencing," she replied. "You need to be more careful, Jem."

"Trust me, you don't have to worry about that," I said. "But the reason I was calling—do you know if Marigny had a connection to the Dorgenois family?"

She was quiet for so long I was beginning to think she'd hung up, but she said, "Why do you ask?"

"If this is awkward—"

"Thérèse Dorgenois is my father-in-law's first cousin," she said finally, "I don't know her all that well, but she's kind of family."

"You never mentioned you were related to Lauralee before," I replied.

"I just assumed you knew," she laughed. "Everyone knows. Oh, yes, you're not from here. I just don't think about it much because it just is, you know? There were a lot of stories about the Judge—

Thérèse's husband, but I was never sure if there was anything to them."

"What kind of stories?" I glanced back at his Wikipedia page.

"The usual awful stuff people say about powerful men," Rachel sighed. "That he had other women, wasn't faithful to Thérèse, that sort of thing, that he drank too much and forced himself on women who weren't interested." She paused. "I always just figured it was because of his civil rights work, you know, on the bench—the racists always love to smear their opponents. Do you know Jerry Channing?"

"I've never met him, but I know who he is." Jerry Channing had written a famous book about a legendary murder case, *Garden District Gothic,* and wrote true crime pieces for *Street Talk* and other magazines. He was good—he always liked to report on crimes of the rich and famous, how money and power can make justice not quite so blind as the founding fathers had imagined. He was older, shaved his head, and prone to wearing black V-neck T-shirts and tight jeans. The story was he'd been a personal trainer to the ladies of the Garden District, which was where he got all the dirt that went into his book. He certainly looked like he'd made a living with his body when he was younger. "Why?"

"He wrote a great piece about the Judge for *Crescent City* a while back. I'll send you a link to it, and his number if you want to give him a call."

"So was Marigny one of the women Judge Dorgenois supposedly was involved with?"

"I think so? I know Marigny and Lee Ann were quite the pair back when they were younger," Rachel laughed. "I feel like I'm gossiping over the back fence with a neighbor. Anyway, yes, people used to talk all kind of smack about the two of them—namely, they'd pretty much sleep with anything in pants. You know, the usual horrible misogynist stuff. I think this was all before Marigny went to Paris to work at Chanel."

I blew a raspberry. "I just find that so hard to believe," I scoffed. "There's no way she worked at Chanel and designed such ugly dresses. Maybe she was the receptionist or something?"

Rachel laughed. "Maybe, but Marigny told that story to anyone and everyone who'd listen to her." There was a noise from her side of the call. She put down the phone to say something, then picked it up again. "Jem, I have to go. But if you want to know anything about Marigny's sordid past, you should talk to Lee Ann. She knows where all the bodies are buried." She hung up.

I moved the cursor to the directory for Marigny's files, clicked on the search bar, and typed Dorgenois into it. The wheel spun again, then several folders— some chapters numbered between eight and fourteen appeared so I clicked on the lowest number.

The document opened, and again I went to the search function, and typed the name.

The first instance came up, with the name Dorgenois highlighted in yellow.

I was thrilled when Tanner Dorgenois asked me to the Newman prom. He was one of the best looking boys in New Orleans, and of course his father was the notorious Judge Harlan Dorgenois. Some of the girls at McGehee were surprised I would go out with a boy from a family like that, but that was to be expected from those empty-headed girls who couldn't form an original thought if they were held at gunpoint. All they did was parrot all the horrible things their daddies said around the dinner table. The worst of them told me if I'd go out with the son of a "n****r lover, then I must be one too. I stood up to them, of course—I'd been standing up to them ever since I entered that horrific torture academy, and wasn't about to back down my senior year to a bunch of narrow-minded bigots.

I skipped ahead to the next Dorgenois mention.

His father drove us, which was both exciting and scary at the same time. Judge Dorgenois was so handsome, and charming, and such a gentleman! I'm afraid he dazzled me, right from the very start. I knew that first time I laid eyes on him that we were destined to be lovers; that my burgeoning relationship with Tanner wasn't going to go anywhere, but it had been worth it to meet the Judge. When he called me the next week and asked me to dinner, of course I said yes. We met at a small restaurant in the Central Business District—and after, he invited me to the suite he kept at the Mon-

teleone Hotel, and our love affair began. I can honestly say the Judge ruined me for other men; I keep trying to rekindle that magic we had together with another man but the truth is there are no others. Five husbands and numerous lovers, all in a desperate attempt to replicate the magic of first love...

I stared at the screen.

Marigny had slept with the Judge?

Blake's father?

I felt light-headed. I got up and walked back into the kitchen. I turned on the faucet and splashed cold water onto my face.

Blake had a conflict of interest in this case. He shouldn't be involved in the investigation at all.

Or maybe he was just making sure suspicion didn't fall on anyone in his family?

It's not like believing a cop was crooked in New Orleans required a huge leap of imagination.

He'd never once mentioned a connection to Marigny.

Was it possible he didn't know?

Would I be making excuses for him if I didn't think he was hot?

Give it up, Jem, he's never going to date you.

Resolutely I walked back into the living room and called Lauralee.

CHAPTER FIFTEEN

Lauralee was more than happy to arrange a meeting for me with her formidable mother-in-law. "Don't let her intimidate you," Lauralee said with a laugh before hanging up, "which is advice I wish I could take. I'll text you once I've talked to her."

"Thank you," I replied and disconnected the call.

Lauralee had told me any number of horror stories about her mother-in-law over the years. Barry's first wife had the right pedigree and had grown up with him. The two families had been thrilled when they started dating and got married once they'd graduated from college. But the marriage had been a mistake right from the start. According to Lauralee, the first wife (whose name I couldn't remember) had been a closeted lesbian with little to no interest in having sex with her husband. "So, of course he cheated on her," Lauralee had said. "and was miserable. But he cared about her too much to out her." She'd finally left Barry when she fell in love with her Crossfit trainer, and they'd gotten divorced. Lauralee had been working as an English Lit teacher at Holy Cross when she met the just-divorced Barry. Barry fell madly in love with her and married her within a year. Lauralee had already been going to Mee Maw's salon when she suddenly became the wife of one of the richest men in the state—and Lauralee was nothing if not loyal.

Even after Mee Maw sold the shop and retired, she kept Lauralee as a client—and eventually passed her on to me.

Lauralee and Barry had been getting ready to go to the Saints game when I called her—the Dorgenois have one of those fancy suites at the Superdome so they don't have to mix with the *hoi polloi*. When I asked her why she'd never told me about Barry's hot younger police detective sibling, she giggled. "When his partner died I thought about trying to fix the two of you up together, but then I remembered what you always say . . ."

I closed my eyes and moved my lips along with her as she said the words ". . . just because we're both gay doesn't mean we'll get along. We don't all like each other and we don't all want to date each other."

It does get old, for the record. If I had a dollar

for every well-meaning straight person who knew someone gay that I should meet . . . hello, people. There's more to us than being gay.

This time, though, I'd shot myself in the foot.

I was lighting the joint again when Lauralee called me back about half an hour later.

"You are expected for tea tomorrow afternoon at three," she said when I answered. "Precisely at three, so if you have another appointment you'd better re-schedule it. I had to promise—well, never mind what I had to promise, but she agreed to talk to you."

"Thanks, Lauralee. I'll give you a free blow out to make up for it."

"Oh, there's no need," she replied. That was how you could tell Lauralee hadn't grown up with mon-ey—she never wanted anything for free or discount-ed. In my experience, people who grow up rich are penny pinchers. Lauralee had waited tables in col-lege, so she always tipped well. "I was a bit surprised she agreed. She wasn't going to until I mentioned Marigny."

"Really? What did you say?"

"I told her you were curious about the murder and you'd been at the fashion show the night she was murdered," Lauralee said. "Then she said okay, tell him to be here for tea at three."

"Do I need to dress up?"

"She is kind of snooty about the way people dress," Lauralee admitted, and I remembered a story she'd told me about the first time she'd met Thérèse, wearing a designer dress she'd picked up at an uptown thrift store where the wealthier ladies of New Orleans recycled their clothes. Thérèse had recognized the dress and known the woman who'd originally owned it.

After that, Barry gave her a Saks credit card.

"And if you're even a minute late she won't allow the butler to let you in. She's a stickler for punctuality," Lauralee was saying. I thanked her and hung up—she was, I reflected, a good friend as well as client.

And I should start pumping Lauralee for more information about Blake.

Forget it, guys like Blake don't go for guys like me.

I spent the rest of the night reading Marigny's memoir and resisting the urge to google Blake.

Who would want to read any of this? I kept asking myself while scrolling down, stifling yawns. Marigny's writing style was what I think they call confessional—lots of exclamation points and run-on sentences. It read like she was excitedly whispering it all in your ear, so it kind of sucked you in to keep reading. There was a lot of gossip about people whose names sounded vaguely familiar but couldn't place.

I could see this being a nine day wonder in New Orleans when it was published. It was one of those books everyone would talk smack about but then read privately.

But who would publish this? Maybe a local small press?

It was also very clear from the beginning that this was all Marigny's point of view, and that she was incredibly deluded about a lot of things. She talked a lot during the early chapters about the stories she'd been told growing up about the Orloff family being descended from an illegitimate son of a Russian Romanov archduke, a Tsar's younger son. She'd become obsessed with Russia and the tragic history of the final Imperial dynasty. The book wasn't written chronologically. She began with the childhood stories and how she's gone to Russia to try to trace the stories and prove she was Imperial royalty.

Hadn't Jackson said she'd failed? That it was all a lie and the ancestor had owned a butcher shop in St. Petersburg?

In the book she said it was too difficult since she didn't speak Russian, but she enjoyed visiting all the places the Romanovs had lived.

By the time we got to her teen years I'd already relit the joint to try to help me get to the end. She went on and on about being Carnival royalty, and how proud she'd been to be Queen of Patroclus when she was eighteen. She'd tell an interesting story about a member of New Orleans society but just the bare bones . . . and then would spend pages describing her ball dress.

Marigny was in desperate need of an editor.

Finally, just before midnight, I reached the part about Judge Dorgenois. It was also poorly written in that same confessional breathless style, like she was whispering to you over drinks at Galatoire's. At first, she'd been thrilled to be asked to her prom by Tanner Dorgenois, and she went on for pages about what an honor it was. But she'd forgotten the Judge's son the moment she met his father, when they'd stopped by the Dorgenois mansion for pictures. The Judge called her the next week ... and that was the beginning of a long-running affair that lasted the rest of her senior year and the following summer. She revoltingly talked about the kinds of things the Judge liked to do in bed, and how he taught her how to (her words) "give a man so much pleasure he'd never look at another woman."

But it finally ended in late August when she accepted the internship at Chanel in Paris: *no matter how much I knew he loved me, there was no way the Judge could leave his wife and family for a woman the same age as one of his sons. The white supremacists would crucify him. So I chose my career over the man I loved, went to Paris and tried to forget my soul mate, my one true love* ...

I pinched the joint out again and went to bed. Just before I drifted off to sleep, I thought yes, forty or fifty years ago that would have been a scandal all right but why would anyone care about that today? Enough to kill her? I don't think so.

At two fifty-five the next afternoon I pulled Mee Maw's 2001 white Buick Skylark up next to the curb in front of the Dorgenois mansion. I got out of the car, staring at the enormous house. I brushed imaginary lint off my dressiest black pants. I'd even put on a nice white button-down shirt and dress shoes—but drew the line at a tie.

How had Lauralee felt the first time Barry brought her here? I wondered as I opened the elaborate iron gate and strolled up the slanted walk to the front gallery. The lawn was emerald green and lush, perfectly manicured—putting the slapdash job I always did on our back yard to shame. A black wrought iron fountain was centered on the lawn, replicas of the Three Graces meeting in the center, the water bubbling out above them and cascading down their faces and their bodies. The sculptor had done a really good job of creating the impression that their diaphanous robes were wet and clinging to their bodies—so good the fountain seemed borderline pornographic.

The house itself was stunning. Somehow the white paint looked as fresh as if it had been given a new coat this morning—no small feat in New Orleans, where our air is filled with dirt and dust. The stairs were built in a half circle leading up to the front gallery, where four columns supported each corner of the gallery. Every five feet another set of two columns supported the gallery. There was deck

furniture on the second-floor balcony as well as el-
ephant ferns. Roses and jonquils bloomed in the
flower bed along the gallery. I climbed the steps to
the double doors and rang the doorbell.

A few moments later the door was opened by
an older Black woman in a maid's uniform. I smiled.
"Jem Richard for Mrs. Dorgenois?"

She inclined her head and opened the door for
me. "She's expecting you. If you'll follow me?"

I have a lot of well-to-do clients, so I've been
inside some truly magnificent homes in the city.
Even so, the Dorgenois house gave me pause. The
hardwood floors gleamed. The Oriental rugs and
furniture screamed antique and expensive at the
same time. The chandelier hanging in the foyer
glittered and flashed fire when its crystals caught
the light. She led me into a drawing room, nodding
again and saying "Mrs. Dorgenois will be with you
shortly. Is there anything I can do to make you more
comfortable?"

I demurred and she backed out of the room.
There was a wet bar against one wall, and the French
doors opened out to the gallery. The room was painted a dark emerald shade, with gold trim. There was
another massive chandelier hanging from an incredibly fancy medallion on the ceiling. Usually they had
very basic patterns, but this one had clipper ships and
fish and mermaids worked into its intricate design. It
was a masterpiece, a work of art itself.

"It's special, isn't it?"

Thérèse Dorgenois stood in the doorway, smiling at me. She was of about medium height, with short white hair perfectly styled and was wearing a pair of gold-framed glasses perched on the edge of her strong nose. She wore a knee-length black silk dress with two ropes of pearls around her neck. She held out her hands as she walked toward me, and I took them.

"Thank you for agreeing to see me," I replied. "I'm Jem Richard—"

"Yes, dear, I know well who you are," she said, her voice warm as she gestured toward two wing-back chairs intimately arranged between the windows with a small table between them. She was a little taller than I was, and her figure was still as trim as when she reigned as Queen of Rex. "Do you want coffee? Tea? Is it too early for a cocktail?" She frowned and pushed her glasses up, peering at the clock on the marble mantelpiece. "I can have a tea service brought in for us, if you prefer? I told Lauralee I'd offer you tea—" her voice slightly altered when she said Lauralee's name, "—but I'd prefer a cocktail, wouldn't you?"

"No, I'm fine, thank you," I replied.

"Do you mind if I have one?"

"Not at all."

She walked over to the wet bar, put some ice in a cocktail shaker and added gin. "Lauralee speaks so highly of you." She smiled at me. "You make her look beautiful." She poured some vermouth into a martini glass, swishing it around before dumping it down the sink. She shook the mixer, strained the gin into the glass, and popped two olives into it.

"She is already beautiful. I just make her feel like she is," I replied as she sat down across from me.

"Wisely said," She toasted me with her glass. "I have to tell you I am most curious about why you wanted to see me? Is there some charity you want me to donate to?"

I took a deep breath. "No, Mrs. Dorgenois, that's not why I'm here." I could tell she was the kind of woman who appreciated directness. "I was at Marigny Orloff's house the other night for her fashion show—I helped with styling it—and—"

"That detestable woman!" She interrupted me with a most unladylike eye roll. "All of her taste was in her mouth—and even that was questionable."

Lauralee had warned me that Thérèse didn't mince words. I smothered a grin. "Not a fan?"

She laughed, a marvelous sounding noise, like tinkling glass. "Discretion is my middle name, after all." She shook her head, the corners of her mouth twitching. "She was an awful woman, just awful. She always was, and she never changed." She clucked her tongue. "But still, no one deserves to be murdered. How dreadful for her boys—no matter what they thought of her, she was their mother." She closed her eyes and took a few deep breaths.

"She had trouble with her sons?" I asked after a few moments.

Thérèse opened her eyes and focused them on me. "One doesn't move to Memphis, Tennessee, because one wants to, dear." She sighed. "Being murdered doesn't make her any less detestable. That whole 'don't speak ill of the dead' is just the kind of hypocrisy I despise. Someone dies, and everyone gets all sad and pretends the departed was a saint? No, I don't subscribe to that notion. I wouldn't wish death on anyone, of course, not even someone as perfectly awful as Marigny Orloff, but I'm not going to pretend she was a lovely person. She most definitely was not.

"I didn't like her myself," I replied, lowering my voice like we were sharing secrets. "She tried to stiff me on a job the last time I worked for her—"

"Let me guess—Lee Ann Vidrine guaranteed your payment for you?" A corner of her mouth went up nastily.

"Well, yes, how did you know?"

"Lee Ann's been cleaning up after Marigny since they were both hellions running around the Quarter going after anything in pants." She shook her head. "I understood that the rules have changed and I'm a dinosaur, as my grandchildren love to remind me, but I just don't understand the appeal of sleeping around. If you're going to just have sex indiscriminately, why not get paid for it?" She laughed at the look on my face. "Are you horrified at my archaic views?"

"No. But you said something about her sons—"

"Oh, you want the gossip?" She gave me a wicked smile as she sipped her martini. "Her oldest, Aramis, dated my daughter Iris, you know." Iris was her younger daughter, an enormously successful photojournalist for National Geographic. She was currently on assignment in Tanzania. "I can't tell you how terrified I was Iris might actually marry him—she was crazy about him." She gave a delicate shudder. "The thought of possibly sharing grandchildren with that horrible woman used to give me nightmares. Such a shame. Aramis was a lovely young man."

"I don't think I've ever met him or the other son, Bonaparte?"

It wouldn't be proper to say a woman of her stature snorted, but Mrs. Dorgenois did it in a very lady-like way. "Who names their son after one of *The Three Musketeers*? At least Bonaparte—" she rolled her eyes, "—his father claimed to be descended from one of the Baltimore Bonapartes, which is why she gave him that ridiculous name, but I suppose he should be grateful she didn't give him some jaw-breaking Russian name. She thought she was a long-lost Romanov, you know."

"I always thought it was odd all her sons took her last name."

Thérèse made a face. "I can't even remember how many times she was married. Four? Five?" She gave a little *who knows* shrug. "She was pretty wild before she married the first time, too. Anything with pants in the Quarter was fair game to her." She said it with disdain, like she was talking about something she'd accidentally stepped in. "You know Marigny was writing a book, don't you?"

"A book?" I feigned surprise. "What kind of book?"

"A memoir." Thérèse's lip curled. She looked over to the painting of her husband hanging over the mantelpiece. Judge Thomas Dorgenois had been deceased about ten years, and she always referred to him at the Judge. He'd been serving on the state Supreme Court when he died. There were some nasty rumors about what exactly he'd been doing when he had the massive coronary. The public story was that he'd died in his judge's chambers. The whispers were that he wasn't alone. "She actually called me—when was it? Last week sometime?" She frowned, pinching the bridge of her nose. "Yes, yes, it was Wednesday. I'd just gotten home from that awful book club luncheon." She gave a little mock shudder. "Terribly stupid women, but it seemed like a good idea at the time. Never again."

"She called you?" I prompted.

"I hadn't spoken to her in years," Thérèse's voice was grim. "She called to tell me she was writing a

book—her memoirs, and just wanted to warn me."
She made air quotes as she said the last two words,
and her eyes were steely. "What she *really wanted*
was money, of course, and I wasn't having any of it.
I laughed in her face. Well, on the phone, anyway."

"Money?" I stared at her. "You mean blackmail?"

She sighed and got a look on her face that chilled
me. "Marigny's been over-extended for years, of
course." She pursed her lips contemptuously. "That's
no great secret, you know. Those dreadful designs she
came up with? She should have gone for the drag
queen market—because no woman with any refine-
ment or elegance would wear those horrors she designed." She made a face. "Sequins and feathers—just
dreadful. She never had any taste, of course, and she
tore through whatever money her father left her—
which wasn't much—and then there were all those
marriages and young men . . ." her voice trailed off
as she looked off into the distance. I was about to
prompt her when she shook her head slightly and
looked back at me. "She thought I'd give her money
if she promised to leave the Judge out of her revolting
book." She barked out a hoarse laugh. "You should
have heard her voice! Of course she called. She knew
if she dared show her face here with her little blackmail demands I would have slapped her silly."

I found my voice. "The Judge?"

"My husband was a wonderful man and I loved
him, my dear, but above all else he was a man."

Her voice twisted into scorn on the last word. She shrugged. "When I was pregnant with Blake, he strayed. It wasn't the end of the world. And Marigny was pretty, then—if you like that common street-walker look, and men always seem to." She smiled. "She didn't age well, poor dear. But then the slutty ones never do. The hard living always shows on their faces in the end—just like their character. I guess she thought I wouldn't want the Judge's name sullied in her nasty little book." She barked out a laugh. "He's *dead*. If anything, people would feel sorry for *me*." She rolled her eyes theatrically. "Which is what I told her. And even if people gossiped and said bad things about me or the Judge, who cares?" She locked her brown eyes on mine. "They burned crosses on my front lawn and fired guns into our windows when I had small children in the house." She laughed. "You think I'm afraid of a little gossip? Why would I give her money so she wouldn't look like the tramp she was in her silly little book?" She waved a hand dismissively.

"I, uh, do you think she was using her book to blackmail people?" I managed to get the words out.

"It wouldn't surprise me in the least," Thérèse replied with a little shrug of her shoulders. "She was like a cat in heat back in the day. She was the same age as my son Tanner—that was how we met her, Tanner took her out a few times—but even then she had a reputation. She went to Tulane for a year before she took off for Paris, you know—there wasn't a pair of pants in the French Quarter she didn't have that last year before she took off. It was disgraceful. But her father never could control her—he drank, you know, and gambled away most of their money. She came back for his funeral. Her mother died when she was a little girl. I always felt a little sorry for Marigny. It couldn't have been easy growing up the way she did." She smiled slightly. "Then she slept with my husband, actually thought he would leave me for her." She emitted a nasty little laugh. "Like that was going to happen while I was still breathing."

The way she said it made me shift uncomfortably in my seat.

"But I'm sure there are any number of men who had liaisons with her that probably wouldn't want them coming to light," she went on with a smile on her face.

"I don't think someone would kill her to keep a past indiscretion a secret," I replied. Maybe twenty years ago, but now? Now, we'd had a sitting senator who'd paid prostitutes to diaper him and God knows what else, who hadn't resigned when his indiscretion became public knowledge—and the good people of Louisiana had even reelected him after his prostitution scandal. Bearing that in mind, I couldn't imagine why *anyone* would pay Marigny Orloff to be left out of her book—let alone kill her to stop her.

I suppose she couldn't be blamed for thinking she might be able to get money out of Thérèse Dorgenois—but she'd miscalculated.

"You never know what people will do," Thérèse replied, setting her martini glass down with a smile.

"You said she was having money problems?"

"That was no secret. The money always runs out for people like Marigny Orloff—there's never enough money for them." She waved her hand again. "She always lied about things, you know." Women like Thérèse don't snort, but the sound she made was pretty close. "Her mother was from Houma. And after she started that design business? Those airs she put on? About working for Chanel in Paris all those years?" She made that not-snorting sound again. "I checked with Chanel. They'd never heard of her. I don't know where she was those years, but she certainly *wasn't* working in Paris."

CHAPTER SIXTEEN

I left Thérèse several of my cards ("in case you know anyone who might need me") and showed myself out.

I doubted she would ever hire me, but it never hurt to try. She probably threw them in the trash the minute I left the room.

Maybe it's time you stopped playing Trixie Belden and got your act together, I thought as I went down the front steps of the Dorgenois mansion. *Go to the gym, make a grocery list, run some errands . . . let the police do their jobs and stay out of the way.*

I'd liked Thérèse and her attitude towards her husband's secrets coming out. Her utter contempt for Marigny's attempts to blackmail her into keeping silent had been obvious. I'm sure she'd prefer the Judge's reputation remain pristine, but not if it meant giving a former mistress cash.

Marigny had to have known Thérèse wouldn't pay up, I thought as I went down the steps. Dark clouds were moving in from the West Bank and I could feel damp in the chilly wind. I hurried down the walk. September weather in New Orleans can be a bit bipolar. Sure, it's hot and sunny and humid most of the time, but when rain came the temperature would drop as much as twenty or more degrees. I wasn't dressed for that.

Why had Marigny been so desperate for cash? What was going on with her that she needed so much money?

Well, the divorces had to have cost her a chunk. And as a small business owner myself, I could understand cash flow concerns. As I knew from experience, she'd also had an issue with paying her bills. I'd thought at the time she was just one of those rich people who don't think they have to pay for things, but maybe she really hadn't had the money. Maybe Designs by Marigny was just a house of cards ready to collapse at any moment.

Not your problem, leave it to the police.

Since Jack Jorgensen was now in custody, I didn't have to worry about any more home invasions, either. I could go on with my life like I'd never heard of Marigny Orloff.

But hadn't Jack denied doing the first one? They had him dead to rights for yesterday, so why not admit the first break-in? *Stop it, Jem, this is none of your business.*

Jack admitted putting her hard drive in my make-up case. Ellis had the case, so it hadn't been there when he broke in the first time. So, no one else could have known where it was, right? Even Jackson, her own son, had said it wasn't his mother's because she hadn't marked it the way she usually did.

Maybe someone saw Jack put the hard drive in my make-up case?

I couldn't stop thinking about it.

I got into my car and drummed my fingers on the steering wheel for a moment. I was in the neighborhood, so driving by Designs by Marigny wasn't too far out of the way home. I started the car and headed further uptown. At the first place I could turn around, I crossed over the neutral ground in front of a downtown streetcar and headed back downriver. I pulled over into an open spot just past the intersection once I crossed Nashville. I got out of the car and leaned against it. It was getting darker as the storm clouds crossed the river and the wind was picking up. I shivered. I could see the upper floors of the big old house over the tilted brick fence. The tent was still up in the backyard. There were no lights on in the house. Crime scene tape on the front gate fluttered...but the gate was open.

Curious, I crossed the street and walked down the sidewalk to the front gate, and stood beneath the awning. I could see the front doors were bisected with crime scene tape, too. *Why hasn't this all been secured?* I shook my head. *You watch too many cop shows,* I reminded myself. I reached out and tentatively pushed on the gate.

It swung wide open soundlessly.

I looked both ways. The drivers passing on St. Charles weren't paying any attention to me. The coast was clear.

I slowly walked up to the front steps, looking around constantly to see if anyone was watching. I flinched every time a car drove past. You're pushing your luck, and coming back to look at the scene of the crime is a serious mistake if not a crime.

The front door of the house opened. Blake pushed aside the crime scene tape and Latoya stepped outside. He followed, closing the door behind him.

Blake made a sour face when he saw me. "What are you doing here?" He folded his arms, and I tried not to notice how both biceps bulged in the tight pink Polo shirt he was wearing, how it stretched across his thick, broad chest. "Isn't it bad enough that you're pestering my mother?"

"How did—" I stopped. Of course, his mother told him I was stopping by, and why. I could feel myself starting to blush in embarrassment.

"We should run you in for interfering with a police investigation," Latoya added in a cold voice.

She was wearing a dove gray pant suit, with a silk salmon blouse and matching shoes. She tilted her head as she spoke, raising her eyebrows. "Can you let us do our jobs?"

"I'm not interfering with your investigation," I replied, knowing it wasn't true. "But after being assaulted in my own home two days in a row, I think you can understand my concerns about how well your investigation is going?"

"We arrested Jack Jorgensen yesterday, didn't we?" Blake replied, his face twisting. "You don't have to worry about him anymore. And we have the hard drive."

"Did he admit to the break-in on Saturday?" I asked.

"He's invoked his right to counsel." Latoya shrugged. "And you need to come down to the station to give a statement."

Blake had told me that. I'd forgotten. "I'm sorry." I muttered. "I will."

"Latoya, can you give us a moment?" Blake asked.

Her eyes went back and forth between us a few times, and she shrugged. "I'm heading back to the station," she said. "Meet me there when you finish with him." She gave me another appraising look, then her heels clacked on the sidewalk as she walked down the sidewalk and out the front gate.

Blake's arms remained crossed. "I didn't want to say this in front of her, but Jem, I know you must have read the files on Marigny's hard drive. You really shouldn't have done that."

"Are you going to charge me?" I said, matching his tone and crossing my own arms to mirror him. "And you can't know that."

"The only way you could have connected my mother to Marigny Orloff was if you read her memoirs," Blake scratched his head and leaned against one of the columns. "And yeah, there's not much we can charge you with and make stick. You found it in your make-up case and naturally you tried to see what was on it." He barked out a little laugh. "Although how you figured out her password—"

"I tried giving it back to Jackson," I retorted. "He told me it wasn't one of his mother's, but he told me she used the same password for everything and sure enough, it worked." Which was probably when I should have unplugged it, knowing it was hers and might be evidence.

I was making a lot of bad decisions lately. Maybe it was the head injury.

"Look, Jem, I know you're just trying to help, and I get it, you're kind of involved in the case, so of course you're curious, but you've got to stop." Blake said, placing a hand on my shoulder and looking me in my eyes. "It could be dangerous! You've already been attacked twice! What more do I have to tell you to convince you to leave it to us?"

God, his eyes are amazing, I thought, feeling weak in the knees. "Look, Blake, I'm not trying to cause trouble, seriously." I walked over to one of the wooden rocking chairs on the gallery and sat down so he couldn't see how shaky he was making me. "I don't even know what I'm doing. But when Jorgensen put that hard drive in my make-up kit, he painted a target on me. He denied breaking into my place on Saturday." Saturday's break-in was the one that didn't make sense. If it wasn't Jack, who could it have been? "If he's telling the truth—"

Blake's lips narrowed. "*If* he's telling the truth."

"What if he is?" I went on. "That means someone else out there is looking for the hard drive." But no, that didn't make sense. Whoever had broken in on Saturday had trashed my place ... "They trashed my place to make it look like a random crime." I heard myself saying. "When he couldn't find my case, he didn't want anyone to figure out what he was doing in the first place. Doesn't that make sense?"

"It also makes sense that Jack Jorgensen simply came back on Sunday," Blake replied through clenched teeth. His face had colored a bit darker, too.

"But he couldn't have known that Ellis dropped off my case—" I stopped myself. Could Ellis—no, that didn't make sense either. Ellis *had* my case, so he had the hard drive all along.

"Someone else could have seen him put the hard drive in my make-up case," I went on. "There were people in and out of the house—and the dressing room—all night long. Any of the other queens could have done it, or any of the party guests. The French doors leading out to the back gallery were never locked, you know."

"Ellis would have seen them," Blake pointed out. "Ellis was in the dressing room the entire time the show was going on."

"But after the show everyone changed out of their drag *and* either went home or joined the party," I said. "Jorgensen said he got into the house and moved the hard drive during the party, not the show. The dressing room was pretty much unattended for the rest of the night. What if someone else after the hard drive saw him take it and put it in my case, but never had a chance to get it back the rest of the night?"

"They'd also have to know it was your case."

"It's hard to miss. It's a Louis Vuitton that belonged to my grandmother, and her initials are on the clasp." I replied. "It was the only Louis Vuitton in the room, which made it stand out, and made it easier to remember."

"You don't have the same initials as your grandmother?" He smiled. "How did Jack know it was your make-up case?"

"All he had to do was ask," I replied. "Everyone in the show knew it was my case."

"Or maybe it was Ellis."

"*What?*" I stared at him. "You can't be serious."

"Can't I?" He held up a big, strong hand. There were callouses on his fingers and palm. He started ticking things off on his fingers. "Ellis had access to all areas of the house all night, Ellis was alone in the house every time all the models were out on the runway, Ellis mysteriously moved to New Orleans just three years ago—out of the blue, he just gave up his home and a pretty successful drag career in San Francisco to move here, and I'm having some trouble getting an alibi out of him for the time you were attacked."

"Ellis wasn't the only person with access to all areas of the house all night, he wasn't the only person who was ever alone in the house—I was, for one—and people move here from other places all the time because it's New Orleans, Blake." I rolled my eyes. "He could buy a house in New Orleans for what a studio in San Francisco costs. And people generally don't have alibis because they don't know they're going to need one. And besides—Ellis had no need to break into my house to steal the hard drive. *It was in his possession from Friday night until Sunday afternoon.*"

"You watch too much television," he grumbled. "I'm not even supposed to talk about on-going cases with anyone, and you're getting all this out of me."

"If I didn't know better, I'd say you like me." I teased, winking at him.

He didn't give that the dignity of a response It

was a bit disappointing but not surprising. Blake was gorgeous and obviously spent time at the gym. He was a member of one of the wealthiest families in town. Blake was one of those guys who signed into Grindr and immediately got dozens of hits from people. He was one of those shirtless guys I'd see every Saturday night at Oz, sweat running down a gloriously defined torso in the middle of a crowd of equally gorgeous men on the dance floor, drawing every eye in the place to him.

He could have anyone he wanted, so why would he want me?

And the way I kept trying to flirt with him unsuccessfully was getting embarrassing.

This is the reason why guys ghost you. You come on too strong.

"What are you even doing here?" Blake asked, shaking his head.

Oh my God, that was even worse. My flirting was so bad he didn't even realize I was trying.

"I was leaving your mom's when I remembered Jorgensen said he didn't break in to my place Saturday." I shrugged. "This was kind of on my way home so I thought I'd swing by here and see if just, you know, being here would remind me of something I noticed or saw on Friday night that I don't remember." It sounded even more lame out loud than it had in my head.

I wished a hole would open in the ground and swallow me.

I resisted the urge to just stop talking and run to my car.

You're such a catch, Jem!

I didn't expect Blake to start laughing. He sat down in the rocking chair next to me, laughing. I hadn't said anything *that* funny—but the longer he kept laughing, I could feel my face starting to flush.

"It's rude to laugh in someone's face." I said stiffly.

"I'm sorry—it's not you, really, I just—" and he started laughing again. I sat there, stone-faced, waiting for him to stop being so amused at my expense. Finally, he got a hold of himself and wiped at his eyes. His voice was still a little high-pitched from the laughing. "Really, I'm sorry," he said. "I probably shouldn't do this—and I will deny it if you tell anyone—but you know what, I'm going to take you inside, why not?" He shook his head. "This whole case has been nuts, so why do things by the book anyway?" He got up, gesturing for me to follow him. He fit a key into the front door, turned it, and held the door open for me. "Come on in—just don't touch anything. The Crime Lab has already processed the entire site—the whole house—but we haven't released the scene yet in case the district attorney's office wants to come take a look around."

I stepped inside the oddly silent house.

Is there anything creepier than a house this size that's silent as a tomb?

Probably just a tomb.

The big open room that took up most of the first floor of the house looked cavernous and spooky. The mannequins in their dresses posed and motionless, staring with blank eyes out in front of them. The big staircase that led up to the living space was chained off, just as it had been the night of the party—but the chain wasn't a deterrent. Anyone could just step over it and go straight up into Marigny's home. I looked up and could see the hallway. I made a face. Yeah, I didn't like that. I'd want there to be a door up there for privacy—and a lock to keep people out.

"Do customers sometimes wander up the stairs?" I wondered out loud.

"It wouldn't surprise me," Blake said, leading me around to the back. There was a second door on one side that I didn't remember, but the door to the workroom—which we'd used as a dressing room— was open.

"What's behind this door?" I pointed at the one I didn't remember seeing.

"That's Marigny's office," Blake replied. "Where Jackson found her Saturday morning. The coroner put her time of death at sometime between one and three in the morning, give or take."

"That puts Ellis in the clear for the murder," I pointed out. "We were at Baby Jane's until at least three in the morning." I couldn't remember. I'd drank too much Friday night to remember what time I went home. "Is her computer in the office?"

Blake nodded. "She had a laptop upstairs, too, but her primary computer was in her office."

I stepped into the workroom/dressing room. The room was deserted. It looked huge without all the mirrors and make-up cases and suitcases and nine other queens. All the sewing tables and fabrics had been moved to one side of the workroom to make room for us on Friday night. I closed my eyes and tried remembering how the room had looked. *Yes, she'd put a drop cloth or something over all of this to hide it.* The lighted three-way mirrors had been set up in front of the covered tables, hiding them from view. "Someone moved all the mirrors and clothes racks we used for the show out of here," I said slowly. "I know we left the party around twelve and it was all still in here when I retrieved my make-up case. Ellis offered me a ride to Baby Jane's, so we loaded it into his trunk and took off."

"No one has admitted to moving anything out of this room Friday night," Blake said with a frown. "But you say all of that stuff was still in here at roughly midnight?" He pulled a pad out of a pocket and made a couple of notes. "Her staff claimed she'd sent them all home once the caterers left." He scratched his forehead. "I can't see Marigny doing the physical labor to move everything, can you?"

"Well, someone had to do it, but you're right, I can't see her doing it." I put my hands on my hips and looked around the room again. Something else was wrong, but I couldn't quite put my finger on what it was. I closed my eyes, trying to remember, but whatever it was just wasn't there for me for now.

"You see or hear anything out of the ordinary?" Blake asked, "Like someone threatening her, maybe?"

"I saw and heard a lot of things." I replied. "But the night is such a jumble. I was doing tequila shots during the show, and then I got a little more tipsy at the party and—"

"It's okay." Blake said with a sigh. "Long shot, but I thought maybe you'd remembered something you hadn't when we originally interviewed you."

I walked over to the French doors and opened them, looking out on Marigny's backyard. The backyard looked abandoned beneath the tent. The fountains weren't on, and party wreckage was still scattered everywhere I looked—empty plastic cups, paper plates with food debris, and cans. The catering tables were gone as was the liquor station. The red runner she'd put down to make a runway through the yard and past the fountains and little seating areas she'd had set up was still there, but the folding chairs were gone. Had I just walked that runway three nights ago in full drag and heels?

I smiled. It had been fun, wobbly as I was on the heels.

I'd felt powerful on that runway, with everyone's eyes on me, listening to the polite applause for the gown I was wearing and my make-up and hair. I'd felt alive in a way I never had before.

Maybe—maybe when this was all over, I should enroll in Ellis' drag school? I was already a make-up and hair artist, and wasn't drag just another natural progression in the development of my art? I already had a major feather in my cap having won the Bourbon Street Awards for Best Drag—something that would gag the other queens—and sure, maybe the mask of make-up and the complete disguise and transformation into another person would take care of my stage fright? I hadn't been nervous on the runway—well, besides worrying about navigating the heels—and so what if I never performed for an audience in drag? Learning how to do it properly was a new skill set, and it never hurt to have more tools in the box, you know?

And if I could make money doing it, why not?

"Reliving your first stint in drag?" Blake said from behind me.

"It was fun," I admitted. "Have you ever done drag?"

Blake laughed. "I've done the Red Dress Run, but never full drag, not even for a costume."

"Why not?" I asked, turning to look at him, surprised to see he was standing so close behind me. "Doesn't fit in with your macho muscle-cop image?"

"No," he grinned, showing off his perfectly straight teeth, and moving closer to me. His lips were full, red, and sensual. "I don't look pretty as a woman, and I'd want to be pretty." He winked at me. "I bet you looked pretty."

"There are pictures," I replied loftily. "I even made the *Times-Picayune*."

He laughed and moved in closer to me, so close I could feel the heat of his skin. "I prefer the real thing to pictures."

He was inside my personal space, but I didn't care. I opened my mouth to say something flirtatious when he stepped even closer to me. He put his hands behind my head and pulled me into an unexpected kiss. Instinctively, I tried to pull back, but he didn't let go and I realized I didn't want him to let go—

He pulled me in closer, tighter, wrapping both powerful arms around me and pressing me against his hard, firm chest. My hands went around his wide, strong back. I let my hands drift down his hard, muscular back while he kept pressing firmly up against me. His mouth tasted of peppermint and he smelled musky, a mix of sweat, cologne and deodorant starting to fail. He hoisted me up and I wrapped my legs around his waist as our mouths remained together, my eyes closed and still not quite believing that this handsome sexy cop that every gay man in New Orleans wanted was kissing me, passionately and hungrily and that meant he was attracted to me, and—

He pulled his head back and said, huskily, "I think we'd better head over to my place to finish this, don't you think?"

All I could do was nod.

CHAPTER SEVENTEEN

As I woke up, I didn't open my eyes. I was so *comfortable*. I didn't want to get out of bed. As my mind swam up from the clouds of sleep, I vaguely remembered this amazing dream. I'd spent the night with one of the most gorgeous men I'd ever seen. It was so vivid, too. I remembered everything about his body, from the treasure trail of wiry black hair running down from his navel, the black stubble in the valley between his massive pectoral muscles, how strong and muscular his arms were, what a good kisser . . . and those deep blue eyes.

I moaned. Why couldn't I have just stayed in that dream forever?

Ah, well, might as well get up and get some coffee.

I kept my eyes closed for a few moments more before giving up.

I opened my eyes as I sat up, yawning and stretching. But as my eyes swam into focus, I didn't recognize my surroundings at first.

This isn't my bed, I thought, looking around the room before remembering I was at Blake's.

I smiled happily and laid back against the pillows. It *hadn't* been a dream!

Blake's bedroom was beautiful. It was painted coral with cerulean trim, sunshine coming through two enormous windows. I could see the branches of a live oak, and the gray side of the house next door. The sheets were also cerulean and appeared to have very high thread count of Egyptian cotton. There was a door opening into a cerulean blue bathroom. The bed faced a mantlepiece that looked like black marble. There was an enormous painting above it in a heavy gilt frame. It was of a steamboat coming down the Mississippi. Blake's partner had been an art dealer if I remembered correctly. I looked around. There was other art on the walls, mostly old sepia prints of photographs of the New Orleans of times past. There were also some abstract looking sculptures on the mantel.

The art was probably worth more than I made in a year.

I hugged myself. I sure hadn't been expecting *this* when I swung by Designs by Marigny yesterday.

What a pleasant surprise.

After he'd kissed me at the crime scene, I'd followed Blake back downtown and parked on the street in front of his house. It was on Coliseum Square, a stunningly beautiful and carefully restored Greek Revival double-gallery house also painted coral.

Blake had pulled his Mustang into a garage around the corner on Polymnia Street and had walked around to wait for me at the gate when I got out of my car. I whistled. There was an enormous live oak right on the corner, just inside the black iron fence. The ancient tree's trunk was painted green with moss in places. Some interesting looking geometric neon lights hung from its massive branches. "If I didn't know you came from money, Blake, seeing this place would make me question your ethics as a cop."

"Don't even joke about that," he replied with a shake of his bluish-black curls and a grimace. He took my hand in his, leading me through the gate. "For one thing, this was my partner's house. He'd just finished having it renovated when we met and started dating." He gave me a sad look. "It's really his place, and I should sell it and move into something smaller, but . . . it's kind of my home and I don't want to move." He looked at me. "I've lived here almost twenty years."

I stared at him. "How old are you?"

He laughed, squeezing my hand as he led me up the walk to the front gallery. "I'm forty-five, if you must know. I was twenty-three when I met Dan." His thick eyebrows knit together. "I don't know, selling his house seems like, I don't know. A betrayal?"

"I'm so sorry. I can't imagine how hard it must be to lose your partner.

"That's sweet." He unlocked the front door and immediately punched a code into the burglar alarm just inside the door. "It was hard at first." He gave me a weak smile. "You never get over it. You just get used to living with it." He pulled me close and kissed me, deep and hard and long. I put my arms around his neck and let him pull me in tight and close. "Let's stop talking about Dan," he said in a husky voice, "and get upstairs."

Blake's partner had owned a gallery on Julia Street for decades, and his exquisite taste was on display throughout the house. Gorgeous paintings hung on the walls, pieces of gorgeous sculptures on every available surface. The side yard was also beautiful, with a gorgeous marble fountain with Diana leading the hunt in the center, the water splashing down out of her quiver. Even as he led me upstairs, I couldn't stop looking at everything. The house was gorgeous, like something out of *Architectural Digest* or some interior design magazine. The house was also spotless, everything in its place. No cobwebs hung from the ceiling in corners, like in my place. I felt my cheeks flush with embarrassment. What must he have thought of *my* place if he lived in this palace?

I felt self-conscious, afraid to touch anything.

Besides him.

I smelled bacon.

I got out of the bed naked. My clothes had been picked up from where I'd scattered them in my frenzy to get naked and were neatly folded in a chair. On top of them were a pair of black Saints sweatpants and a Saints jersey. I slipped on my underwear before pulling on the sweats, which were soft and smelled like fabric softener. I walked into the bathroom. There was a brand new toothbrush, still in its packaging, sitting next to a tube of toothpaste on the counter. I brushed my teeth and washed my face. I tried to tame my hair, finally having to wet it so it wouldn't stand up.

Barefoot, I walked out of the bathroom and down the hanging staircase. The smell of bacon grew stronger and more tantalizing with every step down. My stomach was growling. Oh yes, we'd ordered pizza last night and watched old movies in his bed between bouts of fun. TCM had been running a Rosalind Russell double feature, *His Girl Friday* and *The Women*. Blake had been delighted that I knew both movies.

"Most guys your age don't know the classics," he'd said, before kissing my neck and making me forget about the movies.

"Mee Maw loved classic Hollywood and—oh! Oooooooohhhhh."

I followed the smell of breakfast down the hallway and through a door. Blake was standing at the gas stove, scrambling eggs. There was a small plate with buttered toast sitting on the island next to the toaster. Two more pieces popped up. He was wearing a pair of loose-fitting gray cargo shorts and no shirt. I stood in the doorway for a moment, watching the muscles moving in his back as he stirred the eggs. His shoulders were so broad, and the muscles in his back . . . the way his broad back kept getting narrower on the way down to his waist.

I slipped up behind him and slid my arms around his stomach. He was warm. His muscles were hard, but his skin was baby-soft. I rested my cheek against his smooth back. "And you make breakfast, too?" I asked, running my fingertips lightly over his defined abs. "You may never get me to leave."

As soon as the words came out, I could have bitten off my tongue.

Needy and desperate, party of one, your table is ready.

He reached back and put his hand on my left leg, leaning a bit back into me. "Get some coffee and sit at the island—I don't want you getting burned." As soon as he said it, the bacon sizzled and popped. I jumped back away from the stove. We both laughed, and I poured coffee into the mug he'd thoughtfully set out next to the coffee maker. It was good—a rich dark roast and strong, just the way I liked it. I sat down at the marble-topped island and took in the room. The walls were painted a calm shade of soothing pale yellow. The counters were black and white marble with swirls and curlicues. The island had a sink and a trash compacter built into it, along with numerous drawers and doors. Pots and pans hung on a rack suspended by chains hooked into the ceiling. Two ceiling fans spun lazily on either side of the hanging rack. There was also a fancy espresso machine, a microwave, and every conceivable kitchen appliance and gadget. "I'm not much of a cook," Blake said over his shoulder as he spooned out scrambled eggs onto two plates. "Dan liked to cook, so I never learned to make anything other than breakfast." He laughed. "My waffles are out of this world—but I didn't know what you liked so I figured I couldn't go wrong with eggs and bacon." He gestured with his head to one of the refrigerators. "That silver refrigerator is where all the drinks are, so help yourself to milk or juice—I think's there's orange and apple and grape?"

"Nah, just coffee's good," I replied, taking another sip. He also made a great cup of coffee. I watched the muscles in his back move as he reached up to get plates from a cabinet. *I could get used to this view,* I thought.

And this is the reason why guys ghost you, Jem, you want to get married after the first date.

But he hadn't chased me out of here last night after having his way with me, had he?

That had to count for something.

"*Voilà*," he said, presenting a plate to me with a flourish, a slight bow, and an irresistible smile. He put down an actual cloth napkin and utensils next to my plate before sitting down on the stool next to me. His right leg pressed up against mine under the overhang of the island, and I pressed back. He smiled at me—Jesus, that smile! I felt like melting into a puddle at his feet—and said, "I'm really glad you're here." He winked at me. "Do you still think I'm trying to protect my mother?"

I felt the color creep into my face again. "I'm sorry—"

"I'm teasing you." He replied, bumping me with his leg again. "It's not every day I get accused of being a crooked cop." He shrugged. "I wasn't worried, really. I knew about Dad and Marigny—"

"You did?"

He nodded, picking up a forkful of fluffy eggs—he wasn't kidding about being good at making breakfast—and replied, "Yes, it happened when Mom was pregnant. The Judge—Dad—he had affairs almost the entire time they were married. There are still rumors that people swear are true that he died in bed with one of his mistresses, or a hooker."

"Was it true?"

He shook his head, curls bouncing. "Dad died at home, Jem. He had a massive stroke one night after dinner and was dead before he hit the floor."

He shook his head. "Mom kept most of it from us when we were kids, but when I got older—he died when I was in college—I started finding out the truth about my father. Everyone has clay feet, you know. My dad accomplished a lot of great things, but he was human." He grinned at me. "Admit it, you copied the files to your computer before giving me the hard drive so you could read it." He held up his hands. "I won't tell anyone."

"Wouldn't you have?" I spread butter and strawberry jam on my toast. "I did worry if I was interfering with an investigation or whatever it is they call it on *Law and Order*, but . . . what can I say? I'm nosy."

"I don't see the harm, but I'm not a lawyer." He popped a piece of perfectly crisped bacon into his mouth. "I figured you must have if you went to see my mother. The only way anyone could connect Marigny to my mother is through those stupid memoirs of hers." He laughed. "My mother, for the record, wouldn't kill Marigny to protect my father's reputation. Sure, back when he was serving on the Supreme Court it would have been a big deal, but he's dead. If people find out Dad went through women like Kleenex, would they care now? Does it change the way he ruled, the way he changed

Louisiana for the better?" He winked at me. "Besides, Mom was married to a lawyer her entire adult life. If she was going to kill Marigny, she wouldn't have waited until now to do it. And she's not stupid enough to do it herself." He stared into my eyes. "And you've met my mother now. Can you see her sneaking into Marigny's house at three in the morning with a gun?"

He had a point.

"I got to the part about your father and stopped reading." I admitted, getting up and refilling my coffee cup. "That's when I put two and two together and realized Lauralee was your sister-in-law—"

"How long have you lived in New Orleans?" he teased. "We're all connected here in some way, you know. Everyone knows everyone, or is related to everyone, and on and on it goes. For example, I went to Newman with Bonaparte Orloff, you know."

"No, I didn't know that." New Orleans really was a ridiculously small town. "Were you friends?"

"We were on the football team together, and we got along, but we didn't hang out or anything like that." He wrinkled his brow. "I don't think I've seen him since graduation."

"Your mother thinks Marigny drove Bonaparte out of town," I said, hearing her voice saying *one doesn't just move to Memphis because one wants to, dear.*

"Bonaparte was ... interesting." Blake picked up his clean plate and placed it in the sink.

"Like I said, Bonaparte and I were both on the football team, we were in the same grade, we'd gone to school together ever since we were little, you know? So, I'd see her from time to time, you know, at school functions or picking him up after school, just around. Mom really didn't like her—I found out much later why, and couldn't really blame her once I knew about her and Dad—and I felt sorry for him, you know what I mean?"

"Why? What was Marigny like as a mother?"

"He never talked about her, if that's what you're asking me. He always seemed unhappy, and worse whenever she was around. He paused for a moment, thinking. "You know how teenagers hate having their parents around?"

Did I ever. "Yeah?"

"It seemed like it was more than that for Bonaparte. Marigny used to embarrass him all the time, and she always had to know what he was doing, does that make sense?" He exhaled. "She would always make a scene—like after football games. She'd corner Coach Duncan and yell at him for not playing Bonaparte more, that sort of thing. Mother was always chewing teachers out in front of crowds of people, you know? And he always looked like he wanted to jump off the Huey Long Bridge. She always made me grateful—" he swallowed, "—that my own mother wasn't like that."

I tried picturing Thérèse screaming at a football coach and couldn't. I couldn't imagine a lady like Thérèse ever raising her voice—because women like Thérèse never had to.

"Mom always felt bad for Bonaparte, and she would always say things to me, like 'doesn't she know she's humiliating her child?' But she was glad Bonaparte and I weren't friends. He hung out with some of the other guys from the team, but he wasn't one of what you'd call the popular kids, I guess."

"Were you? One of the popular kids, I mean." I closed my eyes. "Star of the football team, good-looking, old family—yes, I bet you were really popular in high school. Homecoming King?"

He chuckled. "Yes, I was Homecoming King."

"You weren't out in high school?"

"No." He shuddered. "There were kids who got bullied for it. I always felt bad I never said anything but I was afraid—"

"They'd turn on you?"

He nodded. "What about you?"

"High school was high school," I replied, waving a hand and finishing my last bite of breakfast. After I swallowed, I went on, "High school sucks pretty much for everyone. Yeah, they started calling me a queer and a fairy and all that in junior high school. At first it was horrible and scary and I was, you know, afraid it would get violent. By the time I got to high school, though, I figured it was just one of those things, so I started learning how to clap back." I grinned at him. "Never underestimate the power of a sharp tongue."

"I do like your tongue," he came up behind me and wrapped his arms around my waist, pressing his lips to my shoulder.

"Thanks," I leaned back into his body. "So, Marigny was an overbearing mother. How did she run Bonaparte out of town?"

"I don't know the whole story, but she wanted the boys to take over her business, the fashion company, you know. Bonaparte had no desire to do that—they didn't really get along much once he went off to LSU, once he got out from under her thumb—and he worked for Designs by Marigny for a couple of years before getting a job in Memphis and getting the hell out of New Orleans. Jackson is the only one who stuck around. I think Aramis runs a hotel in Miami now?" He shook his head. "Aramis. Can you imagine going through life with a name like that? Bonaparte isn't much better, either." He sighed. "She had a chip on her shoulder, you could tell." He frowned, squeezing me softly. "Because she wasn't, you know, old money. Like any of that really matters."

I loved how that kind of thing didn't matter to him. "Your sister doesn't buy clothes from her?"

"I couldn't say." He thought for a minute. "I think she designed Iris's wedding dress, maybe? I wasn't paying a lot of attention, you know—I know things got tense a lot between her and Mom, but I just chalked it up to wedding tension and nerves, you know." He rolled his eyes. "Iris dated Aramis for a while, you know. He was the second oldest."

"*Really?*" I raised my eyebrows.

"Iris really didn't like Marigny, either." He frowned. "She really loved Aramis...I thought she might marry him. But she fought with Marigny all the time." He made a face. "Weird how as soon as Aramis did get married, he left town."

"I don't know Jackson very well—he used to date my roommate Kyle for a while, which is how I know him—but he seems to have survived okay. And he's worked for her for years now."

"I hate that I have to go into the station when I'd rather stay here in bed with you all day," He kissed the top of my head. "So, what are you going to do for the rest of the day?"

The truth was, I didn't have anything to do. I wasn't booked for another two weeks, but fortunately Lauralee and Lee Ann had paid me well, so I was good for a while before I had to start worrying about renting a chair in a salon again. "I'd rather just hang out with you all day," I replied, "but I should probably go home and see what needs to be done around the house." I made a face. "Check for bullet holes and fingerprint dust we might have missed—you know, your average every day typical New Orleans house cleaning."

He put all the dishes into the sink and pulled me in for another bear hug and a kiss. His skin felt hot to mine, and he was so strong...it was all I could do not just to melt in his arms.

Yeah, I had it bad.

"Well, I'll head on home."

He replied. "You want me to text you when I am done with work for the day?" He kissed me again and nuzzled on my neck. I resisted the urge to pull him down on top of me again.

"I can't think of anything I'd want more," I replied.

`"Next time I have a day off, let's just camp out here," he stretched, and I watched the muscles in his arms and shoulders flex and contract and stretch. He was almost too good-looking, I thought, as I followed him back up to the bedroom. The calves in his lower legs were strong and defined, like everything. As he climbed the steps the waistband of the gray shorts started working their way down, and he wasn't wearing underwear.

Yeah, I need to get out of here soon or I am never leaving, I thought as we got the top of the stairs. He turned on the shower in the master bathroom and leaned against the doorway. "Sure I can't talk you into taking a shower with me?"

"You don't want me to leave, do you?" I winked. "Raincheck on the shower." *Raincheck on everything,* I thought as I pulled on my jeans and my shirt. I looked up from tying my shoes to see him strip out of the shorts and step into the shower. I resisted the urge to go join him.

I also resisted the urge to go stand in the doorway and watch him shower.

It would probably be better than porn.

I called a goodbye into the bathroom as I walked past and down the hanging staircase. It was all I could do to not jump up into the air and click my heels together. I felt—

Happy.

This is what happy feels like.

I hadn't felt like this since that first night with Tradd a few weeks ago.

Tradd. I hadn't thought about him and his ghosting for days now, I thought as I walked past the table in the foyer with the bowl where Blake's keys were. As I glanced into it his phone lit up with a text message across the screen.

MOM: So you have the memoir in hand now?

My heart sank. I looked back up the staircase. Should I take the phone to him and ask for an explanation?

Somehow I got outside, unlocked the Mercury and got into my car. It was a beautiful, warm late September morning, and the sun was out and not a cloud in the sky. Dogs were chasing frisbees in the park or dancing and running as they played with their owners. The fountain was splashing. I started the car and drove around Coliseum Square, my car pointed downtown.

I was pulling onto the highway when my phone started ringing. I touched the phone to answer the car so it would play through my speakers, stopping the Taylor Swift playlist on Spotify that Kyle claimed I listened to far too much.

"Jem, this is Lee Ann." Lee Ann Vidrine, to be exact; I recognized the voice coming through my speakers. "Do you think you could come by my place?" Her voice sounded shaky, like she was upset about something.

Of course, she's upset about something, I reminded myself. *Her best friend was murdered this weekend.* "I'm getting on the highway now to head home," I replied, "I can get off at Orleans and be at your place in no time." I heard another voice in the background but couldn't make out if it was male or female or what they were saying.

"Thanks, Jem," she said and hung up.

I took the I-10 East ramp from Highway 90 and in five minutes was coming down the Orleans off-ramp into the Treme neighborhood. I took the weird looping turn off near Armstrong Park from Basin to Rampart and stopped at the light.

I texted Kyle, *do you think Blake Dorgenois is trustworthy?*

I hesitated before sending it. Maybe I was making too much out of this? His mother's text could have been innocent, and he may have been telling the truth.

"Why couldn't I have been straight?" I asked aloud as I slipped my phone back into my pocket and drove into the Quarter.

CHAPTER EIGHTEEN

When I was a kid visiting for the summers, I thought it would be fun to live in the French Quarter. I loved riding my bike up the back streets of the Bywater and Marigny for beignets and café au lait at Café du Monde or to get a po'boy from any of the corner groceries, where the enormous sandwiches were wrapped in butcher paper decorated with grease spots. Bourbon Street during the day was a lot more interesting to me than it was at night. I've always known I preferred boys to girls, so gravitated toward the gay bars and shops with their rainbow flags proudly flying out front. I used to go into the shops and look at the beefcake calendars I could never buy and take back to Dallas. I loved the waiters and cooks at the Clover Grill, with their finger-snaps and quick snarky clap backs that were meant in fun and were part of the experience. I was always tempted to step into one of the bars but never had the nerve. I'd looked young for my age when I was a kid and still got carded sometimes. I think it's because I'm short.

I still love the Quarter but don't want to live there anymore. There were too many people, too many cars, too much noise, too many restrictions.

Plus, not really a great idea to live in walking distance of so many bars.

It was getting warmer as I drove into the Quarter on Orleans Street. Parking was always an issue in the Quarter even in those few short off-season weeks that seem to get shorter every year. As a local I had an aversion to paying to park anywhere, which made it harder. Free parking was restricted to two hours unless you had a Vieux Carré parking sticker, and it was closely monitored. I turned left on Burgundy and headed into the lower Quarter. Once you're downriver from St. Ann Street, the neighborhood becomes more residential than commercial. This end of the Quarter was surprisingly quiet, even on Fat Tuesday when the entire neighborhood was filled with people in costumes day drinking as soon as the sun comes up. Sure, there were days when I got frustrated living in New Orleans—it was easy, because everything seemed to be designed here to be frustrating, from the potholes marking every street to the stoplights that rarely worked properly to the way City Hall always seemed to favor tourists and tourism over the locals. But it was still a great place to live. The city was beautiful, and the weather good outside of that hellish patch from late May to early September. The gay bars in the Quarter were all grouped near each other, making it easy to move onto another place should you get bored at one and want a change of scene. And of course, I was completely addicted to Carnival. Kyle and I would ride our bikes over to Café Lafitte in Exile at the corner of Bourbon and Dumaine, padlock them to the balcony poles. The parades on Canal Street were about a ten-minute walk from there. From my pocket, a bell tolled—some more emails had been delivered.

It was my lucky day. There was a parking spot near Cabrini Park. I waited for a speeding cab to shoot by before getting out and locking up the car. The park was alive with dogs and their owners. Frisbees and sticks and tennis balls were being tossed for happy barking dogs to chase down and bring back for another round. I strolled the two blocks over to Bourbon Street and ducked into Verdi Marte (aka the Nelly Deli) for a bottle of water. I was already sweating as I turned the corner at Royal to walk uptown to Lee Ann's house. There was a slight breeze coming from the direction of the river. It was such a gorgeous day I almost wanted to start singing. Everything was in bloom, the last gasp of the warm weather before the temperatures started dropping.

A sweet breeze was alive with mix of scents from blossoming trees, vines and flowers. Brick fences hid behind lush flowering vines cascading down to the tilted sidewalk. I stepped down onto the street to get around a walking tour, pasty looking tourists with white skin, their upper left chest adorned by a tour sticker.

This end of the Quarter smelled much better than the other end, closer to Canal. The foul stench of Bourbon Street—a mixture of vomit, piss, stale liquor, and pine cleaner—hung in the air like a miasmic cloud.

I finished my water by the time I reached the corner of St Philip and Royal. I tossed it into a garbage receptable and went inside the CC's to get an iced mocha. While I waited, I checked my phone for texts and emails.

I had a text from Blake: *can't wait to see you tonight.*

I smiled, feeling his strong arms around me again. I could get used to that.

Maybe he'd break my dates-ghosting-me streak.

I spent a few moments fantasizing about Blake, waking up in that four-poster bed, living in that gorgeous museum-like house, going to sleep every night in his arms . . .

But can I trust him?

The young Black girl behind the counter called my name, snapping me out of a most pleasant daydream. I slid my phone back into my pocket and picked up my drink.

So far, so good, I thought as I walked back outside, *I might as well enjoy the honeymoon until he gets to know me better and vanishes.*

There was a street band playing further up the street with an amazing young female vocalist. There were playing an old song that sounded familiar and made me think of Mee Maw. Mee Maw had loved music and always had it on while she worked or cleaned or did anything, really. Her tastes were eclectic. She liked everything from blue grass to country to jazz to hip hop to classic rock.

I really missed her.

As I walked up Royal to Dumaine, I started humming along to the music—and the title came to me: "Edge of Seventeen" by Stevie Nicks. I wished Lee Ann wasn't expecting me because I'd listen to the band for a while. They were quite good. The singer wasn't Stevie Nicks, but she had a style of her own that was haunting and powerful.

You haven't spent much time in the Quarter in a while, I thought as I stood on the corner of Dumaine. Since Kyle had started performing regularly at Baby Jane's, I'd kind of stopped coming to the Quarter bars.

It's easier, I heard Tradd saying in my head. *You don't have to worry about parking or finding a cab and in a worst case scenario, we can always walk back to your place.*

Yes, Tradd had hated the Quarter bars, hated the Quarter, really. And I'd allowed him to get me out of the habit of going there. Yes, Baby Jane's was easier. Yes, Baby Jane's was fun, and it was close to the Phoenix for late night bad decisions after too many drinks.

Maybe Blake will take me dancing at Oz, I thought, picturing him on the dance floor again, sweat running down his bare torso as he swiveled his hips and moved to the backbeat.

You just want to show him off, a little voice whispered.

I laughed. Who wouldn't?

I reached the corner at Dumaine as a buggy ride went by. "Did you know that Grace Kelly wasn't the first American born princess of Monaco? The first was a New Orleans heiress named Alice Heine, and this house right up here at the corner is where she lived. Café Amelie is named after her mother . . ."

When I turned back to look up Dumaine a woman came out of Lee Ann's front door. She was dressed entirely in black, including a large brimmed black hat with a veil. She was tall and slender and something about her looked familiar.

Marigny? I thought, before recognizing her.

She'd been leaving Lee Ann's house the last time I came by.

She'd checked my name off the list at the front gate Saturday night.

As I watched, she pulled a pack of cigarettes out of her purse, shook one out with trembling hands, and cupped her hand so she could light it.

Just like the other day when I'd seen her.

Arabella?

Isabelle.

Isabelle DePew.

The wind caught her full skirt so the black fabric swirled around her and she inhaled, blowing out the smoke before letting the veil fall back into place. She reached the bottom of the steps and started walking towards me. She was slouching a bit, like she was uncomfortable with her height. She was a little taller than me but bone thin. The wrists coming out of the full black sleeves were skin over bone. Her fingers were long and skeletal, the nails bitten down to the quicks. There were no rings on her fingers.

I stood there and let her walk past me, did a mock double take, and turned to call after her, "Isabelle?"

She stopped and turned back to look at me. She lifted the veil again and took another long drag on the cigarette. Her face was bare of make-up, making her look faded and washed out. Her big brown eyes were bloodshot and watery. "Yes?" she asked, her eyes looking me up and down trying to place me.

It was a condescending look. I guess she'd decided that what I was wearing made me less of a person in her eyes, someone clearly beneath her.

I smiled.

Please. I've been judged and found wanting by much better people than her.

"Jem Richard, glam artist extraordinaire," I replied, widening my eyes and making my smile as big and phony as possible. "We just seem to keep running into each other."

"Do we?"

"Well, we met at Marigny's show the other night .... I came on at the last minute to help with the make-up and hair for the fashion show?" *And I wound up walking in it?* "Remember?" I clucked my tongue and gave her what I hoped was my winningest smile. "And I ran into you here the other day, remember? Have you and Lee Ann known each other long?"

Her eyes narrowed and she puffed on the cigarette. "Lee Ann and I met after I went to work for Marigny, they were close friends. She's been very good to me." Her voice cracked and she seemed to struggle for a moment to get herself back under control.

She reminded me of those girls who sit around in coffee shops getting amped on cappuccinos while they scribble incredibly bad poetry in their notebooks. My older brother had been crazy about one when I was a kid—my parents couldn't stand her, because everything was miserable or misery. Most of her friends had been like her too, with their black mascara and black clothes and dark lipstick and white pancake make-up. I think the idea was to show contempt for the societal beauty standards by rejecting beauty in any form. Since beauty was my business, I could only applaud them for this to a point. I mean, if all women eschewed the unrealistic beauty standards imposed on them by a misogynist society and culture, I'd be out of work.

I could relate. The gay male beauty standard is even worse than those for women. We're not all gym gods with no body fat and veins bulging out of our muscles, like Kyle and Blake.

But for girls like Isabelle, everything was high drama. Everything was angst and pain and suffering and being misunderstood.

"How are you handling it all? This must be so rough for you." I managed to shoehorn some sympathy into my voice. Glam artists don't just make women look and feel beautiful. We spend hours with our clients, in what I call a state of invasive intimacy. You have to be a kind of amateur counselor, ask lots of questions, and establish a rapport. I never mistook the rapport for friendship—it was a business relationship, bottom line—but I also like to think that just being a sympathetic ear for my clients was helpful.

"Your clients will tell you things they won't even tell their best friends or shrinks," Mee Maw had told me plenty of times. I'd watched her with her clients growing up and she was phenomenal at it—

which was why the Beauty Shoppe had been such a success. Her clients had loved her.

She took another hit. "Marigny was more than just a boss to me. She was my mentor and my friend." She flicked ash with one hand and wiped at her eyes with the other.

Clang clang clang clang—my bull detector was going off in both ears. Still, it was nice to hear someone say something nice about Marigny. I don't think I'd heard that from anyone else, not even Jackson? "I'm so sorry, you must be devastated."

She nodded again, wiping at her eyes and nose with her sleeve. "Marigny was very admired in the industry, you know. I couldn't believe my incredible good luck in getting a job with her."

"Where else have you worked?" I asked.

"I worked for Calvin Klein in New York for years after school," she replied, slightly raising her chin proudly. "I'd still be with CK if the job with Marigny hadn't come open. Such an opportunity, and to work with one of my favorite designers?"

I didn't think there were many people who would have considered Marigny Orloff in the same category as Calvin Klein, but what did I know about fashion? "I imagine the competition was fierce." No reason not to play along with her delusions.

She agreed. "One of my professors—he was my mentor—he knew her from her days at Chanel in Paris." She sighed dreamily. "The necklines and sleeves, the amazing silhouettes she would come up with ... as soon as I saw some of her designs, I knew I wanted to work for her, learn from her, soak up her knowledge and talent."

Like a sponge? I was tempted to say it but bit the words back instead.

There were any number of responses I could make to that, but they were all sarcastic and or rude, so I just smiled. "Is the business going to continue?"

She nodded. "Jackson wants me to take over the design portion of the business," she said excitedly before remembering she was supposed to be in mourning. "He'll run the business and I'll do the designing." She gave me a chilling smile. "You did a great job on the make-up at the show Friday night—Marigny was really pleased." She reached into her purse and fumbled around finally coming up with an engraved silver business card holder. She flicked it open, and handed me a business card.

"You gave me one the other day," I reminded her, but took it anyway.

"Call me soon—Jackson and I are thinking about doing some photo shoots for the website and you'd be perfect for the make-up."

"I will." I said, tucking her card into my wallet. "I'm always looking for new clients!"

She nodded and tossed her cigarette into the gutter. "Nice to see you again," she said, walking past me and turning down Royal Street.

I watched her go. Something nagged at me—something she'd said was wrong?

But my phone buzzed, and I forgot about it as I looked at the screen. It was from Kyle: *I just heard on the news they've arrested Jackson.*

Jackson?

I wouldn't have thought Jackson capable of killing his mother. You never know what people are capable of, but murder? His mother? If Jackson was going to kill his mother, why would he have waited so long?

It made sense . . . but I'd tried to give him the hard drive back and he hadn't wanted it.

So maybe the hard drive and the break-ins had nothing to do with the murder?

I'd ask Blake about it later. He probably couldn't tell me much, but . . . Jackson?

That couldn't be right. It just didn't seem right.

I climbed up the cement steps to Lee Ann's front door. I pushed the buzzer and could here it ringing inside the house. I sipped my Mocha and heard footsteps approaching the door. I guess her intercom didn't work. The big door swung open.

"Sorry I took so long," I said.

"Oh Jem." She looked like she hadn't stopped crying for days. Her feet were bare, and her graying hair was in disarray. She smelled slightly of stale liquor and cigarette smoke. She grabbed me by the hands and pulled me inside, closing the door behind her quickly and pushing me into her kitchen from the hallway. "Thank you for coming." She ran a hand through her hair and picked up a sweating rocks glass with melting ice swimming in a brownish-gold liquid. She tossed back what was left in the glass and shuddered as she swallowed.

"I just ran into Isabelle—"

"They've arrested Jackson," she interrupted me, walking towards the drawing room, gesturing for me to follow.

"I just heard." I replied, a little surprised. "Is that why you wanted me to come by?"

She gestured for me to take a seat, and shakily wandered over to the wet bar. She was wearing the ultimate fashion disaster—a multicolored polyester muumuu, which hung from her skeletal frame like a tent. Her hands shook as she plunked more ice cubes into her glass and added a couple of inches of Johnny Walker Black Label to it. When she noticed me watching her, she asked, "Would you like a drink?"

I held up my iced mocha and shook it, rattling the ice. "Already got something, thanks."

"I usually don't drink this early but—Christ, that woman." She made her way back over to where I was seated on a cream-colored chaise lounge chair. She sat down in a rocking chair, raising her shaking hand to her mouth and taking a healthy swig. She swished it around in her mouth like she was trying to get a bad taste out of it before gulping it down. She gave me a brittle look. "It's funny, Jem, this morning after I heard the news about Jackson I realized, for the first time, that with Marigny dead I don't really have anyone to talk to about anything anymore." She took another swallow. "I don't know what to do and I need some advice."

"I don't know if I am the right person, but I'll be glad to help if I can."

"I kept her secrets while she was alive," she muttered. "She can't get mad at me for talking about the truth now that she's dead."

"Marigny?"

She smiled at me. "Marigny and I went to school together, we were the same age," she said slowly. "I know a lot of people used to talk about the two of us—I'm sure by now you've heard any number of people talk about what sluts we were when we were younger. And maybe we were, by the standards of the day, but nowadays we'd be considered feminists in control of our own sexuality. Still, we had a lot of fun. Marigny was wilder than I was, of course—but she also wanted to get married."

"Five times, wasn't it?"

She nodded. "Five times. But when she decided to write that memoir—"

Ah, now we're getting to the good stuff, I thought.

"—and I kept telling her she was insane, she was crazy, no one would want to read all that old gossip and no one would care. But she kept saying she wanted the world to know the truth about her life ..."

"The truth about her life?"

"She never worked for Chanel in Paris," she finished the whiskey and refilled the glass. Her hands were still shaking. "She was never in Paris at all."

Thérèse Dorgenois had said the same thing.

"Then where was she?" I asked. "She did leave New Orleans, didn't she?"

"Marigny had an affair with a very powerful very married man when we were in our early twenties." She snickered. "Marigny was so stupid, she actually thought this man would leave his wife and family for her."

The Judge, I thought.

"So, she stopped taking her birth control." Lee Ann went on. "I told her she was crazy for trying it. He was never going to leave his wife for her, even if she got pregnant. *His wife was pregnant*, which shows you how out of her mind she was. He wasn't going to give up his career for her. She was just a—what do you kids call it these days? A side piece?"

"Yes, that's what they call it today." I stifled a grin. "Lee Ann, I appreciate you thinking of me as someone you can confide in, but I'm not sure why I'm here."

She got up to refill the glass again but was weaving a little as well as shaking as she walked back over to the bar. "She left New Orleans because she was pregnant," Lee Ann hiccuped, refilling her glass yet another time. "And she didn't want anyone to know. Her baby daddy—" she seemed fine with that modern slang, "gave her some money to go away and she did, even gave the baby away." She hiccupped again, and put her hand out to the bar to balance herself. "I don't—I don't feel so good."

She coughed and I noticed that she was sweating heavily. Her lips were looking bluish, her eyes bulging. She tried to speak but nothing came out but a grunt. She was struggling to breath, her hands coming up and clawing at her throat.

"Lee Ann?" I asked, pulling my phone out and getting to my feet.

She took a few stumbling steps away from the bar. I could see her pupils had shrunk to pinpoints in the center of her eyes. Still gasping for air, her lips were turning a deeper shade of blue and she started gagging.

My hands shaking, I dialed 911.

She pitched headfirst onto the rug, convulsing and shaking, her breaths coming shallow and rapid. She was foaming at the mouth and gasping for breath, clawing at the air with her fingers. Her skin was turning grayish blue. I reached for her wrist and her skin was cold, clammy, damp. She made a choking, gurgling noise deep in her throat.

"911, what's your emergency?"

I asked for an ambulance, gave Lee Ann's address, and started explaining what I was seeing to her. "Sir, I have an ambulance and the paramedics are on their way. It sounds like she's overdosing from fentanyl. Do you have Naloxone handy?"

Fentanyl? I thought wildly. *Lee Ann was on heroin?*

"Is she conscious?"

"Her eyes are open."

"Try to get her to speak!"

My phone fell out of my hand with a clatter as I reached for Lee Ann and shook her. "Lee Ann, can you say anything? Can you talk to me? The paramedics are on their way, hang in there for me, Lee Ann, you can do it, please hold on." I could hear the 911 operator talking.

Lee Ann was staring at me, coughing and choking and gagging. I rolled her over onto her side and vomit spewed out of out of her mouth, green and chunky and acidic smelling. She gagged again and turned her head to look at me.

"Isabelle . . ." she croaked out. "Ellis . . ."

Her eyes went vacant and she exhaled one more time in a big sigh before her entire body went limp.

Lee Ann Vidrine was dead.

CHAPTER NINETEEN

Stunned, I stayed there on my knees, not comprehending fully that Lee Ann was gone.

I'd never seen anyone die before.

I didn't know what to do. Should I leave her and go outside? I picked up my phone with numb, shaking fingers and said *hello* but the 911 operator had disconnected. I wasn't sure how long I'd been sitting there in shock. I could hear sirens but they sounded far away over the roaring in my ears. There wasn't anything I could for Lee Ann.

Somehow I managed to get to my feet and stumble out of the drawing room into the hallway. I staggered towards the front door on wobbly legs, putting my hand to the wall for support in case my knees gave or something else happened. I could hear my breathing rasping in my ears as I kept moving through slow motion to the door. It seemed to take forever, like the hallway was messing with my mind somehow and getting longer, like some kind of nightmare. I grasped the knob and twisted it, gulping for air once I pulled it open and staggered out into the real world again.

I sat down on the top step and put my head between my knees, trying not to pass out.

Lee Ann was dead.

Dead.

Died right in front of me and I hadn't been able to do anything.

Memories started flashing through my mind like a kaleidoscope. The first time I met Lee Ann, at the Beauty Shoppe when I was thirteen. She'd always been so nice to me, so nice to Mee Maw. I'd always liked Lee Ann. She used to bring me books to read whenever she'd come to the Beauty Shoppe. Like Mee Maw she'd loved crime; they were always talking about some book they'd read or some true crime story they'd seen or were following in the papers. When I moved her to take care of Mee Maw as the cancer slowly killed her, Lee Ann hired me to do her hair. When Mee Maw died, Lee Ann was the once to convince me that starting my life over again in New Orleans was smart and I could put all my dark memories of Dallas and Texas behind me. Lee Ann had helped build my business, referring people to me and recruiting Mee Maw's old client base back for me.

If not for Lee Ann I'd probably be working at a SuperCuts in Metairie.

My eyes were tearing.

Lee Ann had been one of the few ties left to Mee Maw.

It felt like I was losing her again.

I stopped fighting it and buried my face in the crook of my right arm sobbing. I could hear Lee Ann saying again, delighted with how she looked when I handed her a mirror, "Oh, Jem, you're just as good as your grandmother. I can't wait to tell everyone what you can do!"

I couldn't get the image of her blank, staring eyes out of my head.

Things kind of happened in a blur. The sirens got so loud that I couldn't hear anything else, not even my own thoughts. I answered questions, directed EMTS and firemen inside to where her—her *body* lay in the parlor. I thought about her cats—two beautiful Bengals, Napoleon and Josephine—and wondered where they were and who was going to take care of them?

People kept going past me, in and out, and I kept my head down in my arm. I wasn't sobbing anymore but the tears were still coming. I looked up once and saw a crowd of gawkers across the street on the sidewalk, staring and watching.

"Sir?"

I looked up into the face of a pretty young Black woman with long braids, wearing the blue EMT uniform. She sat down beside me and placed her warm hand on my arm. "I'm sorry to tell you that your friend has passed." Her voice was calm, sympathetic, warm.

I looked into her deep brown eyes. "I—I thought so. Thank you for telling me." My voice sounded hollow, like the wind if it could speak.

"It looks like a fentanyl overdose, if I had to guess," she said, her voice sad. "We're seeing more of those these days, unfortunately. Are you okay?" She lowered her voice. "It's a lot to take in."

I just nodded.

Then she was gone, and a police officer was introducing himself to me as Officer Williams, and he stood beside the steps at my eye level. "I need to ask you some questions? If that would be okay?"

"Yes." I said quietly. He started asking, and I answered. Lee Ann was a long-time friend and client. She had called me and asked me to stop by because she needed to talk to me. She'd sounded a bit strange, yes. No, I had never known Lee Ann to take drugs. She drank, yes, maybe more than she should but isn't that everyone in New Orleans? No, she'd never said anything to me about taking drugs other than Xanax. She said she took it for anxiety and post-Katrina PTSD, didn't everyone? I apologized for my tone. Yes I had been in the house before, plenty of times. I came by to do her hair and sometimes to do glam for her when she was going to a special event. Yes, I'd always liked her. She'd been a client of my grandmother's for years and then mine after my grandmother died.

"Do you think this is connected to Marigny's murder?" Blake's deep voice got me to look up from where I'd been staring down at the concrete step. I'd been keeping my head down.

I wiped the wetness off my cheeks and took a deep breath. "How could it not be?"

Blake was standing next to Officer Williams. He was wearing a pair of blue slacks, a white dress shirt, and a blue tie. The shirt was tight—I could see he wasn't wearing a T-shirt—and he had his foot up on the bottom step. I wanted to jump into his arms, bury my face in his chest and just cry until tomorrow. Latoya Picot was quizzing the young EMT who'd told me Lee Ann was gone. "She told me that—" I stopped, remembering the Judge was Blake's father.

"Told you what?"

I looked back down at my shoelaces. "She'd just finished telling me that Marigny had never worked for Chanel, and that the real reason she went away was because she was pregnant by a powerful married man, who'd given her the money to get out of town. And then she—started gurgling and choking

319

and gasping for air—" my voice broke and I took a deep breath.

I hated that he was seeing me cry. Anyone would in my situation, but . . .

Men can cry, Jem. Stop buying into the toxic theories of what is and isn't masculine. You've experienced a trauma and if he can't understand that he's not someone you want to date anyway.

He sat down next to me on the steps, so close our legs were touching. "And the baby's father was the Judge?" he asked softly. "It's okay, Jem, you can say it. I don't have any illusions about my dad anymore." He barked out a harsh laugh. "If I ever did."

"You've arrested Jackson?" I asked. "I think that's why she called me. She was really upset about Jackson being arrested."

"Only on suspicion," Blake replied. "I can't tell you more than that—"

"Fine, okay sure, whatever." I replied with a gesture of my hand.

"Are you okay?" His voice was concerned. "You don't look so hot."

"Someone just died in front of me, Blake." I looked into his oh-so-blue eyes. "My house has been broken into twice over the weekend, I was knocked out and tied up, then shot at, and now this." I buried my face in my hands. "Maybe you're used to this kind of stuff but I'm not. I've…never seen anyone die before." My voice broke again and I exhaled.

"You have no idea how sorry I am I agreed to work that damned fashion show. I should have just said no and been done with it. Nothing good ever came from working for Marigny."

"EMT's seem to think it was a fentanyl over-dose," Latoya's heels clacked on the tilted sidewalk as she walked over to where we were sitting. "Pending the autopsy, of course, but they've seen enough of it to know it when they see it." She tapped her notepad on the steps. "I would have never pegged Lee Ann Vidrine for a heroin user, but just goes to show the opioid epidemic can affect anyone." She shook her head sadly. "Jem, did you know she was using?"

"I don't think she was using, and I don't think this was an accidental overdose." I replied, looking her square in the eye. "So, you just think it's a coincidence her best friend was murdered Saturday night and today Lee Ann overdoses? Seems kind of convenient to me." I shook my head. "Yeah, I know all this time she could have been using, but—"

"Maybe she was distraught about her friend's death and she miscalculated her dose, or it had more Fentanyl in it than it was supposed to, or she didn't know her heroin was cut." Latoya replied. "We'll probably never know."

"She was murdered." I said grimly, not breaking eye contact. "You need to talk to Isabelle DePew."

"Marigny's assistant?" Latoya and Blake looked at each other. "Why?"

"She was leaving when I got here. Lee Ann was upset and was dead a little while later." I closed my eyes. "Lee Ann was drinking. Isabelle could have put the fentanyl in her drink."

"Why would she do that?" Blake asked gently.

"I don't know. Maybe she killed Marigny and Lee Ann knew. Lee Ann was really upset that Jackson had been arrested." I looked at Blake "You really think Jackson killed his mother?"

"All three of her sons hated her," Blake replied. "And the gun that was used to kill her was Jackson's. He claims he kept it in his mother's safe and hasn't touched it in months. There were no fingerprints on the gun—he wasn't that stupid—but it's his gun, he has no alibi, and he has the combination to the safe. If Bonaparte and Aramis didn't have rock solid alibis, I'd suspect them, too, but Jackson also had a nasty argument with his mother that afternoon— she was threatening to fire him and cut him out of her business."

"He admitted to that?" I stared at Blake.

"Well, no, but we have a witness who overheard them."

Things started clicking into place in my head.

No, that couldn't be, I thought in response. But it makes sense.

"Was Isabelle DePew the witness?" I asked.

Latoya and Blake exchanged glances. "Yes, how did you know that?"

I rubbed my eyes. "I told you, Isabelle was here before me. Isabelle worked for Marigny. She probably had access to the safe, knew the gun was there. It's kind of convenient that she overheard this argument, isn't it? And you say Jackson denies it ever happened?"

"Of course, he denies it," Latoya replied.

"So it's her word against his?" I took another deep breath. "Before she died, Lee Ann told me that Marigny left town after her affair with Judge Dorgenois because she was pregnant, not because she was going to work at Chanel in Paris. Your own mother told me she checked with Chanel and they have no record of Marigny ever working there. She left town because she was pregnant and put the child up for adoption." I bit my lower lip. "That child would be Isabelle's age now."

"You think Isabelle is my sister, and that she killed Marigny and Lee Ann—because why? Because Marigny gave her up for adoption?" Blake raised his eyebrows. "Besides, Isabelle isn't the only person in this case who'd be about the right age, either. Ellis Ikehorn is also the right age."

"Ellis?" I thought back to conversations I'd had with Ellis. He'd decided to move to New Orleans because it was smaller and more quiet than San Francisco—which had struck me as odd at the time. He'd had a huge career in drag there, too—why give that up, and then move somewhere and open a drag school? He'd been there on Friday night, too—and hadn't I picked up on some tension between him and Marigny?

I shouldn't have had those tequila shots Friday night, but how was I supposed to know I'd have to remember things from that night later?

But Ellis?

I'd liked Ellis.

This is like how the neighbors of the serial killer always talk about how nice and quiet he was, I thought, shivering despite the warmth of the sun on my skin.

"Ellis was with me when she was killed," I reminded Blake, "and he couldn't have had access to Marigny's safe. But I'm telling you, I don't think Lee Ann was using. She drank too much—like everyone in New Orleans—but I'm positive she didn't do anything else."

"Users are liars, Jem," Latoya said softly.

I gave up. "Do you need me to stay or am I free to go?"

"You're going to need to come down to the station and give a formal statement," Blake replied, "But we will talk to Isabelle DePew."

"Do I have to do it now?"

"It's better when everything is fresh in your mind."

It was about two hours later when I pulled up my car in front of my house and turned off the engine. The shock had worn off, and so had all the adrenaline, and all I wanted to do was just lie down somewhere. I was exhausted, bone tired, wasn't even sure if I had the strength to get out of the car. Kyle was at work, so I'd have the house to myself, which was great. I wasn't really in the mood to talk to anyone about anything right now.

I had liked Lee Ann. I'd considered Lee Ann a friend. My business's success was entirely due to Lee Ann's support. Not only had Lee Ann referred other women to me, she'd introduced me to theater managers and directors all around town, and gotten me listed with the Louisiana Entertainment division of the state so I could get gigs working on film and television.

I couldn't believe I'd never wash, cut and style her hair again.

I was going to miss Lee Ann and her filthy sense of humor.

I sat there behind the wheel for a moment, fighting off the tears.

She'd died right in front of me.

I was never going to get the image of her vacant staring eyes out of my head.

I got out of the car and went inside, locking the front door behind me. But once I was inside, something felt off.

"Kyle?" I called, dropping my keys into the bowl on the coffee table where I always kept them so I could always find them.

The house was silent, other than the air conditioning unit pumping cold air through the vents.

You're just hearing things, I thought as my body relaxed, *which isn't a surprise given what's been going on lately. It'll be a while probably before you feel completely safe inside the house again.*

That was the worst part, I realized. We all live with the illusion that our homes are sacrosanct, safe places that were ours and ours alone. Having that space be violated made you realize how false that sense of safety really was. Instead of viewing the big windows along my front gallery as beautiful and convenient sources of light, now I saw them as easy ways to gain access. Same with the back door—the top half of it was glass. And how sturdy was our fence back there, or the gate with the padlock? Someone could easily scale that fence, or kick the gate in, if they wanted in bad enough.

Stop it, you're just scaring yourself, I thought as I walked through the house, looking around and making sure I was alone inside. I made it back to my workroom—the chain was on the door and the deadbolt was turned, and the door in Kyle's was the same. I breathed out a sigh of relief and got a bottle of water from the refrigerator. I went back into my workroom and booted up my computer. Once it came to life, my calendar opened—I'd set it to default every time the computer woke up, so I would be sure I'd never miss an appointment. The next two weeks were appointment-free. But October should be a good month for me—costume balls galore, and those appointments were more fun than glam because I could explore my creativity. Last year for Fat Tuesday I had painted this super-hot guy named Davey Pettigrew's entire body to look like a leopard—including his brief bikini and the boots. That had been fun and lucrative.

Davey dated Kyle for a little while, and so I doubted I'd ever get to paint Davey's body again.

It had also been a long night. I'd gone over to Davey's at three in the morning to get started and then had to rush home to put together my *Kiss of the Spider Woman* costume for the Bourbon Street Awards.

I closed the calendar and checked my email, but I kept noticing that little folder in the upper right hand of my computer screen—Marigny's memoirs.

I scrolled the mouse over to it—my emails were all junk—and hesitated. *You should just drag it to the trash and be done with it,* I thought.

But I couldn't believe Jackson had killed his mother.

I couldn't believe Jackson could kill anyone.

Marigny had been an awful mother, but he couldn't have been that good of an actor when I'd stopped by to see him, could he? He'd seemed genuinely shocked and upset and grieving—*which didn't mean he didn't kill her—he could have killed her and*

327

grieved, and it was something in the heat of the moment...

It's not your concern anymore, Jem.

But I couldn't shake the belief that Isabelle dePew had poisoned Lee Ann with fentanyl. It would have been easy, wouldn't it, to have dumped the fentanyl in her whiskey bottle? Shaken it up so the powder dissolved? And then—

Someone could have put the fentanyl inside the whiskey at any time—knowing Lee Ann would drink it at some point. She did like her Johnny Walker Black Label.

I shivered. If the fentanyl had been in the whiskey bottle, we were all lucky the only person who was poisoned was Lee Ann.

She'd offered me a drink.

Another call far too close for my liking.

I clicked on the folder.

I opened the pictures folder again and went to the pictures of the nude woman in Marigny's bed with the crown and scepter. The picture in the bed wasn't the only one of the woman, and in all of them she was nude but her face was blurred out.

In the last picture she was standing and posing, nude. Her hands on her hips, with one leg in front of the other and bent slightly, like she was on a pageant runway, proud of her firm breasts and flat stomach and—

Something about her looked familiar.

Where did I know her from?

"Everyone in New Orleans looks familiar," I said out loud. But there was something about the body language, the way she was standing . . . I'd seen her before.

Recently.

I heard Rachel's voice in my head again. *She found pictures of her husband with another woman, both naked, in Marigny's bedroom. The face was blurred out. Marigny threw Tony out and filed for divorce.*

I opened my browser and typed Tony Castiglione Marigny Orloff into the search box.

Not much came up. The marriage announcement to Marigny, the divorce . . . I scrolled down the page looking for something, anything, that looked right.

I found a notice of a marriage—in Covington on the North Shore—between Anthony Castiglione and an Amber Kormann.

I clicked on the memoir folder.

I opened the folder directory and typed "amber" into the search bar.

Chapter thirty five was highlighted, so I clicked it open.

And started reading.

Tony Castiglione had been Marigny's fifth husband.

He'd been the same age as Jackson.

They'd met at a charity fundraiser for Children's Hospital. Tony was a nurse, and in Marigny's words, "one of the hottest hunks I've ever seen." They'd flirted and exchanged numbers, and after a "whirlwind romance" they were married at the casino in Bay St. Louis. And that's when things started going wrong. At first, Marigny was madly in love with him and spent money on him lavishly, so besotted that she even had added him to some of her bank accounts. The honeymoon had lasted six months before she noticed that he was spending a lot of her money—and not depositing his paychecks into joint accounts but instead into personal ones. At first, she thought it was suspicious but didn't care, but as more time passed and his tastes continued to get more and more expensive (wasn't her business always on the brink of bankruptcy?), and she began suspecting him of having an affair.

The nudes of a woman taken in her bed and wearing her crown and scepter from when she was Queen of the Mystik Krewe of Patroclus was the last straw.

But Marigny was nobody's fool. She hadn't moved as quickly as you would think—but then, it wasn't her first divorce, either. She'd hired a private eye named Chanse MacLeod to dig up dirt on them both, as well as independent proof of the affair. It hadn't taken him long, Marigny got her lawyer on it, and the marriage was over. Tony didn't get a dime from Marigny in the divorce, which, per the memoir, had gotten ugly. She'd named Amber Kormann as a correspondent in the divorce, and the judge had ended the marriage and set her free without costing her anything more than her legal fees.

I leaned back in my chair. Sure, Tony and Amber probably hated Marigny, but there was no reason for them to kill her now—the divorce had been three years ago and they wouldn't get a dime from her death.

You need to just delete these files and forget all about it. Jackson killed his mother and Lee Ann was an addict who overdosed. None of this has anything to do with you.

I put the computer back to sleep and stood up, stretching and yawning. Maybe I should take a nap? I was tired—it had been a hell of a few days, and now that it was all over, maybe I could get back to my normal life again.

And Blake was going to text me when he was done with work.

I smiled. Sure, Blake could just be the next guy I dated who ghosted me, that was always possible, but he didn't strike me as the type.

I hope he didn't expect me to make him breakfast when he stays over, I thought with a grin, *because I am a terrible cook.*

My phone chimed and I picked it up.

The message was from Ellis.

Jem, I need you to meet me at my place, urgent, life and death, don't tell anyone. Come around back to the workroom.

I frowned at my phone. I texted back, *seriously?*
The response sent a cold chill down my spine.

If you want to see him alive again, you'd better hurry. And bring the hard drive. No cops or he dies.

CHAPTER TWENTY

Oh my God oh my God oh my God.

I stared at my phone, trying to decide what to do, all these thoughts jumbling together in my head. I started hyperventilating again. I put my hand against the wall to help keep my balance while I bent at the waist and tried to get my breathing under control as my brain started going fuzzy and the edges of my vision grayed out.

Ellis needs my help, I thought, so get it together, man, you don't have time to freak out. Inhale, hold. Exhale slowly. Inhale, hold. My heart rate began slowing as I focused. I repeated the calming exercises several times until I felt my brain starting to unknot itself.

The address was in the Holy Cross district, on the other side of the Industrial Canal. I opened my

Map app and typed in the address. A pin dropped, close to the levee running on that side of the canal. It would take about ten minutes to get there, tops.

Shade jumped into my lap, purring. He started making biscuits on my shirt, rubbing his head against my arm. "No, baby," I pulled him into a tight hug. "Daddy's got to go rescue Ellis."

I stood up, still holding Shade, who squirmed out of my grasp and ran into the kitchen.

But I don't have the hard drive, I thought, reaching for my keys and knocking them to the floor. I picked them up with shaking hands and went out the front door, making sure to lock it. I got into my car and took another deep breath. I put the keys in the ignition and stared at my phone.

They said no cops, they'd kill him if I called the cops. But rushing over there with nobody knowing where I was going—that's just dumb. Resolutely, I called Blake. It went straight to voicemail. I swore under my breath as his deep voice instructed me to leave a message and he'd call me as soon as possible.

When the tone sounded, I talked fast. "Blake, the killer is at Ellis's. They texted me and told me they'd kill him if I didn't bring the hard drive to them. They also told me they'd kill him if I called the cops but I'm not stupid enough to go over there without telling you. I'm in my car and on my way but when you get this you need to send help over there because I don't know what I'm walking into."

I disconnected the call and plugged my phone into my car. I started the car and briefly thought maybe I should just call 911 and let the police handle this, what exactly am I going to do when I get there?

But I dismissed that negativity. A friend needed my help.

I could never leave a friend hanging no matter what kind of danger I might encounter. Mee Maw would haunt me for the rest of my life.

What was I going to do when I got there? I wasn't armed. Maybe I should have gone upstairs and gotten Mee Maw's gun? Not that I knew how to use it or anything. Once this was over, if I made it out alive, I was going to learn how to shoot. I could hear Mee Maw saying, "no point in owning a gun if you don't know how to use it, is there?"

I started slowing as I approached the drawbridge. The red lights were flashing and the bar had come down. I swore under my breath. I didn't have time for this! I drummed my fingers on the steering wheel. I could head up and take the bridge over the canal at Claiborne since it wasn't a draw bridge.... the clock was ticking. Every second seemed to last an eternity.

But they knew I was on my way, so Ellis should be okay. They wouldn't do anything to him until they had the hard drive—

Which I didn't have.

Patience. They don't know you don't have the hard drive and they aren't going to do anything to

Ellis until they have it.

I looked down at my phone while I waited. It felt like I'd been waiting days for the freighter to pass through and the bridge to come back down. If Blake called . . .

The bridge started to slowly come back down.

The delay, though, might have been long enough for the cops to get there before me. If they were there, I could just turn around and head home.

No, I'd have to make sure Ellis was okay first.

The light turned green, and the crossbar went up. The cars in front of me started driving up the slope to the bridge. Finally, I pushed down on the gas pedal and the car moved forward.

Come on, Blake, call me back or send me a text or something.

"After you cross the bridge, in one thousand feet, turn right onto Deslonde Street." The Maps app instructed through the car

I reached the other side of the bridge and watched the street signs.

"Turn right onto Deslonde Street, then proceed another fifteen hundred feet. Your destination will be on the left."

I took the turn and slowed to a crawl. A mangy looking dog ran across the street in front of my car. The houses in this neighborhood looked freshly painted, new. This part of the lower 9th Ward had flooded during Katrina because a barge had been left anchored in the canal. The winds had driven it into the levee, smashing a huge hole that devastated the neighborhood.

"You have arrived."

I drove past and parked on the other side of the street, about two houses down the block, almost to the corner at Dauphine. Ellis's Toyota SUV was parked on the street in front of his house. It was a Creole cottage style house, painted turquoise with coral shutters. A driveway went past to the back, and I could see a building back there. That must be where they were waiting for me. I slowly walked along the street, watching the house for signs of activity, anything.

The street was so empty I kind of expected tumbleweeds to start blowing down the street.

Not only were no cops here, I didn't hear sirens.

Maybe the police weren't coming after all.

Wait for Blake—what are you going to do? What can you do? You're not an Avenger, you don't have superpowers. You don't have the hard drive so why wouldn't they kill both you and Ellis? Get back in the car and call 911.

Sweating, I opened the car door and reached for my phone.

I still didn't hear sirens, and I didn't see flashing red lights anywhere.

I looked at the messages again.

No, I hadn't imagined it. That last text was clearly a threat.

I dialed Blake again, and once again went straight to voicemail.

"Of all times to ghost me," I slipped my phone into my pants pocket and leaned back against the car.

Wait for the cops, Jem. This is above your pay grade by a long shot.

The hairs on the back of my neck were standing up. I started walking down the sidewalk from the corner, that little voice in my head repeating over and over what are you doing leave this to the cops.

The text had said not to call the cops.

Oh well, too late now.

Is this for real? I thought as I reached the driveway. The house was still and silent. I could hear cars driving past on St. Claude. A battered looking Honda Civic turned onto Deslonde from St. Claude. That wasn't Blake, just someone from the neighborhood going about their business. All around me life was going on as normal.

You'd never know someone was being held by murderers inside that back building.

I looked at the back building. Carriage house or mother-in-law house, it was also painted the same colors as the main building. It was two stories, and there was a gallery on the second floor. Mee Maw hadn't rebuilt her carriage house after the Katrina flood. She'd rented it out for years, but her tenant had moved away earlier that summer and it was empty.

I bit my lower lip and slowly started walking up the driveway. The main house was silent as a tomb. The shutters on the side windows were all closed and latched. When I reached the back corner of the house, I paused, listening again.

Still no sirens.

The backyard was a lush tropical garden, with banana trees, a couple of palm trees, and ferns and flowers and grass and a riot of colors from flowers— reds and blues and purples and yellows. It was gorgeous, with two massive live oaks giving shade to the far corners of the lot. There was a stone fountain in the center of the backyard. The water was off, but the statue in the basin was of Divine.

Definitely a drag queen's backyard.

I crept to the front door of the small building in the backyard. It wasn't very big—Mee Maw's had run the length of the back property line. This one was smaller, couldn't have been more than 500 square feet on each floor. The blinds in the windows were closed. I stopped. What do I do now? Knock? They'd want the hard drive and when I didn't have it . . . well, they'd have no reason to keep either of us alive.

Wait for the cops, wait for the cops, wait for the cops . . .

No, I couldn't wait. Ellis was in danger. Crazy as it seemed, I had to get in there and do something— anything—to rescue Ellis, or at least make sure he was safe when the police showed up.

If they showed up.

I pulled out my phone. Nothing from Blake. I quickly typed out a text *something up at Ellis's check your voicemail you need to get over here. SOS.*

In case that didn't sound urgent enough, I added *HELP!!!!*

I hit send and slipped the phone back into my pocket.

I looked up at the second floor. The gallery circled the entire building.

There was a door up there, too.

If I could just get up to the gallery.

I didn't see any ladders. But one of the live oaks had a huge branch that reached for the back of the building.

Afraid to breathe, afraid of making any noise, I walked around planters and massive ferns and picked my way carefully around to the back.

The branch didn't reach, but there was a ladder leaning against the back wall.

It was made of rusty metal. I picked it up and swung around so that it was perpendicular to the ground. My arms and shoulders complained as I maneuvered it so that it was leaning against the house. I jiggled it a couple of times to see if it would hold. It seemed solid. Biting my lower lip, I started up the ladder. It jounced and shuddered with every step I took, but I just grimly gritted my teeth and kept climbing, careful not to look down, careful to not think about whether or not the gallery was rotted out and might not hold my weight—

I reached the top and grasped the railing. I yanked on it. It wobbled but didn't move. I took a deep breath and swung my right leg over the railing, still holding the ladder. The railing held, and I gently pulled myself over. The balcony groaned when I put my weight on it, making this seem even more like an episode of *Scooby Doo Where Are You!* I froze and listened. Still no sirens anywhere. I moved as quickly as I could while trying to make as little noise as possible. I reached the front corner and the door.

If the door's locked, I'm going back down the ladder and waiting for Blake.

I turned the handle and the latch released. The door swung open silently. I crept inside. I didn't close the door behind me completely in case I needed to get out in a hurry. The last thing in the world I needed was to be trapped inside with the killer.

And now to find Ellis.

It was cool inside the house. Some light was getting in around the shutters and blinds, so I could see I was in a workroom. Mannequins wearing dresses in various stages of construction were standing around. One entire wall was covered with wigs hanging from hooks. There was the faint odor of mothballs and expensive perfume. On the opposite side from the door was a staircase leading down. A door led into a large walk-in closet with gowns and dresses hanging from racks. Another wall was covered with shelves holding every imaginable kind of shoes, the heels in varying sizes and styles and colors. A door inside the closet led to a bathroom. This was obviously Ellis's drag workshop. As I turned back to the room from the closet a fabulous electric blue beaded gown caught my eye.

Priorities, I reminded myself, but still thinking how good I'd look in that dress, I tiptoed over to the railing along the staircase and listened. I could hear voices now from downstairs.

The smart thing to do was go back to the car and wait for Blake and the cavalry to arrive.

But I've never been known for doing the smart thing.

I crept to the top of the stairs. I had limited sight of the room downstairs—mostly I could see a sewing machine and bolts of brightly colored cloth stacked against the wall. Every instinct in my body was screaming get out of here, but I ignored those sane, rational thoughts.

I carefully slipped my phone out of my pocket, turned it to silent mode—should have done that first, I'm terrible at this—and then touched the flashlight app. A beam of white light shot out of the back of my phone. I slowly turned it around the room, just to be sure.

No people, just mannequins.

That was when I heard a thump from downstairs.

I switched off the flashlight and crept back to the hanging staircase, hoping I didn't step on a squeaky board or kick something by mistake. When I put my foot on the top step I heard a voice, muffled so I couldn't understand what was said, and then another voice answered.

I felt relief surge through me. Ellis must be alive, right?

How was I going to get downstairs without being seen?

The stairs were open to the room. There was a railing along the side that wasn't against the brick back wall, but there was no way I wouldn't be seen if I used the stairs. I cursed under my breath, straining to hear. All I could be certain of was there were at least two people downstairs.

If one of the voice wasn't Ellis's, I was also outnumbered.

And didn't have a weapon.

Stop that, I commanded the little voice in my brain. *Shut up if you're not helping.*

I needed to find out who was downstairs.

I touched the screen of my phone and pressed the voice memo app button. I turned it on, placing it back into my pants pocket.

I didn't know what its range was, but better to be prepared for anything.

Every instinct was telling me to run, get the hell out of there and wait for the police.

I was the only person who could find out who they were and stop them from hurting Ellis.

Why Ellis danced through my head.

I paused. That was a very good question.

I could hear them talking again now.

The woman's voice was definitely Isabelle—I recognized her high-pitched voice. But I couldn't tell who the man was—but I knew I'd heard that voice before.

I froze. It was the guy from Saturday night, the man I'd heard arguing with Marigny and then bumped into as he was leaving.

"I told you, she was going to call the cops and tell them everything!" Isabelle was saying. "I didn't have a choice. I didn't want to kill her."

"You've bungled this whole thing," the man was saying. "I should have known I couldn't trust you to do anything."

"Maybe if you actually had done *anything* besides kidnapping my brother—"

There was a smacking sound and a cry. "I'll smack you again if you keep it up." The man's voice was coiled and low, tight with anger. "How was I supposed to know he'd let the hard drive out of his hands?"

"Big man," Isabelle jeered angrily. "We shouldn't even be here. This is stupid. You shouldn't have kidnapped Ellis. We could just take the goddamned money and jewelry from Marigny's safe and get out of the country. They already think Jackson was embezzling from the old bitch, they'll just think he stole this stuff, too."

Her voice was harder, more mature sounding than when I'd talked to her before. I knew this was the real Isabelle—whoever the hell she was.

"Honey, you know as well as I do the real money is on that fucking hard drive," the man replied, his voice cajoling. "How are we going to turn these jewels into cash anyway? And there's only a couple of grand in her safe. The hard drive is a gold mine and you know it."

"I wasn't the one who tried to hide the damned thing in his make-up case," she went on, her voice now taking on a whiny tone. "That was you. And you were seen, weren't you?"

He sighed. "I told you Jack Jorgensen took it and hid it in the kid's make-up case. I was going to take it, but Marigny almost caught me. What did you want me to do, Amber?"

Jack had lied about taking it, I thought. But why? And what did they mean by a gold mine? Was there other stuff in the memoir besides the stuff about Judge Dorgenois that no one wanted to come out? Had Marigny been blackmailing people?

They didn't know that the police had the hard drive.

Isabelle's voice became whiny. "Come on, Tony, let's get out of here. It's enough for me that she's dead and her son's going to fry for it?"

Tony.

It had to be Tony Castiglione—and if it was . . . then maybe Amber and Isabelle…

"What about your brother?" Tony replied. "Should we just leave him here?"

Brother? Ellis was Isabelle's brother?

I hoped my phone was picking up all of this. I leaned forward and peeped around the corner. I leaned forward and saw them. They had their backs to me. Isabelle was leaning against the wall on the right. A very muscular man was sitting at a card table, rifling through something.

And there was Ellis, tied to a chair with a gag in his mouth.

He was looking right at me.

I held a finger to my lips and he inclined his head slightly to let me know he'd seen me.

I glanced at my watch. It had only been fifteen minutes since I got out of my car and texted Blake.

I pulled myself back up out of sight.

Even in no traffic with his siren on, Blake couldn't get here fast enough to save Ellis—or me.

"Amber, why you wanna be so goddamned stupid?" Tony said, his voice sounding almost dangerously seductive. "You know the old bitch got a shitload of money for what's on that drive. A couple of grand ain't gonna be enough to keep us in style once we get the hell out of this town. We need a nest egg to set us up."

Amber? Isabelle was Amber?

Another piece clicked into place.

Marigny had twins. Ellis and Amber. Had he been in on it with them?

They wouldn't have tied him up if he was, would they?

Marigny hadn't known what Amber had looked like. Amber had come to work for her under another name, gotten close to her. Jackson hadn't been stealing from his mother—Isabelle/Amber had been framing him all along. What had their plan been? For her to get access to the house, to the safe, so she could steal money?

It hardly seemed worth the trouble.

I couldn't help but wonder if the plan had been to kill Marigny all along.

Tony married Marigny for her money—but she'd found out about his affair and kicked him to the curb.

She'd tried to shake down Thérèse about her affair with the Judge, wanting money to leave it out of her memoir. Thérèse said she'd laughed at her and thrown her out—and the pictures of Marigny with the Judge had been there. Marigny had been blackmailing people, asking for money in exchange for being left out of her memoir.

The hard drive, apparently, had all that damning information on it.

When I'd accessed it, there had only been the

one folder. But I hadn't taken the time to read the whole thing, either.

The hard drive had been in my make-up case, which had been in Ellis's possession for almost a day.

I was still missing pieces. Think, Jem, think.

I still didn't hear any sirens. I couldn't hide in here forever. I slipped my phone back out and touched the screen. No new messages, no missed calls.

It was up to me to save the day. But how?

No heroics, what I needed was to get the hell out of here, and let Blake know what the hell was going on.

Let the police handle this.

But I couldn't just leave Ellis here—and there were two of them.

I closed my eyes. There was nothing I could do for Ellis if they were armed. There was no way I could get down those steps and out the front door—so I had to go back out the way I came in.

I stood up and turned to sneak back across the room, but the floor groaned underneath me.

I froze, my heart dropping to my feet and my stomach flipping.

"What was that?" Tony said as my blood turned to ice.

"I didn't hear nothing," Amber/Isabelle replied.

My hands shaking, I pulled my phone out and pulled up my messages. I touched the message thread for Blake and started typing a text message as fast as I could: *At Ellis's the killers are here get here as fast as you can before they find me they have Ellis* and hit send, whispering a prayer to every Higher Being I could think of that Latoya and Blake would get here before it was too late.

"You're imagining things," Amber went on, her voice dripping scorn. She laughed nastily. "Seriously, Tony, what's your problem? Feeling guilty?"

There was the unmistakable sound of a slap and another cry.

Sweat was rolling down my back. I took another step and let my breath out slowly when the floor didn't groan again. I took another step—

And put my foot down on a board that moaned.

"There is someone up there!" I heard a shout from downstairs.

My blood went cold. Did I have time to get to the door? I could hear someone on the steps. I only had a few moments to decide. Wigs? Hot glue gun? The sewing machine? Why was there nothing up here to use as a weapon?

I grabbed a mannequin with pink silk pinned around it and dragged it to the stairs. By the time I got to the top Tony was halfway up the steps. I recognized his face—and he had a gun in his hand. His face twisted in rage. "You!" He started to bring the gun up . . .

. . . and I threw the mannequin at him. The gun went off. I think I felt a rush of air as the bullet passed me but that could have been my imagination. I watched it happen in what seemed like slow motion. The mannequin hit Tony full on, and there was a cracking sound as he fell backward. His eyes opened wide, and he dropped the gun reaching for the railing. It went off again as gravity finally won the battle and he fell backwards down the steps. He hit his head with a hard thud on the stone floor when he reached the bottom. I went clattering down the stairs behind him. Over the ringing of my ears from the gunshots and the powder smell in my nose making my eyes water, I could hear someone screaming. The gun had bounced over to the kitchen counter and was on the floor next to the dishwasher. I leaped over him and picked it up with my shaking hands.

I pointed it at Isabelle. "Stop screaming and untie him."

She held up her hands, closed her mouth and nodded.

I gestured with the gun. "NOW."

"Okay okay!" She stepped behind Ellis and removed his gag. He coughed and she knelt down to untie the knots.

That was when I heard the sirens.

About time, I thought, as my entire body began shaking from the adrenaline rush.

"Tie her up," I said to Ellis. Somehow, I managed to make it to the front door and out into the fresh air and the sunshine, out into the daylight and I was somehow aware that there were flashing red lights at the foot of the driveway so far away from me. I collapsed into the grass and started throwing up.

"Jem?" I heard a voice as I struggled to breathe. "Honey, are you okay?"

Someone grabbed one of my hands and started talking to me. "Relax, catch your breath, you're going to be all right."

Slowly everything came back into focus, and I started to breathe again.

I looked up into Blake's concerned face and wanted to start crying.

"Are you okay?" he asked me, sitting down next to me in the grass as I nodded. He slipped an arm around me.

"Panic . . . attack." I managed to say.

He nodded. Over his shoulder I could see Tony and Isabelle/Amber being led out of the house in handcuffs by uniforms, Latoya walking along side of them reading them their rights. She stopped, gestured for them to wait, and walked over to us. "Ellis is going to be fine," she said. "We need to have him checked out at the hospital, but he's fine.

I closed my eyes and rested my head against Blake's chest.

Later that night, after I got checked out at the hospital and Ellis was released, we shared a Lyft back over to his place so I could pick up my car. On the way over, he explained to me how he and

Isabelle had found each other. Marigny had given them up but hadn't told anyone there had been twins. They were adopted separately. Ellis had been adopted by a nice family from the Bay Area, where he'd grown up and been happy. Five years ago, Isabelle found him—and wanted to find their mother.

"I wasn't interested, but she was determined," Ellis said simply. "Isabelle—well, she wasn't quite right, if you know what I mean? I worried about her, you know—and so I came to visit, to check up on her. That was when I found out she was sleeping with our mother's husband." His face got grim. "That's why I retired and moved to New Orleans, to try to keep Isabelle out of trouble. When Marigny—our mother—was murdered, I was worried. I was sure Isabelle and Tony must have had something to do with it, but . . . she was my sister. When she called today and asked me to meet her there . . . I knew something was off."

"I don't understand, though." I replied. "Why did they take you prisoner?"

"That was Tony's idea." He shook his head. "They were getting desperate, and were running out of money. I'd make the mistake of telling Isabelle that—well, that you and I'd gone out together after the show and hit it off. I guess Tony thought that was the best way to get you to give up the hard drive."

"I'd already given it to the police," I replied.

He buried his face in his hands. "Can you forgive me for not being honest with you?"

"You'd be surprised at what I can forgive," I replied as we got out of the Lyft. He gave me a hug and I said, as he started to go, "When does your next drag class start?"

He smiled. "A week from Monday."

"I'll call you." I watched him get in his car and drive off.

I got back into my car and smiled. *Why not? I had the free time and I'd had fun at the show—it was all the stuff that came after that was the mess.*

And if I could make some extra money, why not?

I was about to put my car into gear when my phone vibrated. It was Blake.

Almost done at the station, mind if I come by?

Give me a few minutes, I've got to drive home, I wrote back.

I pulled away from the curb.

The future was looking bright for me.

Somehow, I knew Mee Maw was pleased.

KILLER QUEEN
mystery series

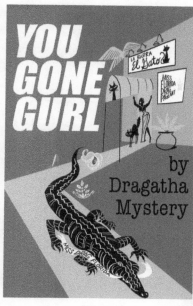

coming in 2024

Enjoy This Sneak Peak of

YOU GONE GIRL

CHAPTER ONE

My edible kicked in just as we crossed the state line into Florida.

I could feel all the tension and stress leaving my entire body and almost sighed in pleasure. I should have taken it the minute we pulled away from the curb.

"They just let us drive right in?" I said, watching the WELCOME TO FLORIDA sign as it approached and then disappeared behind us.

"What were you expecting?" Ellis turned and looked at me from over the passenger seat, a wry smile on his face and one eyebrow raised. "Barbed wire? Guard towers? Immigration patrols with semi-automatic weapons and German shepherds?"

"And hot butch military men in tight green camo. And Army jeeps, too." I laughed, picturing it

357

with cannabis-enhanced delight in my head. There's just something about a butch man in tight green camo. Ellis shook his head and turned back around. "Is that too much to ask for?"

I settled back into my seat and kept watching out the window as we sped past a seemingly endless line of pine trees. We were heading east on I-10. We'd catch I-75 South past Tallahassee at Lake City, and then drive through the scary, beating heart of Florida till we reached St. Petersburg.

I'd like to state for the record that I was against driving from the beginning. I remembered driving with my family once from New Orleans to Orlando for Disney World, and that drive had seemed horrible and endless. Florida just went on and on and on . . . .

Ellis pointed out that we had too much baggage to fly and we'd have to rent a car anyway once we arrived, so it made more sense to just take his Toyota Range Rover. Much as I hated long drives in cars, I had to admit the Range Rover was a smooth ride and comfortable. I had the entire back seat to myself so I could stretch out and sleep if I wanted to, and I had a backpack full of books in the floorboard to read if I got tired of the showtune Spotify station Ellis had blaring through the speakers. I'd never been much of a Broadway queen, but I had to admit the Hamilton cast recording was pretty good.

Why did I ever agree to this? I re-plumped

my pillow and double-checked that the door I was leaning against was locked. I swung my legs up onto the seat and leaned back against the pillow. I must not have been thinking too clearly.

But after dealing with a couple of murders, getting out of town for a while had sounded like a good idea. I still had nightmares of opening the front door to someone with a gun again. I didn't have the dream as much since having an expensive security system installed.

And it was a paying gig, an added bonus. But Florida? Why did it have to be Florida?

The Sunshine State had once been a queer mecca. Queers loved Disney, amusement parks, and beaches. Florida ticked all three boxes. My last trip to Disney World had been for Gay Days two years ago. Florida's economy has primarily been built around tourism, but then they decided to shoot themselves in the foot by making the state as inhospitable for everyone as they could. Their homophobic governor and state legislature had been trying to legislate queer people out of existence since taking power, from banning books in libraries to "Don't Say Gay" laws to targeting therapy for trans kids. Oh, and of course, the ever-popular drag queens are groomers. The same old vomit they've spewed for years. For some reason this time around it gained traction somehow. Their battle cry—"The children! The children!"—would be a bit easier to swallow if they cared about those same kids getting slaughtered by a school shooter, or child beauty pageants, or protested in front of Catholic churches.

Who knew drag queens were more deadly than an AK-47?

Florida politicians and their homophobic base, that's who.

As calls for boycotts, travel advisories, and lawsuits mounted, the Miss Queer America pageant decided not to cancel or move their event from St. Petersburg, Instead, the organizers gave this year's pageant the theme Defiance! and basically dared the state to shut the pageant down. But as we sped along in Ellis's Toyota Range Rover, getting further from the safety of New Orleans and deeper into the Florida panhandle, I was beginning to wonder if maybe it wasn't the best idea to defy the state for the sake of holding a pageant?

It was cold and gray outside, and the sky was filled with dark clouds. All the weather forecasts were saying we would be enjoying blue skies and temperatures in the high seventies/low eighties once we got there. A former student of Ellis's was representing Mississippi in the pageant. "And of course, he's freaking out," Ellis had told me with a shake of his head. "He wants me there to help out, and I told him about your make-up expertise, so he wants to pay you to help out, too. He's rented me a two-bedroom condo near the host hotel—only a few blocks from the beach." Ellis grinned. "It'll be a good experience for you to be backstage at a pageant, you can see what it's like."

"I told you, I don't think pageants are for me," I'd replied hesitantly. I'd just completed Ellis's three-week course in doing drag. I'd performed in our graduation show at Baby Jane's the previous Monday, but the audience had been friends and family. The next thing for me to do, as a working drag queen, was to start booking some gigs. But ... sure I'd managed to get up in front of a crowd of friends and family and lip-synced two numbers, "Tick Tock" by Ke$ha and "We Found Love" by Rihanna. My stomach had been twisted into almost painful knots and my armpits were wet, but everyone swore they couldn't tell I'd been nervous.

I didn't know if I could perform in front of a bar filled with strangers.

"Avery will pay you $1,000 for helping with make-up and wigs, and you can stay in the condo with me for free, all you need is spending money." Ellis held up both hands. "You don't even have to help pay for gas. We can take my car." He'd also invited my roommate Kyle, who volunteered to do most of the driving. He was going to visit an ex who'd moved to Tampa, on the other side of the bay.

I touched my phone screen and pulled up the website for Miss Queer America again. I'd looked at it so many times already I practically had it memo-

rized. It was subtitled An Inclusive Pageant, implying the other pageants weren't. Miss Queer America was relatively new to the pageant circuit, having
first been held about five years ago. Ellis had told
me that talk on the pageant circuit was that found-
er Quentin Carlyle—who had been a longstand-
ing board member and heavily involved in several
other pageants—had started Miss Queer America
because he'd been banned from involvement in all
the others. But based on what I'd found doing my
due diligence, Quentin had built it up into a jugger-
naut in a very short time. Miss Queer America now
had competitions in all fifty states—the first year
anyone who wanted to enter could, while Quentin
was getting the supporting apparatus in place—and
last year's contest had sold out one of the casinos in
Las Vegas. This year's pageant had been sold out for
weeks, and Quentin had landed some major spon-
sors, too—a beer company, a vodka company, and a
gay cruise line, among others. Miss Queer America
also got a cash prize of twenty thousand dollars to
go with her sash, tiara, and robe.

I switched over to text messages and stared.

Was Blake ghosting me now? I glanced at the
back of Ellis's head as I slipped my phone back into
my jacket pocket, proud of myself for not texting
him again. Maybe he was busy. Maybe he had some
family or work drama that was taking up all of his
time so he was too tired or preoccupied to text me

back. Or call. I thought our last date had been kind of magical, to be honest. He'd picked me up and taken me to dinner at Coquette, a lovely restaurant in the Garden District on Magazine, and then we'd headed further uptown to catch the latest Timothee Chalomet period drama at the Prytania Theater. I'd spent the night at his place on Coliseum Square and he'd made me breakfast the way he always did when I stayed over. He had to go to work so I'd taken a Lyft home—and the last thing he said was, "I'll call you."

I texted him on my way home—*thanks again for a lovely evening*—and since then, nothing.

And despite the constant itch to send him another, I was following Kyle's advice and not text-bombing him. "Go ahead if you want to seem desperate and thirsty," Kyle had said, after taking my phone away from me. "How many times did you text Tradd?"

I hate when he's right.

Tradd was the guy who'd ghosted me before my brief whatever-it-was I had with Blake. We'd met over the course of a murder investigation, and there were sparks. Blake is a hot zaddy, somewhere in his mid-forties. He hasn't missed a day at the gym since he was a teenager and it showed. He was handsome, with a square jaw with a cleft in the chin, dimples in his cheeks, blue eyes and curly black hair. He was also a police detective whose long term partner had died a year or two ago. There were plenty of red flags there I ignored—cop, widowed, New Orleans society family—but he was sexy, he was handsome, he was sweet and above all else he was interested in me. Who was I to turn all that hotness down? We'd gone out a few times since I'd helped him catch the killer, and then....

Nothing.

Don't harsh the mellow.

I looked back out the window just as rain started coming down, splatting against the car with random thunks at first, before coming down like a machine gun as Kyle slowed down. I wrapped a blanket around me and slid down in the seat. Shade meowed at me from his carrier in the floorboards. I slid down into the seat and pulled a sleeping bag up over me.

Only about seven more hours to go.

ACKNOWLEDGMENTS

Writing a book can be a lonely process, but I've always been blessed with great friends and support my entire career.

I dedicated this book to them, but I need to thank James Conrad, Wendy Corsi Staub and Alison Gaylin again. This book was their conception, and I cannot thank y'all enough for thinking I was the right person to write it. I would have never thought about writing about a drag queen-in-training and her journey, so thank you so much. There would be no Jem without your encouragement and support.

And a big thank you Carol Ebbecke and Catherine Luttinger at Golden Notebook Press for their hard work on copy and marketing and all the other behind the curtain work.

I am also singularly blessed to have an amazing day job that is not only educational, but makes a difference in people's lives every day. I have amazing co-workers, from my supervisor, Blayke D'Ambrosio, to my fellow team members LaToya Galle, Al Frost, and Danielle Sandifer. The rest of the Prevention department here at Crescent Care is amazing, and all deserve a shout out: Erica Vincent, Sevynn Moss, Kelsie Rhodes, Tamara Hammerman, Celeste Carter, Bryson Richard, Lakarla Williams, Naomi Langlois, Ellis Lee, Tiana Anderson, Leon Harrison, Eric Lightell, Shelby Young, Kyra Kincaid, Charles Darensbourg, Corrina Goldblatt, Piper Avila, Tobas Babilon-Crockett, Jeremy Schroeder, Owen Ever, Patchouco Pieree, Meredith Booth, Diane Murray, Jeffrey Babineaux, Jasmine Davis, Glenis Scott, Diane Murray, Conchita Iglesias-Mcelwee, and Caitlin Boyle—with extra thanks to Ellis, Kyle, Blayke, and Bryson for letting me borrow their names for characters.

No longer co-workers but still missed are Narquis Barak, Joey Olson, Beau Braddock, Jean Redmann, Jordan Probst, and Cullen Hunter.

I have an amazing circle of friends who are incredibly kind and gracious with their time and their advice, even when I'm being annoying or obtuse, so thank you to John Copenhaver, Marco Carocari, Kelly J. Ford, Alafair Burke, Jeffrey Marks, Ellen Byron, Sarah Weinman, Sara J. Henry, Donna Andrews, Art Taylor, Tara Laskowski, Kellye Garrett, Alex Segura Jr, Elizabeth Little, Alan Orloff, Gillian Roger, Susan Larson, Pat Brady and Michael Ledet, Bev and Butch Marshall, Bill Loefhelm, AC Lambeth, Steve and Margery Flax, Oline Cogdill, Laura Lippman, Megan Abbott, Robyn Gigl, Ed Aymar, Jen Dornan-Fish, Cheryl Head, Sandra SG Wong, Susanna Calkins, Amie M. Evans, Stephen Driscoll, Stuart Wamsley, Rob Tocci, Nikki Dolson, Chris and Katrina Niidas Holm, and my Birmingham/Wetumpka family. Love you all very much.

And of course, I wouldn't be here if not for my wonderful partner of twenty-eight years, Paul Willis. You are the center of my world and I am forever grateful I finally found you.

Greg Herren is the award-winning author of over forty novels and fifty short stories, and the award-winning editor of over twenty anthologies. He has won two Lambda Literary Award (from fourteen nominations), an Anthony (out of seven nominations), and two Moonbeam Children's/Young Adult Literature medals. He has also been shortlisted for the Agatha, Lefty, and Shirley Jackson Awards. He has published short stories in markets as varied as *Ellery Queen's Mystery Magazine*, *Mystery Weekly*, *Mystery Tribune*, and the critically acclaimed *New Orleans Noir*, among many others. He was the first openly gay Executive Vice President of Mystery Writers of America. He has also served as a judge for the Hammett Prize, the Edgar Awards, the Stoker Awards, and the Lambda Literary Awards. A co-founder of Saints & Sinners, the world's longest running LGBQT+ literary festival, he lives in New Orleans with his partner of twenty-eight years.